Autumn Leaves

Michael Fountain

authorHOUSE®

AuthorHouse™
1663 Liberty Drive
Bloomington, IN 47403
www.authorhouse.com
Phone: 1 (800) 839-8640

Published by AuthorHouse 01/19/2018

ISBN: 978-1-5462-2522-5 (sc)
ISBN: 978-1-5462-2521-8 (e)

Library of Congress Control Number: 2018900687

Print information available on the last page.

Any people depicted in stock imagery provided by Thinkstock are models, and such images are being used for illustrative purposes only. Certain stock imagery © Thinkstock.

This book is printed on acid-free paper.

Epilog

History of the Family

Joseph, Douglas, Bosworth's father was livid upon hearing from parents of a thirteen year old girl, his son impregnated their daughter two weeks before marrying Bessel. Being a peaceful man, he stifled his discontentment, and swallowed his anger. He feared the reaction of his prospective daughter-in-law. Chances were there would be no wedding, or something worst. Bessel had a reputation for attacking women who flirted with her prospective husband. There was no telling what she might do to the young girl carrying her fiancé's child. He felt compelled to smokescreen Joseph's infidelity.

When he told Fanny, his wife of thirty years, she reminded him Bessel was insanely jealous. *"She forbid Joseph from looking at other women, let alone conversing with them. How he managed to sneak around getting a teenage girl pregnant is a mystery to me. Every step he procure, Bessel's there. And we've both seen her viciously beat women she perceived as a threat to her relationship with Joseph. I shudder to think of what she might do if she knew our son got another woman pregnant."*

Recently Joseph built an industrial plant with financial backing from Bessel's mother, Victoria. Douglas refused to sit by idly watching his son's dream crumble. One word from Bessel, Victoria might withdraw support. Many times Bessel threaten to persuade her mother to cease funding Bosworth when his son did something contrary to her wishes.

He recalled a birthday party for Joseph in his backyard under a huge tent. Bessel had a conniption when a female friend greeted his son innocently with a kiss on the cheeks. Bessel was about to strike the girl when Fanny intervened by pulling her to the side and making it known she would not tolerate any of her shenanigans. She scolded her by saying, "If you can't behave herself, then you're welcome to leave." Bessel shrugged her shoulders in defiance, collapsed into a nearby chair, and mellowed down. After the party, he overheard a heated argument between Joseph and Bessel.

"If you ever cheat on me, I swear, I will make sure your plant fail. I'll convince mother to stop financing your company," she yelled, exploiting her influence, and he resented it.

Even though they were monetarily comfortable, neither he, nor his wife, retain sufficient capital to maintain the operation of a factory. Luckily for Joseph, his future mother-in law held controlling stock in an esteemed Black Insurance Company in Baltimore; a company her family launched during the turn of the century. Her parents were immigrants from Nigeria who came to America with a vision. They created a company from scratch establishing a colossal empire when all odds were stacked against them. Della Indemnity was the first, black, insurance company in the country offering colored people an alternative for purchasing life, automobile, and home coverage.

Confident Joseph would pay her back many times over, Victoria gladly investment in his son's business. He was a pioneer in the corporate world, making a mark for his race, and she wanted him to succeed. A quarter of a million dollars meant nothing to her. It barely dent her bank account.

Victoria was a short, hefty, homey looking woman which contributed to her spinsterhood. She moved gracefully on her feet, and was as limber as a child. Her midnight complexion enhanced her roaming cat eyes, and crystal white teeth. Even though she was obese, she dressed impeccably, and Fanny, his wife, speculated she ordered her flashy outfits from magazines geared to full-figured women. There was no store on the shore where she could purchase fitting clothes.

Douglas summoned the young girl, and her parents, to his spacious office connected to his fifteen room rancher on Quantico road. He was their ticket to wealth. He would do anything to avoid a scandal, and salvage Joseph's company.

The girl was built like a college student instead of a mere adolescent. Small breast protruded through her low cut blouse arousing him. A tight dress accented her boney legs which were gapped advertising her undergarment. One thing for certain, she was a temptress. No wonder his son was weak. She was asking for it. Nevertheless, he knew better.

Her parents wore dingy clothes. Apparently, they were laborers who retired from a tawdry day in the fields. Her mother wore a scarf wrapping her braided hair hiding monster plats. A dilapidated straw hat protected her father from the sun when he harvested crops. Their shoes were ripped, exposing dusty toes. Obviously, they were poor negroes struggling to make an honest living to support a wayward daughter.

For their silence, he offered a quarter of a million dollars with the stipulation their daughter leave town. With her absence, Joseph could go forward with his plans.

The parents looked at each other grinning from ear to ear, and Douglas surmised what they were thinking. (*He's our pass out of poverty. A quarter of a million dollars. Just think of all we can do with the hush money. Pay off bills, and get a decent place to live with running water, and an inside toilet.*)

For the girl, he vowed five hundred dollars monthly for child support until the child turned twenty-one, provided she kept him supplied with photographs of the child maturing, and liberal visitation rights. He promised never to appear without advanced notification. Bonding with his grandchild was imperative.

The young girl, Melissa, moved to New York, rented an apartment near relatives, and raised her son alone. Her parents remained on the shore, bought a house, a new car, invested in stocks, and lived comfortably for the rest of their lives.

Ten years later, Joseph enquired the whereabouts of Melissa. At the time Bessel was carrying his third son. He knew his father was responsible for her disappearance. Both of his parents were wealthy, and wanted for nothing. His father, a prominent lawyer, and his mother, the Dean of University of Maryland Eastern Shore in Somerset. Alone, his father was worth millions.

His mother, Fanny, was seated at an oblong kitchen table skimming through the newspaper when Douglas confessed how he made his mistake vanish. "I offered her parents a good piece of money for their daughter to leave town. They took the bait. She moved to New York where she raised your son off the money I paid monthly."

"If you ask me, they got over like fat rats," Fanny complained sliding her reading glasses to the tip of her nose. She was a studious woman with gray hair. *Paying a quarter of a million dollars to strangers for their silence, and the assurance their child left town was ridiculous. And then to pay the girl five hundred dollars child support to raise her own child was going above and beyond the call of duty. But it was Douglas's money. It was his choice.*

"I want to see my son." Joseph said bravely.

Fanny peered over her glasses. She anticipated he was up to no good. "Don't do anything foolish," she warned. "You have a family, and thriving business. Leave the girl alone." Her words were harsh and assertive. "That young lady doesn't deserve to meet with the furry of your wife," Fanny warned him.

"Just want to see my son," Joseph insisted.

"Ok. I will give you her address," Douglas surrendered. He looked ten years younger than his wife even though they were the same age. His even temperament, and calm disposition, accounted for that. Stress he avoided at all expense. "Please promise me, you will not disrupt their lives," Douglas pleaded meekly.

He grew fond of the Melissa, and his beloved grandson. He wanted no harm to pledge either of them. Shielding them from the wrath of Bessel was his chief priority.

The boy bore a striking resemblance to him when he was his age. They shared facial features, and body structure.

Temptation to bring his grandson home for the weekends pressed his thoughts knowing it unwise. If Bessel discovered her husband fathered an outside child, she might leave him, or do something terrible to Melissa, and her child. If she divorced him, there would be no plant.

When the boy was seven, he enquired about his father. The kids on the playground badgered him about his daddy. They wanted to know who he was, was he staying with him, what he did for a living, and so on. The boy had no answers, so he kept silent, but the kids continued harassing. They were relentless, and he dreaded going to school for fear of being bullied. His mother explained his conception, and birth, but it did not remedy his problem. If anything, it made it worse. He could not tell them what his mother said. They would not understand.

When Douglas visited, Melissa updated him concerning the children at school pestering his grandson about his father. He sat beside his grandson on a lumpy couch, and told him the assorted story about his birth, and the role he played. He figured if he was old enough to ask, he was old enough to hear the truth. In conclusion, he advised him to tell anyone who asked about his father, that his parents separated before he was borne, but he had a grandfather who loved him very much, and saw he wanted for nothing. The boy was pleased. Hearing the story from him, and the advice given, made a big difference. His grandson hugged him as tears rolled down his face; a sight he would never forget. The next day his grandson told the kids at school what he said, and they never pestered him again.

Secretly Joseph drove to New York, and went to the apartment where his son lived. A young boy, about ten at the time, with nappy hair like his, staring through his inherited gray pupils, answered the door. Melissa yelled, "Who's at the door?" The boy said, "A man." She was about to ask for his identity when Joseph stepped inside the cozy flat as he entered the room, sipping coke, only to discover her ex-lover standing there in a three piece suit; The man she slept with whenever he beckoned. The man who blessed her with a handsome boy who stood in his presence.

"What takes you here?" Melissa asked. Joseph was the last person she expected to see.

Joseph was impressed by her appearance. She was gorgeous. But he was there for his son, not to flirt with his mother. He stuck to his mission. "Want to see-"

"Who is he momma?" The young boy interrupted exchanging glances between both parents, not realizing he was the topic.

"Nobody important. Go to your room, and do your homework. I'll check it later."

Being an obedient child, the boy did as told.

"I just wanted to see my son," He finished his sentence when the boy was out of range.

Melissa was hostile. *Joseph had a nerve. Ten years later, and now he had the audacity to appear at her doorstep unannounced. Where was he when she brought the boy into the world? Where was he when he graduated from kindergarten? Where was he when he got into his first fight? He never called, or wrote a letter, or showed any interest. His grandfather played dual roles. He was there when he took his first breath. He was there for every birthday, and every holiday, especially Christmas. He was there countless weekends, picnicking in the park, riding subways, touring the city, exploring Connie Island etc. Whatever his grandson wanted to do, they did. Joseph was a man not known, not seen.* "He doesn't need a father. Go home to your family!" She ordered. *He could have called, and made inquiries.*

"Does he ask about me?" He was curious.

"I told him his father had another family. Your father told him likewise. He accepted that." Melissa was thankful her son reframed confronting her about Joseph. He was content with her love, and frequent outings with his grandfather.

"And that's enough for him?" Joseph was doubtful.

"Yes." She grabbed a cigarette from a cocktail stand, and lit it quickly filling the room with smoke; a bad habit she acquired. "He's a smart little boy. Something he inherited from you." She accredited him.

"Look. I'm not going to stay. Just wanted to see him." He backed to the closed door. "If he needs anything, let me know." He reached into his pocket handing her a business card. "This is my private number."

Years later Joseph heard from his son's mother when she called seeking college intuition. He mailed her a check. Weeks later she telephoned his private line thanking him for his contribution.

Victoria had a heart-attack shortly after Bessel birthed her third child. She spent three weeks in Peninsula General Hospital recuperating from a double heart bypass operation. She was scheduled to be discharged when she suffered a stroke and died. The doctors and nurses were baffled. Nobody saw it coming. Medical reports indicated she was recuperating perfectly, and the operation was a success. A clot mysteriously developed damaging her heart which triggered a massive stroke leaving her lifeless.

For weeks, Bessel mourned the sudden death of her mother. She stopped eating, and suffered from insomnia. Her nights were tormented with reoccurring dreams of Victoria's funeral. Weeks turned into months. Daily she lounged about the house crying whenever she thought about her mother. Accepting her mother's death was difficult. Eventually she neglected caring for her children, and Joseph hired a fulltime babysitter for his sons. Finally he reached the point where he could not watch Bessel suffer. She needed help snapping out of her depression. It was also stressing him. He sought professional aid making provisions for his wife to attend an Mental Health Clinic in Virginia.

During the week, Joseph ran the plant, missing his wife beside him. She had a knack for business, and made wise decisions. Something she inherited from her mother. On the weekends, he stayed with Bessel at the clinic. He watched her gradually come out of her depression. By the fourth week, she was back to her normal self, and anxious to return home. She resumed her mothering responsibilities, and business partner to Joseph. They were a team again.

Years later Joseph learned his middle son, John, attended the same college as his half-brother. They became good friends. He learned their college peers presumed they were twins due to their staggering resemblance. Faculty had trouble distinguishing them apart and they found boundless pleasure in passing off for each other. The only thing that separated them were their age difference. John was a freshman and his brother was a graduate student.

When John returned home for spring break, and informed Joseph about his lookalike friend, he dismissed his concern by saying, "Everybody has a twin". He knew John had befriended his brother, but he was not ready to expose his identity. Bessel was not the forgiving type.

Fanny died from an aneurism when she was in her late seventies leaving Douglas devastated, and heartbroken. They had been married since high school; Fifty-Plus blissful years. Without Fanny, life was empty. Fourteen months later Douglas contracted pneumonia, and joined his wife in death.

Stanly and John were buddies in high school; a relationship stemming from elementary grade. Football was their game of choice, and they were credited the team's most valuable players. Stanly was swift on his feet, and was notorious for scoring countless touchdowns. No one could tackle, or catch him once he caught the ball, soaring down the field like a hawk leaving a trail of antagonist behind. John was good at defense. If anyone was in his path, prepare to be blocked or tackled. There was no penetrating his barricade. Together they were an awesome combination; A reckoning force.

But Stanly had a dark side. He brainwashed naive girls to sleep with him. A trade he learned from his Indian culture. He was a master of manipulation. With drugs and hypnosis, few girls could deter his motive. John never apprehended why Stanly resorted to the black arts being voted the sexiest guy on campus thanks to his football reputation and popularity. Half the female population would gladly succumb, and consider it an honor.

A few times he watched Stanly slip a powdery substance into unsuspecting girls' drink or food. Through hypnosis, he convinced them to meet him in a secluded place where they unknowingly surrendered their body. Upon satisfying his sexual appetite, he instructed them to return from whence they came. When they came to themselves, they had no memory of what occurred.

John usually avoided Stanly when he anticipated he was going to seduce an unsuspecting girl. Countless times he begged him to call off his mission proclaiming it was wrong, and illegal, but Stanly possessed a one track mind. If he saw a girl he desired, he pursued her permitting nothing to hinder him. His hormones were in charge.

John almost choked the day Stanly decided to seduce a new girl at school. She was cute and shy. He felt sorry for her. What Stanly had in mind, made his stomach quiver?

It was the end of the day, and the girl was standing in front of the school, alone, awaiting her ride. Stanly spotted her upon exiting the building.

Stanly hunched John. "I'm going to get some of that."

"No Stanly, don't do it," John pleaded. "Look at her. She'll probably run and hide if you speak to her." John dreaded what was coming next. *If only he could persuade him to dismiss his scheme, but he was not listening.*

"You wouldn't mind tapping that would you?" Stanly asked as he reached into his pocket retrieving a stick of gum.

She was adorable with small boobs, plump hips and curly hair hanging loosely over her round shoulders. Thoughts of caressing her milk, chocolate, skin aroused even him but he suppressed the feeling. Taking advantage of a person was sinful. "No Stanly. This can't be right," he reiterated.

"Watch this my man."

John tried holding him back. "Don't do it Stan!"

Stanly jerked free, and approached the girl clutching her books.

"Hey, what's your name?" The game was on.

The girl looked at Stanly. *He was handsome, no doubt. Just like her friends claimed. His Indian ban wrapping his forehead, dreadlocks dangling down his back, his pale complexion, and thick eyebrows, all the markings of an Indian. But he wasn't her type. Now his colleague was more her speed.* "Stella," she said eyeballing John bodily. *Why didn't his comrade speak?*

"Piece of gum." Stanly offered.

What harm was there in accepting a gesture. She accepted the gum, unwrapped it, stuffed it into her mouth, and littered the pavement with the wrapping. *It tasted good. Just what she needed for her dry mouth.* "You're the star player on the football field." Stella zipped her jacket. A cold breeze ironed her body.

"I never see you at the games." Stanly reminded her.

"People talk." Stella's focus remained on John.

"Where're you from? I know you are new here."

"Philly." *His buddy had an endearing smile, broad shoulders, bulging muscles, and bowlegged as hell, but a terrific looking guy. Why didn't he communicate to her instead of his Indian pal with his lame smile, smelling of a cheap cologne?*

"City slicker." Stanly teased.

Stella fingered her hair back hoping to attract his silent partner's attention. "Where are you from?" She finally acknowledged her pursuer. "I have never met an Indian before."

"From around here. I stay with my grandmother."

Suddenly Stella felt dizzy. Her world began to fold as a silhouette of colors enveloped her, and she felt vulnerable, and helpless. The Indian asked for her number, and she willingly gave it to him, watching him scribble it in a book. Then he walked away, laughing, but his friend was mute. She wondered if he could talk.

Seconds later everything reverted into prospective. Her mother pulled in front of her, and she slid into the station wagon. Her mother questioned her about her day, but she did not hear her. All she knew was the Indian would call. She was under a diabolical power.

That evening after she finished her homework, the phone rang, and she stared at it, afraid to answer. After the second ring, it stopped. Her mother yelled from downstairs, "Stella, phone call." She edged to her princess phone resting on her nightstand. Nervously she picked up the receiver.

"Yes," she mumbled quietly.

"Come to the park. It's on the street where you live."

Stella wanted to say no, but she was compelled to obey. A force inside took charge. She slipped into her shoes and coat and went downstairs to confront her parents sitting at a small kitchen table conversing quietly. Her mother was peeling potatoes for dinner, and her father sipped coffee while watching the news on a small black and white television positioned on a distant counter.

"Mom I'm going to the park for a few minutes. Some of the kids at school are going to meet me there, if that's ok." Stella felt guilty lying to her parents. It was not her character.

"Make sure you're back in a few hours. Dinner should be ready by then." Her father said removing his thick glasses, and placing them on the wooden table.

Stella left her cozy two bedroom bungalow, and headed to the neighborhood park a block from her house. Upon approaching the park, she saw Stanly leaning against a tree smoking a cigarette which he tossed to the ground, and squished with his foot. *The smell of nicotine made her sick. What boys saw in cigarettes was a mystery to her. Smoking was repulsive.*

"Have any trouble getting away?" He asked.

"No. But I can't stay long," she managed to say. *Why was she there? What power did he hold over her? Why was she drawn to him?* She relaxed when she saw his buddy rising from a nearby swing hidden by a bush.

"Let's go into the woods. I want to show you something." He grasped her tiny hands leading her into a wooded area of the park, absent from public view.

John's assignment was to keep watch, alerting them of visitors; an assignment he took to protect Stella. Stanly could be aggressive, and have been known to leave bruises or marks from rough handling of his victims. If he went ballistic, he would intervene preventing Stanly from hurting her. Contusions and scars on her beautiful body was not acceptable.

Chances of patrons dropping by was improbable. It was a chilly evening, and in a few hours, it would be dark. His only worry was cops patrolling for vagabonds lurking for shelter in the public rest area.

Reluctantly Stella went with Stanly. He ushered her into an uncultivated section of the park crammed with trees and shrubs, a distance from John. Everything within her said, run while you can. Split before it's too late. Again her ecosphere became fuzzy. Whatever he requested, she was obligated to obey. She was under his influence, his slave.

Stanly gently caressed her neck as her heart pounded in her chest making her legs week. Chills creased her body as he unfastened her warm, winter coat and unbuttoned her blouse enabling him to nibble her petite boobs. She shivered as the gravity of his teeth sank into her flesh, and sought to retaliate, but was helpless. He was hurting her. Then he tilted her gently onto the frozen earth, using her coat as a cushion against the pine shacks, and removed her wool skirt, and silk underwear simultaneously revealing her hairy midsection. Next he unbuckled his jeans dropping them to his ankles with his baggy briefs exposing his huge erection. She wondered why he elected to go bareback. Panic struck as he approached fearing she was unequipped to handle what he offered. Nervously she closed her eyes, and bit her lips as he mounted himself between her quivering legs penetrating her tight flesh, abolishing her virginity. Tears clustered her eyes, and she sobbed quietly as the pain increased, and she groaned in agony praying for relief as he plowed deep inside her, exploring untouched territory. She wanted to scream, but was unable to comply as he ravished her. It was if invisible hands muffled her mouth. As Stanly pranced over her like a beast in heat, she felt a substance dripping down her thighs. She thought the boy had ripped her insides apart. She pleaded for him to stop, but he ignored her. She struggled to shove him off, but he was too powerful. As she squirmed to free herself, the harder he packed his manhood inside her. Suddenly he quivered, and pinned her to the ground spreading her legs apart with his legs until he climaxed. Afterward he stood tall, pulled up his briefs, and trousers hiding his limpness, and facilitated her to her feet. Horror gripped her discovering blood streaming down her legs. *What terrible thing had this awful boy done?*

"Don't worry. Today you became a woman," he said nonchalantly zipping his pants.

John abandoned his post when he heard Stella whimper, and observed from a distance as Stanly devoured her virtue like an animal seeking retribution. Swiftly he pranced toward the crime scene, but when he reached them, they were on their feet. The damage had been done. He saw blood dripping down Stella's legs, and discerned Stanly violated a virgin. He felt sick, almost vomiting. Immediately he offered advice. "Go to the bathroom and clean up. There are towels and stuff in there. I will walk you home." That was the least he could do.

Stella rushed towards the public restroom gripping her belongings covering her spoiled body with her long coat. She found paper towels in a dispenser, and a bar of soap on a dingy sink. With soap and water she lathered her private parts, and wiped away the excess seaman and blood as best she could with paper towels. Then she stuffed dry paper towels in her panties and dressed. She prayed there was no stains on her clothes. That would be difficult to explain. To avoid persecuting questions, she would wash her clothes, disposing the evidence before her parents caught wind of what had happened.

When she exited the dimly lit bathroom, Stanly was gone but John was waiting as promised. He apologized for his friend's depraved behavior feeling guilty for not intervening. For the moment, his fleeting conversation was comforting, but when she arrived at the street leading to her house, the memory of the seduction had faded. She had no recollection of what occurred. Her mind was blank. Still she felt dirty and cheap, and necessitating a shower.

When she crept inside the house, her parents were in the living room watching television while dinner cooked. The smell of roast in the oven made her hungry when she passed through the kitchen. No one saw her go upstairs to her bedroom where she took a quick shower, and slipped into her pajamas. Afterward she went downstairs into the basement carrying her soiled clothes, poured half a bottle of bleach and two cups of detergent into a running washing machine allowing it to fill before tossing in her clothes and closing the lid. For the life of her, she wondered why she was washing her clothes. Yet she knew it was something she had to do.

As she laid in bed waiting for dinner, she thought about the evening. *Why was John, the man who seldom talked, escorting her home? And what was he escorting her home from. Whatever the reason, she enjoyed his company. She yearned to see him again. She liked being near him. He made her feel warm and fuzzy inside. And then she remembered his girlfriend who watched him like a hawk. Ellen made it known John was her man, and off limits.*

The succeeding day when Stella awakened for school, she dismissed the incident of the previous day as a dream; A nightmare. Stanly gnawing her breast, ripping her insides apart, telling her, "Today you became a woman"; a dreadful dream she hastily forgot, and never evoked again. But the pain of losing her virginity lingered: A pain left unexplained.

John distanced himself from Stanly after he violated Stella, and wanted nothing to do with him. His behavior was deplorable and evil. But Stanly valued their friendship, and refused to let it falter. John was there when his peers poked fun of him, and teased him about his ethnicity. He protected him from bullies, and defended him from harsh criticism. He was there for him all through life.

For weeks John ignored Stanly, avoiding as best he could. If he saw Stanly coming, he went in the opposite direction. But Stanly was persistent. One day he cornered John in the library at the close of the day as students prepared to leave. He begged John to forgive him promising to never drug another woman. John mellowed and agreed to exonerate only if he honored his covenant. The men shook affirming their treaty and hugged. Their friendship was rekindled, and Stanly was content. He kept his bargain with John for years.

John and Stella became good friends, but Ellen resented it. John never told Stella what Stanly did, and she never asked. They kept their relationship mutual and never associated off school premises. Ellen witnessed how close John and Stella were becoming and feared Stella might steal her boyfriend even though John insisted she was not a threat. John claimed they were good friends, nothing more. He assured Ellen he loved her.

Ellen sought to believe him, and was cordial to Stella despite her reservations. She was thrilled when Stella left the school eight months before graduation. The plant where her father worked as foreman shutdown. He was transferred to another factory in New York forcing the family to relocate. At last the rivalry for her future husband's affection had vanished.

John and Ellen married following graduation, and she blessed him with a beautiful daughter sealing their commitment. Stanly worked fulltime at Vernon Powell, a local shoe store, hoping to salvage enough money to start his own business. He dreamed of owning a jewelry store

He dated local black girls, but it never amounted to anything. He found most black women to be demanding, or saddled with a slew of children. After sewing a few wild oats, he moved on to the next prospect.

John loved his daughter unconditionally, and saw she wanted for nothing. Whatever she desired, he got for her. He was her sugar daddy, and Ellen, the disciplinarian.

Shortly proceeding graduation, John's father persuaded him to attend college to obtain a business degree. Even though he was away at college, John was there when Stanly's grandmother passed. He altered his schedule enabling him to be present at the funeral, and accompanied his friend at the burial site. He called frequently, making sure he was coping well. He knew Stanly's grandmother was like a mother. She raised him when his parents died.

John graduated with a business degree, and returned home to work with his father. Years later, Joseph, erected a plant in Wilmington Delaware leaving, John, and his wife, in charge of the Eastern Shore factory. With his father absent overseeing a new factory, John granted himself liberal leave granting his wife more responsibilities. Something his father would not permit under his helm. Joseph had John working seven days a week, learning the business inside out, and forcing him to put his education in practice to stimulate growth. With his father absent, John was able to resurrect an old tradition. The two of them started fishing again; a hobby from boyhood; a bi-monthly function Stanly treasured.

When John's daughter, Edith, turned seventeen, the two men drove to Virginia Beach to purchase jewelry wholesale. With what he salvaged from his job, and the money John gave him, Stanly had enough to acquire an abandoned jewelry store on the plaza. Still he needed start-up inventory. The former store proprietor tipped him about a place in Virginia Beach where he could purchase bulk jewelry dirt cheap. It was an offer Stanly could not pass up.

John borrowed a company van, and they set out on their quest. They arrived at their destination in no time. John pulled in front of a huge warehouse near an abandoned railroad track. A short, stocky, white man with a pot belly escorted them inside the building crammed with boxes of jewels ranging from elegant rings to exquisite necklaces and bracelets. Stanly scouted the jewels, questioning prices as he picked out what he desired. Two hours later, they made a transaction, loaded the van, and prepared for the trip home. Stanly was very pleased with his purchase. He had enough to stock his shelves and have inventory.

They were two miles from the Virginia Maryland Line when a man driving a dump truck ran a stoplight crashing into the driver's side forcing the van off the road tumbling on its side. The two men went crashing into the windshield, and knocked unconscious.

When John awaken, he was in the hospital, and Stanly was sitting beside him with bandages covering bruises sustained from the accident. John's head was wrapped in a gauze. His side ached with pain from the impact. His pelvic was sore. From what, he did not know. Perhaps his pelvic area was jammed into the steering wheel when he was thrown from his seat. He felt like hell. His vision was blurry. If only he had not volunteered to drive back, he would not have been in this predicament. He would be sitting where Stanly sat.

"My God, I feel like shit." John commented.

"Thank God we're both alive. They had to pry us loose."

"I don't remember a thing. I am sore from head to toe."

"I came to when a fireman pulled me from the car. You were still out cold when they put you on a stretcher. For a minute there, I thought you were a goner." Stanly updated him on what transpired.

A doctor wearing a white coat, holding a clip board, came into the emergency room from behind a curtain, and stationed himself beside John's bed blocking Stanly's view. "I don't know how you two survived without occurring any broken bones." He flipped through medical records. "You Mr. Bosworth, is suffering from a mild concussion. I will prescribe medication for that. In a couple days you should be fine." As he continued studying the records, he frowned.

John detected an unsettling countenance on the young man's stubby face. "Doc what is it?

"Sir you have hypertension. Are you being treated for that?"

Hypertension. His doctor never mentioned it. But then his last visit was a year ago. Whenever he planned to see his doctor, something always took preeminence causing him to reschedule his appointments; appointments he rarely kept. Besides he felt terrific. No aches or pains. Not until now. "How bad is it?" John wondered.

"Pretty high. The nurse will give you something to bring it down. But I want you to see your family doctor as soon as possible. This is something you can't take lightly.

"I'll see my doctor when I get back to the shore."

The young doctor took a deep breath. "I know you're sore and dizzy but I am going to release you into the custody of your friend." He turned recognizing Stanly. "I believe he's capable of getting you back to the shore."

Stanly was apprehensive. He thought the doctor was acting prematurely. "Are you sure he will be able to make it home safely?"

"Once he start moving about and getting dressed, he will be fine. That gauze around his head may be deceiving. It's covering cuts and bruises sustained from his head going into the windshield," the doctor explained. "I am going to leave so he can get dressed. I am discharging him as of now." He disappeared behind the curtain.

John eased himself to the side of the bed. The dizziness evaporated. Stanly helped him dress while they talked. The more he moved, the better he felt as the doctor prophesied.

"The van was totaled. They towed the vehicle to a lot about five miles from here. A place called Berry's Towing Yard." Stanly started the conversation.

"I'll contact the insurance company and let them handle it." John said stirring about. "What about the jewels?"

"I rented another vehicle, and paid some guys to transfer the merchandise to the rental."

John slipped into his briefs and pants. "When did you do all this?"

"The minute the doctor released me, and was able to get to a phone." Stanly helped John slip into his socks and shoes. He noticed he hand trouble bending over. "You've been out for several hours. You slept through a battery of exams and test. That's probably because they had you sedated."

"Where is the rental van now?" John asked.

"In the hospital parking garage. The guys who made the transfer parked it there, and left me the keys."

Ninety minutes later Stanly dropped John off at his doorstep, and went to his recently bought store where he unloaded and stocked his shelves. Ellen was shocked when her husband walked through the door with his head wrapped in a gauze, taking baby steps. The pain was receding, but it still hampered his mobility. Immediately Ellen escorted him to a plush, comfortable recliner in the parlor propping up his feet. He told her about the accident.

"Thank God you're OK." Ellen was grateful her husband was alive.

A week later John made arrangements to see his doctor at Pine Bluff Medical Center. His doctor, a Nigerian, fellowshipped in the examining room after a nurse weighed him, calibrated his height, and procured his vital signs. The elderly, bald headed man fashioning designer jeans accented with a dashiki knowledge John with a handshake. It had been months since he last seem him. He sat on a stool, glanced at a chart, and then concentrated on John.

"I see you have high blood pressure." The doctor remarked.

"That's what they tell me."

The Nigerian scooted to John, and started unwrapping the gauze. "I see you were in an accident." He removed the gauze and tossed it into a nearby trash can. "Looks good. A few scars, but they will vanish."

"What about my blood pressure?" John changed the conversation to his immediate concern.

"I see what the doctor at the hospital prescribed, but I feel you need something far stronger. We have to get this under control." He replied.

"Ok. What do you want to do?"

The doctor scratched his bald head. "I want you to try this for a few months." He scribbled something on a slip, and handed it to John. "I want you to go to the lab and get blood work." He quickly checked items on a form, signed it, and handed it to John. "I want to see you in two months."

John went to the lab in three days later after fasting for twelve hours. He took the blood pressure medication as prescribed. Three weeks later his ability to sustain an erection became prevalent. He was not able to please his wife as often as he desired. Their love making session dwindled from three times a week to once a week. When he saw the doctor two months later, he told him about his impotence. The doctor prescribed another type of medicine and scheduled him for a follow up appointment three weeks later. John's sexual life improved dramatically. Everything was back to normal so he thought. Suddenly he was overcome by throbbing headaches, and he could feel his heart pounding in his chest when he rested at night. When he went back to his physician for a checkup, his blood pressure was worse than before. He was on the brick of having a stroke. Without hesitation, the doctor instantly placed him back on the medicine he administered previously. He explained how important it was for him to remain on the recommended dosage.

"I know the medicine is impairing your sex life, but if you don't take it, you will certainly stroke out. And I know you don't want that." He went over the side effects in depth. "What's going to happen is this. There will be times, you will be able to have sex. Perhaps not as intensely or as frequently as you wish."

John didn't want to hear that. He called Stanly and abreast him of his condition. "What am I going to do?" John asked. "Ellen is a high strung woman. She likes to have sex on a regular basis."

"Well, in the past few weeks you haven't been able to grant her desires. Have she complained?" Stanly was curious.

John thought. *No, she had not complained or expressed dissatisfaction. She had not pressured him. If they made love, fine. If not, that was fine also. Perhaps he was placing more emphasis on their sex life than she was. Maybe his ego was at stake. Maybe it was more about him than it was about her. His manhood was in jeopardy. He felt inadequate because he couldn't please himself through his wife. There was only one solution to his problem. He knew his responsibility. When the conditions were ideal, and he was fit to have relations with his wife, he would give it his best shot. He would not hold back. He would make love to her until he was exhausted. He would please her as best he could. He would please himself as well.*

As Stanly's business thrived, John habitually invited him to his house for various celebrations. As a result, Stanly frequently encountered Ellen. They became acquainted on a personal level. Stanly found her to be pleasant, cordial and titillating. But she was not a housewife. He never saw her dust or mop. She hired a maid for that amongst other assigned duties. But then she was wealthy and domestic matters were insignificant. Running the business was her priority.

Stanly was cajoled by his best friend's wife, but struggled to control his feelings. Ellen was gorgeous and alluring. It was awful his friend was lacking in the bedroom. Aware of John's dysfunction, made it arduous to regulate his urges. His hormones were in overdrive. The more he saw Ellen, the more he hankered her, but she never encouraged him. She kept their association formal, and he constantly reminded himself Ellen was banned.

Stanly acquired a bad habit a year after opening his store. Customarily he had a few beers, and a couple cigarettes before retiring, enough to relax and unwind. He hired an associate, an elderly white woman with a stern face and silver hair, to assist with running the store while he spent countless hour writing ads promoting his products, and searching for unique jewelry pieces to sell. He kept himself superfluously busy.

Soon one drink turned into bottles of liquor, and two cigarettes turned into a pack. Before he knew it, he was a drunkard, and a nicotine addict. Still he remained sober enough to oversee the operation of his store. Weekends he was drunk from sunrise to sunset. Alcohol, the devil's brew, sparked his desire for the forbidden fruit. He lusted a woman not his own. The demon in his head said, "Go ahead. Take her. He can't please her like you can." Dreams about her naked body revolved in his imagination like a carousel. Often he awaken perspiring heavily and feeling Horney.

John hitched the boat to the back of his truck, and they journeyed to Rehoboth fishing pier with fishing gear and earth worms in the trunk. Hours later they pulled onto the pier and set the boat lose in the water. They jumped aboard and prepared for a relaxing day at sea. When they were deep in the ocean, John turned off the motor allowing the vessel to drift while they slung rods overboard. John sipped on one bottle of beer for hours while Stanly guzzled down Colt Forty-fives nonstop. Luckily he was not the designated driver. Fish began biting, and they took turns reeling them in, dropping the squirming catch into a cooler packed with ice, and reeled up for another catch. After stocking the cooler with spot and trout, they headed home.

John took the fish to his house. Ellen was sitting at the kitchen table reading a novel when John walked in with Stanly staggering behind. He dumped the fish and ice in the sink taking the cooler with him. Stanly sank into a chair across from Ellen.

"Who do you think is going to clean them? It certainly won't be me." Ellen fussed.

"I'll scale and prep them when I get back," John promised. "I'm going to put the boat in the garage and then take Stanly home. Fix him a cup of coffee to sober up." He left for the garage.

"Sure." Ellen whispered as her husband departed. Then she studied Stanly. He was definitely drunk. A sight she grown accustomed to. She went to the brewing coffee pot and poured coffee into two mugs. "Stanly how do you want your coffee?"

"Black," Stanly slurred.

Ellen placed a mug before Stanly and left one for herself. She filled Stanly's mug halfway for fear of spillage. His eye to hand coordination was off, and she did not want him to burn himself. At that exact moment, the phone rang. She abandoned her coffee to answer the phone. It was her secretary with an update concerning a scheduled with the union. "So that's what they want." She listened for her response.

While Ellen talked on the phone, Stanly reached into his pocket retrieving a small packet, poured a powdery substance into her drink, and stirred it with her spoon. Then he laid the spoon on a napkin. A few minutes later Ellen returned to her chair and sipped her coffee.

The next day was Sunday. Stanly called Ellen requesting she meet him at his plaza store. He knew John was away on a business trip with his mother. Ellen went to the store, not knowing why. Stanly escorted her inside, closed the door, and bolted it. Without whispering a word, he led her into a back room where a cot was set up, a place he napped during the day.

Ellen undress without being asked. Her hands were being manipulated by an invisible force. Stanly did likewise. Her perfect, and luscious breast, aroused him. He gestured toward the neatly made cot, and she laid there without hesitation. Then he straddled himself between her long legs shoving his monstrous erection inside her succulent flesh. He sucked her stiff nipples, and ran his hairy hands down her enthralling hips. He was in heaven. No woman delighted him like Ellen. He held out for as long as possible before erupting. He wanted the magic to last forever. It was better than his fantasy.

He told Ellen to go home, and forget about what transpired. She did as instructed. Stanly felt guilty seducing his friend's wife. It was a stupid move. He swore to himself never to seek Ellen's services again. Then he flushed his mind altering drugs down the toilet.

Ellen forgot about her first encounter with Stanly. Yet, she worried about her marriage when her husband failed to seduce her for weeks. She figured he was seeing another woman. And then she harnessed the courage confronting him about his lack of interest. He confessed he was taking blood pressure medicine that affected his ability to perform as frequently as she desired. Ellen understood but was left sexually frustrated. She grown accustomed to having sex at least twice a week. She was attracted to Stanly. She caught herself watching as he climbed into the truck beside her husband before departing on fishing expeditions fashioning a muscle shirt exposing his curly chest hairs, and tight shorts revealing his muscular legs. Her eyes traveled to the massive bulge between his thighs titillating her curiosity. The more she saw him, the more she lusted for him. The evil spirit within said, "Go for it. Your husband can't do anything for you. Enjoy yourself while you can."

Late one afternoon, she paraded into Stanly's store after he dismissed his last customer, and embraced him vehemently with a kiss before he could catch his breath. Stanly was shocked, but quickly bolted the door, and lowered the closed sign. She could no longer restrain herself from touching him. She ripped his shirt lose exposing his hairy torso. She sought him in the worst way. That kiss was the inauguration of a consenting affair that would linger for months.

Edith was seventeen when her grandfather died. It was a day she would never forget. Her grandpa Joseph, and grandmother, Bessel, attended her graduation at the Wicomico Youth & Civic Center. Her mother, Ellen, and her father, John, were seated on the fourth center row from the stage beside her grandparents when she walked across the stage to accept her diploma. Her grandpa, Joseph, snapped pictures, blinding nearby spectators, while the rest of her family applauded, and stood honoring her achievement as she rejoined her class hugging her diploma. They were proud of her, and by right, they had just cause.

After the ceremony, her family connected with her in the congested lobby, and took turns showering her with hugs and kisses. It was their special day. A celebration they would never forget. She told them, she was going to a graduation party with her classmates before coming home. Ellen understood, and informed her, the family was going to Ponderosa Steak House before retiring for the evening. Her grandpa Joseph insisted on taking snapshots of her with the family with his Polaroid camera. He wanted photographs for the family album. She obliged by posing with each member of her family.

Later she learned, on route to ponderosa, her grandfather sustained sharp pains in his chest, and they rushed him to the hospital where he was admitted. Sometime during the night, with his wife, son and daughter-in-law at his bedside, he slipped into a coma and died. The doctors proclaimed he had a heart attack.

Bessel took her husband's death hard. Joseph was an epitome of good health. His last physical was glowing. No hypertension, blood work was perfect, weight within the ideal range, nothing out of the ordinary. How could he have a heart attack? What triggered this disease? It was an instant replay of her mother recuperating from a successful surgery, and them sudden death.

It grieved her immensely when they lowered Joseph into the ground. She thought her heart would burst. Flashbacks of her mother being lowered into her vault taunted her. She wept uncontrollably and was taken from the graveyard by her son. Nothing anyone said or did could ease the loss. They were together for fifty-plus years. She could not imagine life without him.

As time passed, she learned to cope with the emptiness, accepting the reality her companion was gone. This time she was stronger than before. She was her own therapist. To compensate for the hollowness, she returned to Wilmington Delaware, took an active role running the plant Joseph created, and appointed her son president of the Eastern Shore Division.

Chapter One

On August 22, 1970, Edith Bosworth walked into Blackwell Library through automatic doors. She was on a mission. The campus bookstore sold the last copy of a philosophy text she needed. A freckle-faced girl at the register, promised a shipment was expected in a few days, but she was impatient. She searched the periodical cabinet. Bingo! There it was. She scribbled reference numbers on a sticky, and mounted spiral stairs to the second floor.

Edith enrolled in Salisbury State College against her parents' wishes. They preferred she attended University of Maryland Eastern Shore, a prominently black college. But as long as she earned a business degree, they were lenient. Most of her friends registered for Salisbury State College, and she wanted to be with them.

Rarely did she date or participate in social functions. Education was her priority. Evenings were spent in libraries studying for test or reading textbooks. Her parents expected great things for her, and she refused to be a disappointment.

It was a humid afternoon. Perspiration sprinkled her forehead. Soon the central air would sponge moisture from her face leaving her cool. She scanned rows of literature halting where the edition was filed, and mounted a footstool attempting to seize the book from the top shelf. A hairy hand grasped the textbook presenting it to her. When she swirled about, she was greeted by a distinguished man with hazel, blue eyes, curly black hair, a pleasant smile, and smelling of old spice.

"Thank you." She was appreciative.

"You're Edith Bosworth," the man said, recognizing her.

Recently he read an editorial in the Daily Times identifying Edith Bosworth as the granddaughter of the late Joseph Bosworth, the founder of Bosworth Industries. The article stated her father, John Bosworth, was appointed President of Bosworth following the death of his father. Bosworth Industries was celebrating forty-eight years of operation making the Bosworth's the wealthiest black family on the Eastern Shore.

She recognized Thomas Guy from an autobiography on the back of his book. He was a famous author who frequently appeared on the Dinah Shore, and Mike Douglas show promoting his latest novels.

"And you're Thomas Guy, the writer," she commented. "My cousin is a fan. She has a collection of all your books."

Thomas was impressed. "Well, it's not that many. Five to be exact," he pointed out.

Together they paced to the elevator.

"May I ask what brings you to the shore?" She was curious.

Thomas sighed, and replied, "Do research for my book. Salisbury will be the stage for my novel."

"I see," she remarked. Seeing Salisbury in print would be inspirational.

"Are you going to class now?" he asked as he pressed a button summoning the elevator.

"No. I am off for the day," she confessed. *Thomas was extremely handsome. His photograph did him no justice.*

"Would you accompany me to the student union for a bite?" he asked. "I would like to ask you a few questions, like, where people hang out for fun."

She giggled boarding the elevator. If he desired to know the trendy spots in Salisbury, she was the last person to consult. She came to college to learn, not to socialize. When she graduated from James M Bennett High, her mother convinced her there would be ample time for romance after she obtained a degree; a degree to run the family business.

"Well, I do not hang out as you put it," she emphasized. "I am a homebody. But I can give you a tour of the city."

"I've been to the Ecclesia," he informed her. "But I wonder how aristocratic people entertain themselves. I'm sure you have fun despite the fact you claim to be a homebody."

She smiled, and thought silently. *Thomas was charming as well as handsome. It was awful he was older than she. But then, should age matter.*

"I suppose you have a point."

Weeks following their coincidental encounter, they quickly graduated from guide and tourist to close friends. She put aside her former priorities, and lowered her standards to accommodate a friend.

Frequented they went to Boulevard Theater where they discovered they shared a love for historical films. There she introduced Thomas to her Cousin Bernard, a short, chubby, dark-skinned man in his late teens who was accompanied by a skinny, light complexion girl who looked old enough to be his mother. She told Bernard Thomas was new to the area, and she was familiarizing him to the shore.

Bernard greeted him with a handshake, and replied courteously, "Glad to meet you man."

His companion tugged his shirtsleeves, getting his attention. It was their turn to purchase tickets and go inside.

She drove him to skate-Land, and gave him skating lessons. He swore he never skated a day in his life. He was a city boy, and the sport was alien to him. For the first hour, he stayed in the floor instead of on his feet. As the evening progressed, he mastered his balance and rolled about smoothly. He accidently bumped into her cousin Joseph almost knocking him on his buttocks. Joseph was holding his fiancé's hand as they circled the inner ring dancing to music under flashing carousel lights.

"I'm sorry sir," Thomas apologized.

Quickly she introduced Joseph, and defended her friend. "Thomas is new in town, and has never staked before. I was teaching him to skate. So don't be mad with him, be mad with me."

The men talked briefly getting acquainted, and then Joseph skated into the crowd with his future bride.

Twice a week they feasted at Pappy's Pizzeria. There she introduced Thomas to her cousin Sarah, a stout lady in her mid-twenties wearing a small afro with bushy eyebrows. Sarah made it her business to serve them whenever she worked. She called her after she met Thomas inquiring the seriousness of their relationship. She insisted they were friends, but she knew Sarah chose not to believe that, and it was a matter of time before she called her mother.

At the Salisbury Park, they ran into her cousin Alex. He was scouting the area on feet when they ran into each other as they crossed the bridge over a tiny stream. Alex had little to say. He was on duty. He asked her about school, and who was her friend. She told him, and the men exchanged a high-five palm slap.

Alex was a tall, slim, high yellow man who could pass for a model in his uniform; a uniform he loved wearing. Alex suggested they get together sometime over a few drinks before sliding into a parked squad car with a uniformed young lady in the passenger seat, and drove away.

She made provisions for Thomas to tour Ocean City before it closed for the season. They rode every ride in the resort, laughing and carrying on like teenagers. It was there Thomas met her cousin Eddie. He was operating the Fairest Wheel. It was a busy night. Eddie shoulder hugged him, and kept moving. A crowd materialized at the ride waiting keenly to board. Later she informed Thomas her, and Eddie, were like brother and sister instead of cousins.

Upon his request, she drove him to the Ecclesia Nightclub where they encountered her cousins sitting around a table snickering and laughing. When they saw her with Thomas, they beckoned them to their table. Everyone was shocked seeing her in a club with an attractive, mature, escort; she was diffidently out of her element.

Her cousins introduced themselves. Charlene gestured a welcoming handshake identifying herself. She was short, petite, fashioning a jury curl, and two dimples that surfaced when she smiled. Ethel was tall, and massive, wearing a tight, leisure outfit, showing imperfection in her shape. She introduced herself as she sucked a screwdriver through a straw. Lastly he met Cherry who favored her. They could pass for twins. The only thing that separated them was her cousin Cherry had red hair.

She and Thomas, were like teenagers enjoying each other's company. Subconsciously she housed romantic feelings for him. She sensed he wanted more thank friendship, but was reluctant to pursue his intentions. Perhaps the age difference was a hindrance.

She was reluctant to introduce Thomas to her parents. Her father was no problem, but her mother was another issue. She required time to fathom the energy to confront Ellen. She was extremely protective, and there was no telling how she might react learning her precious daughter was keeping

4

company with a man eight years her senior. She might throw a conniption forbidding her from seeing him. That was the last thing she wanted.

As their sightseeing dwindled, they got to know each other personally. Thursday evenings they bowled at Cherokee Lanes, and dined at Johnny & Sammy's Restaurant. It was there Thomas presented her a synopsis of his childhood.

He was the product of an interracial marriage. His mother was a short, feisty, redheaded Irishwoman who loved jogging, and playing tennis. His father was a slim, black man from Harlem who loved tennis, and jogged every afternoon after work. His parents met on a tennis court in the Bronx. Their courtship was brief, and had led to an expedient marriage.

They procured a house in Long Island, where he was born. He spent his childhood in the city streets playing stickball with the boys in his neighborhood. He attended a public school where his father taught English. His mother was a registered nurse who worked the third shift at a state hospital. Before he went to school, his mother saw he had a nutritious breakfast. He had scrambled eggs with melted pepper jack cheese, toast buttered with strawberry jam, three strips of crispy bacon, and a small glass of freshly squeezed orange juice. At night, before he fell asleep, she recited fairy tales from a huge Mother Goose Book on his nightstand.

When he started elementary school, his mother hired a black woman to cook and clean. She started missing time from work. His father accompanied her to routine doctor visits. Eventually, she monopolized her free time in bed reading magazines, or relaxing in a recliner watching soaps. The feisty woman he called momma dwindled before him.

When he turned eight, her health progressively worsened. She quit her job, and became a hermit. Her vision was poor, her walking was unsteady, and she had frequent accidents. His father assisted with her daily living skills. She became a cripple. Her appetite diminished. He watched her lose weight, and he worried. She became a skeleton; a small picture of existence. He prayed for a healing. Each day she grew weaker, and less mobile. When he questioned his father about her health, he simply said, she had a rare blood disorder, but the doctors were doing everything they could to help. Soon she became an invalid. She stopped talking, and refused to eat. She was hopeless, fighting a losing battle. Still, he expected a miracle. His mother taught him God could do anything.

His father hired nurses twenty-four seven. Eventually she became unresponsive with a distant stare in her weak eyes, and lost contact with the people she loved. A year later she died. He stopped praying, and believing. How could a loving God take away his mother? It was not fair. He became an atheist. His father was devastated. His aunt Bell, his father's sister, sacrificed her apartment in Queens, and moved in with them. She was a spinster. She was more than delighted to support her brother in his hour of sorrow. She became his foster mother. On his twelfth birthday, his father decided to abandon New York, and launch his career in another state. They reestablished roots in Virginia. His aunt accompanied them. In a new state, his father got a fresh outlook. The place where he lost his wife was miles behind him; he began a new life. Time and distance eased the emptiness. He submerged himself in his teaching, and focused on being a terrific father. He took him on countless fishing trips, and accompanied him on special school functions. During the summer, they toured numerous recreational resorts across the country.

He became a popular teacher; the students adored him, and he cherished them. He spent his afternoons tutoring students. There was scarcely enough hours in the day to achieve all his goals, but he was happy.

When it came for Edith to divulge her past, she was hesitant. Thomas's life was moving and sad. She was an only child with the world at her disposal. She craved for nothing. Whatever she sought, her father got. She was a rich, spoiled kid. All she could remember was playing in the backyard of their big house on Jersey Road with her cousins who spent more time at her house than they did at home. Her aunt Bessie supervised them while her parents worked. As long as they played quietly without fussing of fighting, Bessie had no grumbles. Her only requirement was they had to be in the house before dark. Her mother had a thing about children being outside when the sun went down, and her aunt Bessie honored her demands. Her grandfather visited frequently bearing treats like ice cream sandwiches and soda pop. On cool summer afternoons, he would play baseball with the boys in the huge lot behind their house. He was the referee calling all the shots. For the girls, he constructed a gigantic play house where they could escape, and play housewives. The house was furnished with an electric stove that worked, and a kitchen sink with running water, and small furniture. Edith and her female cousins prized the house. It was a miracle, a wonderland of fun; a place where the girls could hide, and practice being women.

At times her grandpa Joseph gathered his grandchildren along with other children in the neighborhood in the back of his huge Chevy truck, and took them crabbing or fishing in Quantico or Crisfield. Afterward they brought whatever they caught home, cooked it outside under the huge pavilion, and invited the community over to feast. Joseph considered himself to be a stupendous chef, and this gave him the opportunity to flaunt his culinary skills.

Finally she could no longer hide Thomas from her mother. Friends and relatives seen them patrolling Salisbury like an inseparable couple. Gossip was she was dating a famous author. The rumor reached her mother's ears. Ellen revealed she was cognizant she was courting a young man several years older than her. Her exact words were, "I hear you've been seeing an older man. A young author by the name of Thomas Guy."

She was lost for words. "We're friends. He's new in town. I was just showing him around," she managed to say evenly.

"Friends you say." Ellen was apprehensive. "You've been spending a lot of time together for just friends. Your cousins tell me you're a twosome. They say you're devoted." The cousin she was referring to was Sarah.

"Mother we're friends, nothing more," she insisted, and headed upstairs to her bedroom when her mother blocked her path.

"Edith, don't do anything you might regret. You have your whole career ahead of you. Be careful. Yes, I know he's cute, and charming, and all that, but, you're still young. Don't be foolish," she lectured.

She knew what she was implying. She was questioning her virginity. Secretly she wanted to seduce Thomas, but she always played it safe. Per her request, they met in public places. If they were alone, she might succumb to temptation, and bare the guilt. "You don't have that to worry about." She left her mother standing at the foot of the stairs, and went upstairs to her bedroom.

Ellen was an attractive black woman in her forties who always sported pantsuits and rarely wore a dress. She liked her husband, but she loved Bosworth Industries. Bosworth was in her blood since she was a child. Her husband was a part of the package. In the beginning she thought she loved John, and maybe she did, but circumstances changed. They lived in the same house, and she played the role of the good wife. Since John was a quiet man, she was uncertain of his feelings. At times he was affectionate, but she wondered if it was genuine.

Ellen studied the photograph of Thomas Guy on the back of his latest novel, and smiled to herself. He definitely was a striking fellow, a gorgeous prospect. No wonder Edith was attracted to him. Hell, half the women in Salisbury would die to have him as a trophy. But Thomas's timing was wrong. College was her daughter's first priority. It was her obligation to obtain a business degree, and ultimately coup the family dynasty. No one or nothing could hinder that. Thomas might be the ideal prize for the moment, but tomorrow a more suitable suitor might appear; someone to help her run the dynasty.

She muddled her spacious vestibule, and grasped the phone fastened to the wall. She contacted an old comrade. "Todd, I have someone I want you to check out. His a famous writer by the name of Thomas Guy."

Chapter Two

Edith and Thomas decided to take a trip to Sight and Sound in Lancaster, Pennsylvania, a three hour drive from Salisbury. They would spend a night in the Steam Boat Motel, and attend the morning show. She was so excited about the invitation, she forgot about her safe code.

The question loomed, could she suppress her desires? It stunned her, Thomas requested her company. It probably shocked him when she accepted.

Weeks prior to their trip, she hungered to kiss, and embrace him. She lusted for his touch, but was cautious. She valued their friendship, and was afraid to jeopardize it.

What if he was playing her for what he could get? He was an older man, and she a young, inexperienced, attractive, naive girl. Immediately she dismissed her negative thoughts. Thomas was a gentleman. He would never take advantage of her. Sure he desired her. She could tell by the bulge in his pants when they cuddled. Equally her flesh burned for him, but she ignored her attraction. If he desired her, he would have to be the initiator. Even if he did, she might be reluctant to give in.

When they arrived at the motel, it was late in the evening. Thomas suggested they dine at the Cracker Barrel Cafe a block from the motel. She was famished. The last good meal she ate was a big breakfast entree from Me Donald's before leaving Wicomico County.

They tossed their suitcases into the closet, and raced for the car. She jumped behind the steering wheel. Thomas drove to Lancaster. It was her turn to chauffeur him. Not only that, she loved maneuvering his Cadillac through city traffic. He tossed her the keys, and navigated her to Cracker Barrel.

9

The café was packed. They waited in the lobby for a table. She rested her head on his broad shoulder, and rubbed his knees. Thomas draped his arm around her shoulder, and drew her close. Being near Thomas bought her warmth and tranquility. The journey to Lancaster was lengthy, and she almost dozed off waiting for a table. A hostess wearing a red dress escorted them to a booth, and handed them a menu. Later a young girl with an accent, and a pin in her blond hair, took their order. Thomas instructed the waitress, they wanted their drinks served with their order.

She permitted Thomas to order for both of them since she was indecisive. He ordered a half rack of ribs with French fries and turnip greens. The ribs were delicious but lacking in comparison to her Grandpa Joseph's barbecued spareribs.

After dinner, they revisited the motel. She noticed there was two king size beds, something she overlooked earlier. She would sleep on one, and Thomas would sleep on the other. They would not share a bed. Temptation of being together was resolved. Thomas made the reservations. Obviously he had no intentions of testing fate.

She waited patiently while Thomas showered, and changed into his pajamas. When he came out, she smiled. He was cute in his flannel pajamas and slippers. She wanted to finger his chest. Instead she plucked a gown from her luggage, and took her turn in the spacious bathroom.

She stripped, dumped her clothes into a hamper, lathered with liquid soap, hosed herself with the shower nozzle, and dried off with a bath towel. Then she slipped into her gown, brushed her hair a hundred strokes, and rejoined Thomas.

He was lying across the bed watching the news. She scooted underneath the comforter. The room was chilly, and her bare feet were cold. She felt heat, seep into the room, but she was still cold from the shower.

"Anything interesting?" she asked not caring.

"Interest rates still high."

She remembered her mother. She deserted notifying her pertaining to the trip with Thomas to Pennsylvania. Instead, she misled her to believe she was going to Sight and Sound with a few girls from her sorority. They were always going places together. She coached her cousins to validate her lie.

When the news went off, Thomas turned the volume down, and sat on side the bed facing Edith. "What time do you want to leave in the morning?"

She almost fell asleep waiting for the news to go off. "What time is the first show?"

"Ten o'clock, I believe," he said.

"Nine o'clock, I guess. If that's alright with you," she replied.

Thomas smiled and gazed at her. She could tell by the gleam in his eyes, he lusted her. She was tempted by his muscular structure, and hypnotic eyes. The scent of his body stimulated unsettled desires. They shared many things together, but not their feelings. The subject was taboo.

"I'm glad you came," Thomas renewed the conversation.

She sat up leaning against her pillow. "I always wanted to come here. Mom and Dad come here a lot. They said the shows are marvelous."

Thomas took a deep breath mustering the courage to make a request. "Would you mind if we cuddled. I see you're shivering. Let me hold you for a few minutes until you warm up. What do you say?"

She debated if his intentions were honorable. *What harm could there be in cuddling? She was always clinging, and leaning against him anyway for warmth and support. Often she referred to him as her teddy bear. How was this any different? Besides, if he got fresh, she knew how to fend him off. The question was, would she?*

"Sure. Why not," she granted his wish.

He crawled in bed, and drew her close to his chest. The fuzziness of his body hairs, and firmness of his muscles, excited her. He massaged her back with his free hand, and rested his chin on her head.

"Does that feel better?" he asked as he covered them with the comforter.

"Feels good," she responded as she drummed her fingers down his thick thighs.

"So you've never been here before?"

"No." She whispered enjoying the texture of his body.

Thomas took a deep breath. "Edith, I've become fond of you in the last few weeks. I like being with you."

"I enjoy being with you," she confessed. She sat up unexpectedly, and kissed him briefly on the lips. "I'm sorry," she apologized. She acted in a moment of weakness.

He drew her close, and kissed her passionately. He held her in his arms for several minutes before letting go.

"We better stop before it's too late," he suggested.

He started to leave when she pulled him back. "Don't leave," she managed to say. "You stay on your side of the bed, and I will stay on my side. But don't leave. I want you beside me tonight."

They both rolled to the opposite side of the bed, and buried themselves underneath the bedding. They closed their eyes listening to the television. As the night progressed, they fell asleep with the urge to unite.

When morning came, the sun penetrated the room through opened curtains. She opened her eyes finding Thomas sitting in a chair, fully dressed, and scribbling in a notebook.

"What time is it?" she asked, wiping sleep from her eyes.

"Almost nine. We still have time," he assured her.

"Let me get dressed. I don't want to be late."

She jumped from the comfortable bed, and dashed into the bathroom where she showered, dressed and groomed in one hour. Then she joined Thomas who slipped into his coat, and assisted her into her coat, before going into the autumn air.

As they drove to the theater, she could not resist rubbing Thomas's thigh. "About last night," she started.

Thomas found it difficult to concentrate with her caressing him, yet he relished the stimulation. "Edith I want you. You know that. Yet I don't want you to do anything until you're ready. Besides, I get the feeling you've never been with a man."

Thomas was correct. She was innocent. Sure she courted a few boys in high school, but she kept their relationship platonic. When they sought more, she axed their affiliation. When she gave herself to a man, it had to be someone she adored; someone like Thomas. "Is that so terrible?" She asked innocently.

He squeezed her roaming fingers. "No. I love your innocence. I love you," he confessed without realizing it.

The words spilled out, and she knew then his feelings were sincere. That twinkle in his eyes, his gentle touch, and the warmth of his presence made her realize he was the chosen one. His confession was comforting and assuring. Now it was her tern.

"I love you too. I think I fell for you the first time we met," she said without curtailing her affixation.

They drove to the theater in silence enjoying each other's Company, aware of each other's cravings. Her breast hankered for his touch, and she knew he thirsted for her eager hips.

The lot was swarming with buses and cars of excited tourist. Thomas parked the vehicle close to the entrance and together they went inside amongst the mob holding hands. Following a ten minute shuffle in a long line, they presented their tickets to an elderly lady who gave the ticket back with directions.

Edith loved the show, Noah, a biblical play. She was impressed by the actors, and how well the animals cooperated. It was a breathtaking performance. Thomas had been there before, yet he too was still impressed by the special effects. It was difficult to imagine how the cast could pull off such a terrific performance year after year with few if any mistakes. Not to mention most of the actors were college students making their premier appearance.

It was late in the afternoon when the show concluded. They went to a smorgasbord restaurant close to the theater. As anticipated, it was filled to capacity. They waited fifteen minutes to be seated. They aborted their winter garments on the back of their chairs, grabbed a plate, made a selection from the food bar, and returned to their table. The food was delicious. Thomas ate until his stomach cramped, and she ate until she could not eat another bite.

It was dark when they returned to the motel. He drew her into his arms and kissed her until her breast popped out of her blouse. Then he tilted her across the bed, straddled himself between her legs, fingered her hair, and fondled her excited nipples.

She pushed him up, slipped out of her bra and unbuttoned her dress allowing him to bury his head between her breasts.

She wanted him. He stood up and she unbuckled his pants watching his slacks drop to the floor. A huge erection inflated his briefs. She removed his underwear revealing a gigantic penis. Quickly she slipped out of her clothes and nestled on the bed naked.

He mounted himself on top of her, and slid his erection inside her soft virgin body. She screamed lightly as he held his hardness inside, ripping her apart, causing great pain. She froze taking deep breathes hoping the discomfort lessened. Gently he pranced over her until her hymen opened saturating his manhood. Each time he penetrated exploring untouched territory, she jerked and moaned as she squeezed his vibrating butt praying it would end soon.

She felt him exploding inside refusing to pullout. He remained inside her warm flesh until he was exhausted and broke out in a sweat. Then he rolled on his back gasping for breath. His penis was limp and moistened with her innocence.

At once she dashed into the bathroom to wash. She knew what happened and it did not frighten her. Thomas took her virginity. Now she was his property.

As she showered, she recalled what her cousins said. The first time you do it, it will hurt. How right they were. When Thomas entered her, it hurt something terrible. The pain was excruciating even though he was gentle. She was relieved when he rolled off her quivering body allowing her to convalesce from the orientation. Her cousins promised it would not be as painful the next time. She hoped they were right.

That night they laid in bed naked holding each other. Thomas did not seduce her even though she knew he wanted to. She wanted to give herself to him, but her body needed rest.

The next day, she awakened at the crack of dawn, and packed her belongings in a suitcase while Thomas remained in bed with the sheet pulled back revealing his hairy body and limp penis. As she looked at Thomas, her body grew warm with lust. Then she remembered the pain. Was she ready for the experience again? Perhaps her cousins were right. Maybe it would not hurt as badly the second time. There was only one way to find out.

She removed her robe, and crawled into bed next to Thomas. She caressed his hairy chest, and kissed the corner of his mouth.

He opened his eyes. Instantly his midsection inflated. She drew him close to her excited body encouraging him to enter her. He pulled to his pounding chest. Then he rolled on top of her taking charge. He repeatedly penetrated her and she held firm to his vibrating buttocks. The passion and magic lasted for twenty minutes, and then he climaxed. But this time she held him close to for five minutes before allowing him to rise, and go to the bathroom. A few minutes later she joined him in the shower, and they washed each other with the same soap, and dried off with the same towel.

She slept on the ride back to Salisbury. It was a memorable vacation. She parted a girl, and returned a woman; a woman for Thomas. She belonged to him. Whenever he beckoned, she would come. They were an item; partners forever. It was wonderful being in love.

They passed autumn leaves littering side streets and meadows on the journey to Salisbury.

Chapter Three

It was midnight when they reached the eastern shore. At a rest-stop in Easton, she telephoned her mother from a phone booth alerting her she would be home within the hour. She prayed her cousins reiterated the fib pertaining to an alleged trip with her sorority girlfriends. If she had an inkling of the truth, she would be furious. As it was, she was not thrilled about her courting an older man.

Thomas dropped her off in front of a dorm. They both agreed to leave her vehicle there as a ploy to substantiate her story. She kissed him, not wanting to leave, and pledged to meet at English Grill for breakfast, Thomas' favorite place. She slid into her car and drove home which was five minutes from the college.

When she got home, the house was dark. She pondered if her mother was peering indiscreetly from behind a curtain. She turned the car off and made her way to the porch leading to the decorated door.

Indiscreetly she unlocked the door, crept into the dimmed foyer, tiptoed upstairs to her bedroom, and shut her door. The room was tidy and clean thanks to the maid who visited three times a week. She undressed and crawled into bed. She dreamed about sleeping in Thomas's arms.

Morning came abruptly triggering her to awaken tired and evil. It had been a long ride home. She wanted to close her eyes and sleep for another hour but that was not possible. Another semester was rapidly ending and she had to study for upcoming exams.

A light knock cracked her silence.

"Who is it?" She prayed it was not her mother.

"Me," her father whispered.

She flopped back the thin sheet. "Just a minute."

"I just want to let you know breakfast is ready."

"I will be there shortly," she promised.

They usually had breakfast together before her parents went to work and she went to school. It was a tradition.

She showered in her private bathroom, dressed for the day, and finished grooming at her vanity. She remembered her prior engagement with Thomas. She would a glass of juice and toast. That would suffice her parent's morning communion.

She procured her place at the prepared dining room table. Her father was hidden behind the newspaper, and her mother studied her as she nibbled her toast.

"How was the trip?" she asked calmly.

Evidently she was preferring to her sorority outing. "It was wonderful. We enjoyed it."

"I am sure you did." Ellen awkwardly commented.

"Mom I really have an early class this morning. I'm going to have a piece of toast and call it breakfast. I hope you won't mind."

Ellen cleared her throat. "Before you leave, there is a piece of advice I have for you," she said evenly without removing her eyes from her daughter.

She was nervous. "What is it mother?"

"I want you to concentrate on your studies, and less on other curricular activities, such as Thomas Guy. I know you say you're just friends, but I think it's more than that. I want you to stop seeing him."

She was shocked. "Mother I am eighteen. You can't dictate my life. I am not a child." She was surprised she had the gumption to confront her mother.

"I know you and Thomas went to Sight and Sound together. If he can con you into spending an elicit week-end of God only knows what, what else will he lower you into?" Ellen said in a firm, scolding voice.

John, her father, peeped from behind the paper but said nothing. It was a mother daughter battle and he declined intervening. He acted as an invisible bystander, and resumed reading his paper.

"He did not con me. I went willingly." The secret was out. The question was, who squealed.

"Are you curious how I knew?" Ellen asked.

"Yes," she mumbled afraid of the answer.

"When you told me about the trip, I contacted the girls you vacationed with last year. They were oblivious of what I was talking about. Your loyal cousins did not render your secret. After snooping, I ascertained you and Thomas were both missing in action." Ellen testified.

"Ok mother, I am sorry," she apologized. "I deceived you."

Ellen reiterated her former request. "I want you to terminate your affiliation with Thomas." She chose her words carefully. "He's too old for you."

"Oh come on mom. What's a few years? It's not like his an old, old, man," she pleaded her case emphasizing old.

"You know where I'm coming from Edith. I want you to finish college before getting romantically attached. Think about your future. Don't jeopardize that." Ellen bid persuading her to rethink her actions.

"Mother, I love you, but I will not axe our friendship. I will minimize our time together for your sake." She sipped her juice and stood up. "I really must go." She seized the unfinished toast dashing from the kitchen.

"Friendship?" Ellen reverberated as Edith escaped her howling presence and shook her head in disgust. *Her daughter had a one track mind.*

Edith lurched to her car and sped to English Grill where she spotted Thomas waiting patiently with the windows rolled up, and his radio blaring. She parked beside him and together they addressed the restaurant.

As usual, the Lobby was crowded, the central retreat for senior citizens, the dominating census. Thomas ordered his usual two for two special which consisted of two eggs over easy, two crisp strips of bacon and two pieces of evenly brown toast with a cup of black coffee. Edith got a bowl of oatmeal, and a small glass of chilled orange juice.

She told Thomas about her morning. Thomas was glad her mother knew about their rendezvous. He hated keeping secrets. At least they could be honest about their affiliation even though Ellen opposed it. After breakfast they went their separate ways not by choice but obligation. Edith had three classes scheduled for the morning and two labs that evening. She would be lucky if she finished by five. Thomas had a commitment with his manuscript. His publisher was hounding him about marketing his book by the start of the New Year.

Chapter Four

The season of lights, family reunions and smiling faces blew into Salisbury. Department stores were decorated for Christmas the day after Halloween. Old timers nagged about the Holidays being too commercial and starting prematurely. During the first week of November 1970, the heavens sprinkled snow over the entire region. Children frolicked the streets with snow ball fights. The elderly peeped from windows praying it would stop. A south wind froze the lakes providing teenagers with an afternoon skiing resort. Churches prepared fruit baskets, and held fundraisers for poverty stricken citizens in the community.

It was snowing profusely when Thomas Guy crossed Main Street leading to Cohn's Jewelry Shop on the Downtown Plaza. He promised Stanly he would seal the last installment on his account by Friday.

Store bells charmed as he entered the store with glass counters housing elegant jewelry pieces, and jerked flakes from his trench coat.

Stanly, a short man with black hair, which he kept in a ponytail, displaying two dimples which lit up his pale face when he smiled, greeted him. He heard Stanly's parents died in an automobile accident when he was young leaving him to be raised by his Indian grandmother.

He removed his gloves resting them on a glass counter. "It's cold."

"You're telling me," Stanly confirmed. "So you're here for the necklace."

"Correct." He retrieved a tattered wallet from his coat pocket. "How much?"

"Let me see." Stanly opened a brown book locating a receipt. "Here we are. That will be ten dollars."

He anticipated a higher balance. "Are you sure?"

"Positive." He accepted his twenty dollar bill, typed it into the register, and gave him his change. "Why don't you look around while I get your necklace?"

"No harm in looking I suppose."

As Stanly headed for the stockroom, he hesitated, and faced Thomas. "By the way, how's the book coming?"

He sighed. "Still a working process."

"I understand." Stanly said, and went into the stockroom.

The jiggling of the door caught his attention. Another customer came in. He turned to see who it was. It was Mrs. Ellen Bosworth, garnished in a two piece pantsuit.

According to the local tabloids, she was voted the best dressed lady in the county, a pioneer for the betterment of black youth on the shore, and the treasurer for a prestigious Afro-American Epistle church in Fruitland. Her family donated proceeds for the construction of the new edifice when the old chapel on Sunnyside was torn down in August 1967.

Ellen joined him at the register, and laid her large pocketbook on the glass counter. Then she faced him, recognizing him instantly. "You're Thomas Guy, in the flesh."

"And you're Ellen Bosworth, the famous black matriarch of the area," he managed to say.

"I would not call myself that." She was modest. "But I do have clout around here."

"No doubt."

Ellen changed the topic. "I understand you've been spending time with my daughter."

"We've been out several times. "He wondered what she was insinuating.

"Let me get to the point. I want you to **leave my daughter alone!**" She spoke distinctively. "She needs to concentrate on her studies instead of parading about with you." She was blunt.

"She has made me aware of your reservations, and I respect your concerns, but I will not stop seeing her until she tells me so. I love Edith, and I would never hurt her." He was brutally honest.

"You love her for what you can get —

Thomas resented her implications and interrupted, "I would never take advantage of her. She knows that."

"Yeah, like when you whizzed her off to Lancaster for the week-end. I dare think what happened," she insinuated.

He was caught off guard. "We saw a show, and came back the next day." *If she knew what really happened, she would have him arrested.*

"You're going to stand there, and tell me, you spent the weekend alone in a motel with an attractive, vulnerable girl without adequate supervision, and nothing happened. What kind of fool do you think I am!" Ellen snarled.

"Don't you trust your daughter?" he said as a last attempt to stifle the conversation.

Stanly returned carrying a little box.

Ellen whispered in a low, but threatening voice. "Stay away from my daughter!"

Stanly bagged the item and presented it to him. He walked out without looking back. He was relieved to escape the fury of Ellen Bosworth. One thing for certain, she was protective of her daughter, and adamant he terminate their relationship. At the same token, they were sincerely in love, and it was too late to turn back.

The laughter of children engaged in a vicious snowball fight, and the hustle and bustle of elderly folk shuffling through snowy streets approaching the plaza merchants eager for their business, brought him back to the season. He went to his car, which he parked on the side street, only to find it covered with white dust. He brushed the flakes from his windows, and climbed into his vehicle. Suddenly the heavens bombarded earth with an intense snow shower. As he made way to his apartment, he switched the wipers on high enabling him to see. The announcer on the radio forecast ten inches by midnight before tapering off.

When he arrived at his Parkside Apartment, a block from Bennett High school, the wind intensified making driving conditions hazardous. He almost fell ascending steps to his apartment. Luckily he made it safely inside without incident. He hung his coat in the closet and removed his soggy sneakers. If he knew it was going to snow, he would have worn his boots.

A light was blinking on his telephone indicating he had a message. At once he activated his answering machine. It was Edith.

"I know the weather is bad, but there is a play at Wicomico High School. My cousin Sarah is in it and I was wondering if you would accompany me. Please call me back." The machine cut off.

Going to a play was not his idea for the perfect evening. Personally he yearned spending a quiet evening watching tapes, sipping coke and sharing a bowl of buttered popcorn. Obviously she had another agenda.

He called Edith and she answered after the first ring. "I got your message."

Edith just stepped from the shower and was sitting on her bed wrapped in a towel. "It's a religious play put on by our church. I thought it would be a good idea to support her and the church. Another of mother's fund raisers for the youth. She's attempting to raise enough money to send them to Walt Disney World this summer."

"Your family could send the whole church and not miss it."

"You're right but this is the way she selected to do it. Besides, this affair might recruit new members to our congregation."

He walked into his kitchen and grabbed a cold Pepsi from the refrigerator. "By the way I saw your mother today. I went to the jewelry store on the plaza to pick up something. She came in." He took a swallow and collapsed on the couch. "She confronted me about whizzing you off to Lancaster and taking advantage of her vulnerable daughter. And she insisted I stay clear of you."

"That sounds like mother."

"Will she be at the function tonight?" He wondered. "I don't want to encounter her again. Once is enough."

Edith grabbed a comb from her vanity and commenced stroking her wet hair.

"Mother will not leave the house in bad weather under no conditions even if somebody took her. So don't fret about that."

"Ok. Where should I pick you up?" He asked. Picking her up at her home was unorthodox. It was forbidden.

"I will be there in an hour. The show starts at seven. I have the tickets."

He thought about the forever worsening weather. "It's getting pretty rough out there. It's not safe?"

"I'll drive father's truck. He won't mind." She approached her huge wardrobe searching for an outfit. "Love you. I've got to get dressed."

"Love you too." He hung up.

The school was crowded despite a major winter storm was brewing. Every seat was occupied or flagged for a guest. Ushers constantly added extra chairs to accommodate the overflow. Edith and Thomas was escorted to their seat in the middle of the auditorium on the right side beside an elderly couple skimming the program they received in the lobby. As soon as Thomas relaxed and glanced around the noisy, populated theater secretly searching for Edith's mother despite the assurance she would not be present, the lights dimmed and the assembly became quiet. It was show time. He was relieved knowing Ellen was absent.

The show was terrific. It was a religious masterpiece about a black family becoming Christians following a series of domestic calamities. Sarah played the minister who led the family to the Lord. Her performance was splendid. Edith applauded frantically following each solo. The audience gave a standing ovation following the performance. Sarah won the hearts of many fans.

After the curtain closed, Edith rushed to the stage to greet and praise her beloved cousin with Thomas close behind. "Sarah you were great. I didn't know you could sing like that."

Sarah was modest. "Oh cousin it was nothing. The show sold itself."

"That may be true but you were good."

Another member of the cast grabbed Sarah by the arm. "Sarah we have to go back stage for a group picture and leave. Weather report says it is almost a foot deep, and slippery. We have to leave before it gets any worse," the young boy who played a teenager said.

"OK John. I am on my way." She turned to face Edith as she backed to the side exit. "I am glad you both could make it. Call me later and we can talk."

"Ok Sarah."

The ride to his apartment was treacherous. Edith slid twice. He volunteered to drive but she claimed she was fine. Besides, if he had an accident with her father's truck, he would be furious. If she had an accident, he would be sympathetic. After all, she was his daughter.

It took thirty minutes to reach their destination opposed to ten minutes under normal traveling conditions. After parking in front of the department, Edith decided to stay over for a few minutes. He tried convincing her to go home before it got worse, but she promised she would not stay long; a half an hour at most. Instead of arguing, he escorted her into the building.

Edith removed her coat, rested it on a rack beside his, and sat on the leather sofa. He prepared two cups of hot chocolate. They sipped the hot beverage which warmed their chilled bodies and gazed at each other. Before they realized it, they were embracing. He lusted for her but she shoved him away.

"What's wrong?" He asked.

"It's that time. I can't do anything," she replied.

He knew what she meant. Experiencing the pleasure of her body was undoable. He sorted to holding her. What was intended to be a half an hour turned into an hour? Reluctantly Edith made provisions to depart. She already stayed overtime.

As she descended the last step toward the truck, she slipped, collapsing onto the snowy pavement. Instantly he assisted her to her feet. She complained about her ankle hurting. He scooped her into his arms taking her back into his warm apartment, and laid her on the couch. Then he removed her snowy boots and damp stockings. Her left ankle commenced bulging. When he touched it, she moaned. Something had to be done to reduce the swelling. Silently he prayed it was a sprain but feared it might be broken. He searched his apartment retrieving a towel, stacked a couple of ice cubes inside and applied it to her bulging ankle.

"I guess I won't be going home tonight," Edith said.

"How are you going to explain that?" He wondered.

"Give me the phone. I will tell dad I am going to spend the night with Sarah due to the weather. He'll believe me." Edith accepted the wireless phone from Thomas. "Maybe by morning, I will be ok and can return home."

"I hope so." He kissed her on the forehead.

"Daddy, I won't be coming home tonight. I am going to spend the night with Sarah." She was becoming a professional liar. "The roads are pretty bad."

He could hear her father's response. "I was hoping you would. Weather man says it might be twenty inches by morning. It might be best you wait until late tomorrow afternoon. By then the major highways will be clear."

"Probably so, "she agreed.

"I hear the play was a success. The pastor called your mother. He said they had a full house. You know your mother was glad to hear that."

"I know. I went to support Sarah, and she did a marvelous job."

"You know Sarah is a good actress."

Edith changed the subject. "By the way, where is mother?"

"She had one of those sinus headaches, and retired early. She didn't even ask about you." He sighed, and then said, "You know she had to be feeling awful."

"I'll see you tomorrow. Give mom my love."

"Ok baby. Love you."

The phone buzzed. He accepted it from Edith and replaced it on its receiver.

"I am going to turn on the television, if you don't mind," he said as he pressed the remote activating the floor console.

Ellen abandoned her cluttered office. It had been a horrible day. The snow prevented one third of the employees from reporting to work. Shop Stewarts hounded her on revising the pension plan. Workers complained about malfunctioning machines. Her secretary called out sick forcing her to play dual roles. At noon, her husband relinquished his secretary for relief which was a blessing. The phone rang continuously. The last straw was when they suffered a blackout, shutting down the plant. A power line knockdown from an accident cut off electricity for the entire region. Frustrated, she closed the plant early. There was nothing else she could do.

She trudged through the melting snow cautiously for fear of falling. Her vehicle was in the front row outside her office. If she could maneuver through the freshly plowed parking-lot safely, she would be fine. The major highways were clear.

Stanly called before she left. He summoned her presence and she keenly accepted his invitation. He closed his store early due the inclement weather. There were few customers lurking around. Nobody in their right mind would ventured out in treacherous weather unless they had to.

She made a pit stop at a local liquor store, and purchased a fifth of wine. As she drove into Princess-Ann, she wondered how long John would remain at the plant before leaving. There was only but so much he could do without power. Then she began to think. She had to devise an alibi explaining where she went after she left the office. The roads were drivable, thanks to the snowplows. It stopped snowing and the sun was melting the residue. It was Thursday. Bible Study was scheduled for 6:00pm. They rarely cancelled Bible Study. She would say she went to Sister Thelma's house for Bible Study. Thelma lived in Pocomoke. If he asked what she did for two hours before Bible Study, she would say she visited the Wicomico County Library to research a new machine they were entertaining purchasing. He would never check her alibi.

She turned onto a slushy Deal Island road trudging to her secret destination. Glare from the setting sun hampered her vision causing her to lower the sun-visor. Classical music soothed her guilty conscience as she searched for Stanly's dwelling.

She pulled her car into a muddy driveway behind Stanly's Chevy truck. There before her rested an old, rundown, bungalow with a dilapidated porch badly needing repair. It was a miracle anyone survived in that shack without being frozen to death in the winter, or tortured by flies in the heat of summer. Certainly Stanly did not have to live like that. His store was profitable. But he was determined to live out his life in the house where he was raised.

He rarely had visitors. His home was off limits to the public.

Nervously she approached the dilapidated dwelling and wrapped lightly. She prayed nobody saw her. The door creaked open and she handed him the liquor wrapped in a brown paper bag. She stepped inside the drafty building and shut out the winter air. A single lamp dimly lit the room. A wood stove crackled heating the uninsulated house.

Stanly uncorked the wine and took a big swag. "Just what I needed."

"I have a few minutes." Ellen removed her gloves. "I know you were raised by your grandmother but do you have any other siblings. It must be lonely at Christmas without any family." She paused at a picture of his grandmother on the wall. It was a dimly lit room making it difficult to ascertain her features.

"My father had a son before he married my mother. He introduced us before he died. We communicate by mail. A matter of fact, he sends me a Christmas card and gift every year. It's nothing etravagent. A tie, shirt, whatever. Matter of fact his card and gift from last year is on that shelf over there." He pointed to a bookshelf in the corner of the room.

"Would you mind if I looked at it." Ellen asked politely.

"Help yourself."

Ellen removed the card from a decorated Christmas bag, leaving the plaid shirt intact with its store wrapping. There was a letter inside the card. She read it silently. Then she faced Stanly. "You have a nephew studying to be a lawyer."

"He calls me at the store. I have seen him a few times. He loves his uncle. I don't know why but he does." Stanly replied before taking another swallow.

"It's good to know someone loves you." She was glad to hear Stanly had a relative that cared. He was a loner without much of a social life. Outside of her husband, and herself, there was nobody.

"Enough talking about me." He hated being the center of her conversation. Stanly pulled her close. "Where is the big man?" He asked not really wanting to know.

"I left him at the office."

Stanly kissed her neck. "I've been wanting you all day." Even though he felt guilty, he allowed his flesh to override his morals.

She dropped her coat in the floor. Stanly rested his bottle on a nearby table and swooped her into his arms hauling her into his dark bedroom.

He helped her remove her clothes, and she facilitated him out of his. Gently he stretched her across his squeaky bed and made gentle, slow, love to her. Every moment with Ellen was the taste of a forbidden treat he could not get enough of. He feared one day he would pay for his sin.

Outside the sun descended, the moon ascended as the wind whistled a warning to the horizon.

Ellen returned home from her secret rendezvous and went to the lavatory where she immediately undressed and took a shower. The tingling water splashing against her warm body did her justice. She scrubbed thoroughly with ivory soap cleansing herself of Stanly's scent rinsing away the evidence before joining her husband. She grabbed a bath towel, dried off, wrapped another towel around her waist and then went across the hall into the master bedroom.

John was in bed naked with a thin sheet pulled up to his chest reading a science fiction novel. "How was Bible Study?" He asked without peering from the book.

"It was great," She replied as she opened her wardrobe, and selected a gown.

John tossed the book on the nightstand. "I checked on the expansion of our sister plant. Mother said it should be finished in a couple months," he informed her watching as she prepared for the night.

"That's good." She slipped into her gown. "What time did you leave?" She was curious.

"About an hour after you."

She slid into bed beside her spouse leaving the towel on a hanger in the closet. She anticipated by the stare and elevated sheet he lusted her; a sight she had not seen for several weeks. Her husband clicked off the lamps leaving them in the dark. The bed vibrated as he mounted himself on her stomach and unbuttoned her gown. She held her breath as he caressed her sensitive breast and chewed her nipples leaving teeth marks. Stiffness gripped her when he pried apart her aching legs and crammed his manhood inside her. A pardon prayer pressed her lips as he pounded her savagely ordering her to move as he thrashed his thick tong down her throat. She froze when he penetrated her, and twitched when he withdrew. She wanted him to do his thing fast. She knew he was making up for lost time. It had been awhile since they had relations. He rode her for twenty minutes before jerking with satisfaction. Relief pillowed her soul when he climaxed and rolled on his back exhausted. When she heard him snore, she knew it was safe to sleep. She closed her eyes and dreamed about Stanly. Stanly was gentle and patient. John was rough and demanding. It was awful he was unable to satisfy her as often as he once did.

Luckily for Edith, the swelling dissolved and the pain vanished restoring a healthy ankle. There was no need to fabricate another lie. It was another secret admits a pool of many. The less her mother knew, the better. Thomas was not her favorite topic. If anything, he was an irritant in her flesh.

Thanksgiving crept on the scene quickly, leaving her a series of uncommitted choices. Traditionally her parents visited her mother's family in Philadelphia for the holiday returning late Sunday evening. Personally, she preferred spending Thanksgiving with Thomas but her mother would never consent. Not only that, final exams were on the horizon and she wanted adequate time to study. Perhaps if she presented her academic request, she could avoid a long trip to Philadelphia where her father got intoxicated and her mother argued with her siblings on how to prepare, quote, the proper thanksgiving meal with all the trimmings. Meanwhile her grandmother bored her with trivia talk while watching ancient thanksgiving movies on TV she seen a thousand times no doubt. Proceeding the feast, the men crowded in a station wagon, travelled to a friend's house in the country where they played cards, leaving the women behind to clean up. Fridays everyone left at the crack of dawn to go shopping for Black Friday specials. She usually slept in until midday.

Saturdays, everyone lounged in pajamas, ate brunch at noon and prepared for the afternoon. The men gathered in the basement playing pool, sipping liquor and reminiscing about their youth. Her mother, and her aunts, and grandmother would escort her to one of Philadelphia's biggest malls where they shopped until they were exhausted, had lunch at a food court, and topped off the adventure with a movie and butter flavored popcorn. That was the highlight of the trip for her.

On Sunday, the entire family spiffed up in their best outfit and went to church per grandma's divine rule. Grandma Mabel was thrilled to introduce her family to her church buddies. This gave her the opportunity to brag about their accomplishments. Bible School was brief, forty-five-minutes at most, which continued to a lengthy morning services lasting for hours. The pastor, a heavy set elderly man, was reluctant to cease preaching until his congregation heard his entire sermon. It was his mission to save everybody's soul.

Usually by three in the evening, her parents were packed and equipped for the long journey to the shore. Her grandmother Mabel was teary eyed when it came time for her children and their spouses to depart. She relished their company.

Edith mustered the courage to challenge her mother about breaking a family tradition. Ellen was seated at the kitchen table rumbling through business documents when she approached her,

"Mom, I know you and daddy visit Grandma Mabel every other Thanksgiving but I don't want to go this year. Exams are coming up and I need time to study."

Ellen faced her beautiful daughter. "I would prefer you come with us. Mother would love to see you."

"I know. But I really need to study. You know how hard it is for me to grasp things."

Ellen knew her child struggled to earn good grades in high school. It took long hours of studying before she was able to retain what she read. College was no exception. Yet her persistent and determination showed on her final exams. She would never make the Dean's list, yet her grade point average was a solid B which was good enough for her. At the same token, she knew her daughter was infatuated with Thomas. Every chance she got to spend time with him, she would take advantage of it. Nevertheless she entertained Edith's request and replied, "Provided you study, and not shack up with Thomas, you may stay. Is that a deal?"

She was shocked. It was hard to believe her mother was granting her request. It was a miracle. "Thanks mom." She hugged her.

"I meant what I said about Thomas," she reiterated strongly.

Edith left smiling.

Ellen mumbled under her breath, "The minutes we're gone, she'll be at his side." Keeping Edith from Thomas would be challenging; perhaps impossible. When she returned, she would develop a strategy. Perhaps by then, Todd would have ammunition to crumble their affiliation.

Thanksgiving week, Edith spent most of her days at the County Library studying with Thomas's help. Periodically he drilled her requisitioning how much she retained from notes and text. As a reprieve, succeeding tedious studying sessions, they retreated to the plaza where they snacked on cushier hotdogs from a vender.

Thomas devoured his snack in three bites while she nibbled precariously and swallowed it with sips of coke. It was a beautiful autumn day. Festive Christmas décor garnished the plaza. A brisk wind shuffled fallen leaves about making a mess for the town parishioners. She observed Thomas spinning about inhaling the frigid air into his lungs. She failed witnessing the expression when he slumped over from a sudden debilitating pain penetrating his stomach. She assumed he was kneeling from the joy and excitement of the holidays.

"What are you doing for Thanksgiving?" she asked discerning he was disoriented.

After catching his breath, he sat beside her on the bench. "I really have not thought about it. I'm sure you will spend time with your parents."

"I told you my parents are spending Thanksgiving in Philadelphia with my mother's mother and her siblings," she reminded him. "I opted to stay home and study."

"What about your relatives here?" He was referring to cousins.

"I want to spend Thanksgiving with you," she insisted.

He smiled and held her pretty face in his hands." And what about the turkey. If you spend Thanksgiving with me, I insist we have a turkey and all the dressings. Can you cook all that?"

The truth was she was a lousy cook. But she had a back-up plan. "You will have a perfect Thanksgiving meal. I will see to that," she promised.

"This I must see." Thomas sensed she possessed no culinary skills to prepare a Thanksgiving meal but he was curious of how she would pull it off.

Unknowing to Thomas, she contacted her cousin Sarah requesting her assistance in preparing a meal for two.

"Girl are you crazy. Thanksgiving is tomorrow. How can I pull this off and spend time with my family?" Sarah complained.

"Please cousin. I will pay $100.00 for your time and services."

Sarah thought it over. A hundred dollars would come in handy for Christmas. She could purchase a race track for her seven year old son. That would make his Christmas. "Ok, I will do it. But you know you have a lot of stuff to buy. Goo to Safeway and pick up a few things and bring them to my house tonight! Can you do that?"

"Sure thing."

"Ok, get a piece of paper, and write this down."

Twenty minutes after Sarah dictated her catering supplies, Edith was in the grocery store stacking a cart. Panic struck perceiving an empty turkey compartment. No turkey at Thanksgiving was un-American. Then a porter strolled from nowhere with a bucket of birds to replenish the cubicle. All was not lost.

When she arrived at Sarah's two room bungalow on Delany Avenue, down the road from Green Giant, a canning factory, her son parked his bicycle in the driveway, and ran to greet her forsaking his two playmates who continued racing down the street.

"Can I help you?" He asked as she opened the back car door to gather grocery bags.

"Sure baby." She passed him two light bags and seized the heavy bags while shutting the door with her foot.

Sarah stood in the doorway providing easy access. When they were safely inside, she allowed the screen door to close and guided them into the kitchen directing where to dispose the food.

Edith thanked Corey for his assistance and fisted him a five dollar bill. Corey thanked her grinning from ear to ear. He had not seen that much money in a long while. He dashed toward the screen door anxious to spend his fortune on foolish gain. Sarah yelled after him, "Put your hood on and fasten that coat. Last thing I need is for you to catch a cold." Corey promised hastily as he exited the house slamming both doors, keeping the cold air out.

The smell of rising yeast rolls on a counter covered with a towel brought back memories. Edith remembered her grandmother Bessel preparing rolls for special occasions when she was young. That was before she moved.

"He sure has grown a lot since I saw him last. Must be in the first grade by now," Edith said as she unfastened her coat and sat at the kitchen table.

"Yes he is. And a good boy at that. Has not given me a moment's trouble." Sarah removed an apron from the back of a chair and tied it around her waist.

Edith reached inside her purse retrieving a brand new hundred dollar bill which she handed to Sarah. Sarah grabbed the bill, crumbled it and shoved it into her apron pocket.

"Don't lose that." Edith warned being apprehensive to where she placed it.

"Oh believe me I won't. That's my Christmas shopping cash."

"Cousin I really appreciate this." She reared back in the chair. "This is Thomas and my first Thanksgiving together. I want it to be special."

Sarah caught Edith's eye. "You really love that man."

"More than I will admit to myself," she confessed.

Sarah took a deep breath and grabbed her cousin's hands. "Cousin you know I've given my life to Christ. And yes, I've made mistakes, and Christ forgave me."

Edith wondered if she was going to question her salvation. "If you're asking me if I have accepted the Lord as my savior, I am working on it. Am I walking holy, no." She was young and wanted to be free. She dreaded being confined by her beliefs.

"I am worried about you. I want you to be careful." Sarah prophesized. "I see things in your future, and I want you to know, whatever happen, God is in control." She shifted her feet and continued, "I know you've been with Thomas, but sometimes what we think is best, is not good for us. So again I say, be careful."

The intensity of her cousin's conversation chilled her spine. She altered the conversation. "Those rolls smell good."

Sarah went to butter her risen yeast rolls. "Your parents usually go to Philadelphia this time of year. How did you manage to get out of that?" She was curious.

"I told mom I needed time to study, and she said ok, provided I stay clear of Thomas."

"Aunt Ellen mellowing a little perhaps." Sarah remarked.

"Maybe."

"You know why Auntie Ellen is so possessive of you?" Sarah asked.

"I know." Edith was tempted to uncover the rolls but feared they might fall.

"She wants you to run Bosworth Industries. Any man you see or become interested in is a threat to her plans for you. Cousin Edith my aunt will do everything in her power to separate you and Thomas."

She knew her cousin spoke the truth.

Sarah changed the topic. "After I cook this dinner, where shall I deliver it?"

"This is what I want you to do." Edith explained.

Chapter Five

Early Thanksgiving Morning, Edith eagerly knocked on his door. Thomas just finished showering and slid into his sweat suit. His intentions were to drive to the park, jog around the premises, and dock at McDonalds for breakfast; anything to stimulate his creative juices. His typewriter craved descriptive paragraphs creating another scene in his manuscript. Edith led him to believe she would be spending the day preparing his Thanksgiving dinner. Of course he disbelieved her.

"Why aren't you home cooking?"

"I did most of it last night." Again she lied. "I'll have it delivered when the time is right." She shoved her way in. "Where are you going this morning?"

"I was going for a run in the park, and then stop by McDonalds for breakfast, if that's ok with you?"

"Mind if I tag along?" She kissed his shaven cheeks.

"Love your company."

Thomas grabbed his jacket. Together they climbed into his Cadillac and headed to the park.

The only straggler in the park was an elderly gentlemen walking his Shepard with a short leach. Apparently everyone chose to stay home for the holidays.

It was a brisk morning. Thomas wished he brought his gloves and toboggan. As he accelerated, his hands warmed up and his forehead perspired. At the end of the lap, they collapsed inside the car and relaxed until they mustered enough energy to ride to the next pit-stop. It was almost nine-thirty when they finished breakfast at McDonalds. Under her suggestion, they went to the Salisbury Mall to carouse and window shop. Most of the Stores were closed with the exception of the Pantry Pride grocery store, and the English Grill Restaurant. From there they went to the Boulevard Theater and caught a matinee. Thomas assumed Edith was deliberately stalling but went along with her scheme.

It was almost three when they unlocked Thomas' apartment. A prearranged table dressed with a multicolored laced cloth greeted them. On the table was four lit candles, smelling of pine cones, surrounding a hand crafted centerpiece, crammed with traditional Thanksgiving treats sheltered from the elements with plastic lids and aluminum foil.

Thomas was surprised and impressed. "I'm not going to ask how you pulled this off. I am just going to enjoy." He kissed her briefly. Together they rushed into the tiny bathroom, took turns washing their hands, rested their coats on a coat rack in the corner, and then sat at the prepared table.

Thomas blessed the food. They ate until they were comfortable. Sarah did a fabulous job. Everything was perfect. The food was scrumptious and filling. After the feast, Edith cleared the table, carefully tucking leftovers in Thomas' bare refrigerator while he retreated to a section of his apartment set up like an office and commenced working on his manuscript while the football game raged in the background from the television he left playing. She wondered how he concentrated with the television blasting.

When her domestic duties were satisfied, she changed the channel. Thomas was so absorbed in his work, he was ignorant of her action. She watched White Christmas, a classic movie. She snuggled on the couch resting her head on a soft pillow. Before she knew it, she fell asleep. When she awakened, she was covered with a thin blanket, and Thomas was sitting in a recliner snoozing with the remote laying on his belly. The wall clock charmed 10:00pm. She had to get home. Her parents would be returning in the morning. Without so much as a kiss, she grabbed her coat and tiptoed to the door glancing at her lover. She was tempted to kiss him. He was cute and sexy. Her teddy bear. She fastened her coat and left. It was a wonderful Thanksgiving.

When John and Ellen arrived at the plant, the Monday following their short vacation, the plant was in an uproar. Folders clouded their desk necessitating signatures. John summoned foremen to the boardroom with instructions to do whatever necessary to satisfy pending orders. No sooner had John abandoned the boardroom, Ellen summoned the designing crew to an unprecedented conference. She presented sketches of new furniture and inquired the earliest date they could present a prototype. The small group of four young men, two black and two Hispanic were reluctant to respond anticipating it would take several weeks to create a prototype. They also knew whenever she wanted a new line, she expected swift deploy, no excuses. Cannot was not in her vocabulary.

The spokesman for the crew, a short Hispanic man with a beard, leaned back in his chair after viewing the designs and said, "Maybe two weeks tops."

"I want it done before the New Year. I want it in the stores by February." She was adamant.

The spokesman was surprised. He thought she expected results by Friday. "Ok Mrs. Bosworth, if you can get a rush on the materials, we'll have it ready before Christmas."

"I will get on it immediately."

That afternoon, she contacted a major fabric providers insisting they deliver her a truck load of supplies by mid-week. They said they would try but could not make any guaranties. Their drivers were on strike. She contacted another factory and got the same response. Still she was determined to launch her a new furniture line. She was confident it would be a bestseller.

Her husband dropped by at noon informing her he would be out of town for a few days, and he was leaving her in charge. Employees on the assembly line at the Wilmington Plant had complaints about safety issues. His mother wanted him to negotiate an agreement with the union to avoid a strike. She told him about her fabric provider reluctance to deliver materials need for a new furniture line due to their drivers being on strike.

"Don't worry. Truckers are striking all over the country. I'll call in a few favors." He told her his game plan.

"Tell me what needs to be done?" She asked cordially.

"I've requisitioned several shipments of lumber for today and tomorrow. I've granted the managers permission to schedule people to work overtime. We have several loads of product to ship in two days. We have back orders waiting delivery. There's a new Hotel in Ohio wanting us to furnish two-hundred bedroom units. Hopefully our drivers won't be striking anytime soon."

"I've got it under control," she assured him. "Go, do your thing,"

John laid documents on her desk and said, "If you have any problem, let me know."

She visited various departments making sure they had ample supplies to do their job. She contacted the maintenance crew making sure every piece of equipment was functioning properly. She spent hours in her office, studying requisitions, making sure the inventory was congruent with the products going out and materials coming in. Everything had to flow smoothly. Before retiring, she checked the quality of products waiting to be shipped. She was pleased with the finished merchandise. Her workers did a marvelous job. Staff took pride in their work and it showed.

Chapter Six

Ellen awakened early the day before Christmas Eve flipping through the vanilla folder Todd faxed to her office. John slept on his belly with a pillow burying his head muffling his acidulous snoring. The last few weeks were hectic, stressing his patients, forcing him to exercise his Presidential authority. Machines were constantly malfunctioning necessitating being repaired or replaced, workers protested company policies, foremen and the truckers threaten to strike for a dollar raise. She tried appeasing disgruntled employees through shop stewards but they wanted input from her husband and were reluctant to bargain with her. Pertinent complaints were settled when he resumed his post. Following days of negotiations and policy modifications, the plant was back on track. Union grievances were resolved financially, granting the employees their request. Company goals were achieved, meeting the demands of their clients. The rest could wait until after the New Year.

The workers cheered when Bosworth closed for the holidays. Each employee received a two hundred dollar bonus in their check. Policy was the plant shut down from December 22 to January 1. This gave the employees time to celebrate the holidays with their family; a well-deserved break for everyone.

Quietly she slipped from the bed, wiggled her feet into her puppy slippers, wrapped her fuzzy robe around her flimsy night-gown, read the report, and placed the folder inside her night-stand. There was nothing supporting her revulsion for Thomas. Disappointed, she tied her robe firmly and went downstairs.

In a few hours her family would arrive. Her maid, Eleanor, cleaned thoroughly, decorated the house for Christmas, and stocked the refrigerator.

She wanted her guest to lack for nothing. Customarily the visiting family prepared most of the meal for the Christmas feast and she supplied the food. She would season the turkey and stuff it in the oven and prepare a pan of dressing. Outside of that, they were on their own. Cooking was not her forte. Usually the women had a cooking contest, and the men were the judges.

She found her daughter sitting in a chair staring at the Christmas tree with a blank expression on her face.

She deciphered her daughter's thoughts and felt obligated to remark. "Honey what is on your mind?"

"I want a favor of you?" Edith asked without making eye contact.

"Before you say another thing, I want to wish you a happy birthday." She hugged her daughter.

Edith forgot about her birthday. Her battle with her mother pertaining to her involvement with Thomas, overwhelmed her thoughts. "You know I'm not into big celebrations. Let's keep it simple."

Ellen removed an envelope from under the tree, and handed it to her daughter. "What do you give a child who has everything?" She sighed. "In this envelope is a card bearing a signed check. You fill in the amount."

Edith hugged her mother. "Thank you so much." She did not open the envelope. "I'll open this later."

"Now what is it you want from me?" She asked.

"May Thomas spend Christmas with us?"

She wished Todd had more information on Thomas. She knew his mother died when he was a young boy. His father was a teacher. Thomas graduated from a Virginian college with a Bachelor's degree in journalism. He was single and virtually a loner. Financially he was worth a million dollars from published works, but lived a middleclass lifestyle. Living extravagantly was not his thing. An opportunist, he was not. That fear could be buried. He was a good steward of his money.

"Baby you spent Thanksgiving with Thomas, even though you told me you had to study," she said evenly.

"I did study." Edith insisted.

"I am sure you did, together, but I do not want him here. That is not too much to ask. Besides, this man must have a family. Let him spend time with them."

Then she remembered the report. Thomas was a loner traveling the country writing books about each state he visited. With the exception of Edith, there was no long term record of any romantic entanglements. He was committed to his craft. His aunt raised him following his mother's death. His aunt died five months after celebrating his twenty-first birthday. All he had was his father.

"Mother, he's miles from home. He does not know anybody here." *In all the time they spent together, the only family members he mentioned was his father and aunt.* "He's new in town."

"Edith, look." She stood in defiance. "You were with him Thanksgiving. Please let him stay where he is," she pleaded. "I want you to spend time with your family." She attempted to persuade her to listen to reason.

"Mother please stop being so bent on keeping us apart?" Edith begged.

"I do not like him." She was brutally honest. "For God's sake leave Thomas where he is." She spoke harshly.

"Once you get to know him—

She remembered their first encounter. He was brass and smart tongued. "I saw him once and I do not care to meet him again," she interjected before Edith could finish her sentence.

"You cannot blame Thomas for taking me to Lancaster. As I said, I deceived you, not him," Edith prevailed.

"The bottom line is, Thomas is not welcomed here for Christmas. So to answer your question, the answer is no."

As she started to leave, she perceived her husband descending the staircase in his pajamas.

"I want Edith to invite Thomas over for the Holidays. My daughter has been spending a lot of time with this man, and, I want to see him." John spoke shattering the tension. "That is my birthday gift to her."

"I have met him, and it was not pleasant. Christmas is not the time for you to acquaint yourself with him. Especially since your family will be here."

"I do not care." He approached his daughter. "Edith, bid him to Christmas dinner."

Edith left her parents confronting each other, and went upstairs to dress.

"John, I do not appreciate what you did." She was angry.

"Our daughter is nineteen. You cannot dictate who she sees or dates. And yes, I know you're grooming her for the business. I want the same. But it has to be something she wants, not just us. So what if she pursues another career instead of running Bosworth Industries. There are other people in my family who would be willing to take over, given the opportunity." He reminded her.

"Look. It is Christmas, and I am not going to stand here and argue with you." She approached the stairs. "I'm going to work."

"What about our family?"

"You entertain them until I get back."

"What are you going to do at the office?" John wondered. "The plant is closed."

"Always something to do," she said sarcastically John rubbed his head, and entered the kitchen searching for tea bags.

Chapter Seven

Edith walked into Johnny & Sammy's restaurant. A hostess escorted her to the table where Thomas sat stirring a cup of black coffee. After draping her coat over the chair and resting her pocketbook in the floor, she sat across from him. She apologized for her tardiness. "I had to do some last minute shopping. Please forgive me."

"I haven't been here that long," he confessed.

"You said you had something important to discuss." She was curious.

The waitress, a young blond chewing gum wildly, took their order. She promised to bring their drinks before departing.

Thomas retrieved a box from his starched shirt pocket revealing an exquisite diamond necklace. Personally he preferred offering an engagement ring but it was too soon. They barely knew each other, four months tops.

Gracefully she accepted the necklace. It was expensive, probably cost a fortune. Immediately she put it on with Thomas's assistance. It fit perfectly. She loved it. "It's beautiful."

"Merry Christmas and happy birthday."

She was shocked Thomas realized it was her birthday. She certainly did not tell him. "How did you know that?"

"I read the newspaper this morning and your mother posted in the birthday section," he told her.

"You couldn't wait until Christmas to give me this. I know it was intended for a Christmas gift." She was fascinated by the diamonds and kept admiring it.

"I figured you would be spending Christmas with your family. Just in case I didn't see you until after the holidays, I wanted to make sure you got it."

"It's stunning."

"I am glad you like it."

She changed the subject. "Speaking of the Holidays. You've been invited to Christmas dinner by my father. He wants to meet you." She added.

"And your mother went along with that?"

"No. Father overrode her decision." She informed him.

Thomas sipped his coffee. He had reservations about the invitation. "Look. It is Christmas. I have no desire to damper the Holidays for your mother. I am going to stay home and work on my book."

"Please come for a few minutes," she begged. "You don't have to stay long. I want to introduce you to my family."

He twitched nervously. Perhaps he could tolerate Ellen for a few minutes being how important it was to her. "I will come for your sake," he agreed reluctantly, "but if your mother ask me to leave, I am out of there."

"Fair enough."

Stanly entered Ellen's spacious contemporary office jerking snow from his trench coat. She instructed him to lock the door. Stanly did as instructed and greeted her with a kiss. The aroma of her expensive perfume brought a pleased smile to his unshaven face. He slung his damp coat across a chair.

"I see it has started snowing," she said peeping through open blinds. "Perhaps we will have a white Christmas." Huge snowflakes littered the parking lot.; A sure indicator it would not last long.

"What takes you here the day before Christmas Eve? You should be home with your husband." Stanly scolded.

"I am pissed with John." She shut the blinds. "He deliberately invited Thomas Guy over for Christmas. He knew how I feel about him." She expressed her displeasure.

"I figure you've investigated Thomas by now." Stanly scoped the office for a bottle of wine. It appeared there was none on the premises. "What have you discovered?"

She sighed. "That's the problem. His record is squeaky clean. No dirt."

"He seems like a good fellow. I think your daughter and him make a nice couple." He voiced his opinion.

"Don't say that!" She snapped. "There is something about that guy that disturbs me."

"First impressions perhaps. I know he ruffled your feathers, especially the way he addressed you." He remembered her telling him about their first encounter in his store.

"Probably right." She anticipated Stanly craved a drink. Alcohol was his best friend. Alcohol was his remedy to get through the weekends. She opened a cabinet revealing a bottle of liquor. "Here's something for you."

Stanly grabbed the whiskey, twisted off the top, and took a deep swallow. It appeased the thirst stabilizing his trembling hands. Then he concentrated on the temptation before him. Not only was he addicted to the spirits, but he was a slave to her alluring body. No woman could gratify his carnal misgivings like her. It was awful she was the wife of his best friend.

"Let's not talk about Edith or John. Let's concentrate on us." Stanly drew her into his powerful arms. "Sure nobody is here?" He felt edgy being in restricted quarters where anyone bearing a key could walk in; anyone like John.

"We're alone. Nobody is here but us," she assured him while removing the empty bottle, leaving it on her desk and led him to a leather couch often used during her lunch breaks. Stanly made love to her, but, he felt edgy. He feared John would storm through the door full of rage. They were testing fait and gambling with their lives.

Bessel Bosworth, John's mother, was a stout woman with curly gray hair which she kept cut afro style. She tossed her luggage on a zebra pattern comforter and walked through a sliding door leading to a stained deck overlooking the backyard. Snow crowned the landscape with white sprinkles. Huge pine trees and fallen pine cones accented the tranquil stream.

She and the late Joseph Bosworth raised their children there. She treasured the estate and hated surrendering it to her son and his wife. The split-level mansion sat on acres of land with the Wicomico River as a bonus. The rooms where massive with wooden floors and eggshell walls with a border. Once upon a time, it was her dream house.

Bill and Luther expressed no interest in the company, and Joseph was disenchanted. They opted other careers. Luther became a lawyer establishing his own firm in Long Island New York, and Bill became a chief surgeon at a private Hospital in Brunswick Virginia. They left the shore forfeiting their inheritance to their brother.

Bosworth Industries' fate rested in John's hand. Her husband knew the girl his son dated in high school esteemed the plant. Often Ellen visited Bosworth to see her father who was a foreman and Joseph's best friend. Constantly she questioned her father about the operation of the plant. He told her all he could and referred her to Joseph for additional information. Joseph was honored to in-service her concerning the overall functioning of Bosworth trusting she would fuel his son's interest in the business.

It was no surprise when John proposed to Ellen. They were sweethearts since childhood. She knew Ellen resided with her father during the school season and spent summers with her mother in Philadelphia. According to her father, her mother was against her daughter attending school in the city. She figured she would get a better education in the country. The truth was she had other children by different men, and she could not afford to keep Ellen all year. Her father had no complaints. He adored his daughter.

When Edith was away for the summer, her son was miserable. He was lost without her. When she returned in September, his eyes sparkled like firecrackers. He was happy.

Ellen got pregnant with Edith during their senior year. She speculated Ellen became pregnant to trap her son into marrying her and ease her way into the business. Her husband counted on Ellen drawing John into the family business. He knew his son hated the business but he trusted with Ellen there, it might stimulate his interest. John was his last hope.

They married after graduation. She made it a festive affair, inviting friends, relatives and influential people in the community. She hired the best decorators and coordinators to organize the event. She spared no expense. It would be a memorable wedding. Three huge tents and a platform for the orchestra blanketed the backyard. One tent served for the wedding ceremony with a trellis entwined with roses. The other two tents served for the recession. English Grill catered the occasion. It was a June wedding with the River serving as a backdrop. Joseph blessed the newlyweds with a two week vacation in Hawaii. When they returned from their honeymoon, he gave them keys to a split-level rancher on Jersey Road in Salisbury as a wedding gift.

The following September John enrolled in Harvard where he was expected to earn a bachelor's degree enabling him to run the dynasty. While John was in college, Ellen had their daughter. She hired her sister to raise Edith while she worked at the plant. Joseph sieged this as the opportunity to train her to be acting CEO. When his son came home, he would share ownership of Bosworth with his wife.

Ellen was a quick study. John was pleased when his father bestowed his wife the CEO tittle. After John obtained his bachelor's degree, he appointed himself chief manager of the designing division; a place he selected to be. Designing furniture was his niche. Other aspects of the company did not intrigue him. Nevertheless Joseph forced John to play an executive role in the company outside of what he choose to do. Years later her husband decided to expand and open another plant. One plant was unable to meet the growing demands. They made a product the world loved. He left John and his wife in charge of the Eastern Shore Plant. With his father out of the picture, John concentrated his focus on designing furniture leaving his wife the opportunity to exercise her CEO duties at maximum capacity. When his father died, she appointed John president. Again he was forced to take an executive position overseeing the entire operation of the plant, and his wife became his assistant, second in command. She knew he resented managerial responsibilities. He had to leave his comfort zone and be a captain, the president of a growing industrial enterprise.

She remembered when her husband yielded their fortress on Riverside Drive to his daughter-in-law as a gift for managing the Eastern Shore Plant. Joseph knew Ellen adored their residence and its location. They bought another house and moved to Wilmington Delaware where he oversaw the construction of a new plant.

She knew Ellen had designs on Bosworth industries since she was a little girl, but it was not hers to possess. It was her husband's legacy. She could supervise the Eastern Shore Division, but she would never possess exclusive ownership. Her son would be the president. She would have to answer to him. He would have the final word.

"Mom, what takes you out here?" John beckoned his mother into the warmth of the guest quarters and closed the glass door. "Thinking about dad I guess."

She hugged her son and kissed his cheek. "Your father loved the Holidays. We spent so many wonderful Christmases here."

"How could I forget?"

Bessel sat on the bed with her son. "I was remembering the past. When you married Ellen, the birth of my grand-daughter, you becoming president-

"Mom let's not talk about that. You know my feelings about Bosworth." He gripped her small hands.

"I know but it's your father's legacy. Take care of it for my sake," she pleaded.

"Ok Mom. I will for your sake," he said to appease her.

"Looks like I'm the first one." She rose to her feet.

"They'll be here shortly. By the way how was your trip from Wilmington?" he asked.

"Traffic was light. When I saw the snow, I thought the worse but thank God it stopped." She was relieved.

"I checked the plant a few weeks ago. It appears things are moving along. I presume you had something to do with that," John remarked.

"Well son you placed qualified people in key positions and they are doing a marvelous job. I trust them explicitly."

John changed the subject. He despised shop talk, yet he knew his mother was delighted he displayed interest. "Are you hungry? The maid left a roast in the oven. It smells delicious. Let's go check it out," John suggested.

"Ok son, I am right behind you."

Chapter Eight

Edith escorted her Thomas into the festively decorated foyer with garland, and a colossal Christmas tree near the stairway banister, and introduced him to her visiting relatives. Her aunt Bessie, a stout lady with dreadlocks gazed at him.

"Child bring that sexy thing over here," she hollered broadcasting her intentions.

She waved him to her aunt. Aunt Bessie sluggishly rose from a wingchair and embraced him. "My you're handsome, and smell good too. Where did you locate a handsome specimen like this?" She joked.

Thomas was embarrassed.

"I met him in the college library," Edith replied. "He was doing research for a book and we became friends."

"How old are you son?" Bessie was curious.

"Twenty-six."

"Well I'm twenty-six," she repeated.

Florence, Bessie's sister, who was leaning against the fireplace, rudely interrupted, "You're a twenty-six liar." Then she laughed as she continued sipping a Pepsi clutched tightly in her fingers.

"Who asked you to put your two cents in? Here I am trying to make time and you come jumping in my business," Bessie scolded playfully.

"Honey you heard that," Florence warned.

"I did." Edith commented. "But I am not worried." She secured his arm.

"If I were you, I would keep my eyes on him. There's no telling what old desperate women might do," Florence said grinning.

Bessie looped her arms through Thomas's other arm. "Say." She studied his hazel eyes for a name.

"Thomas."

"Why don't I introduce you to the family while Edith chat with Florence a wee bit, that is, if it's alright with you Edith?"

"Of course. Just don't forget he belongs to me," she reminded her.

Bessie led Thomas into another room where men were gathered around a table smoking cigarettes, drinking beer and playing a friendly game of cards.

Florence finished her drink, and beckoned for Edith to join her on a vintage divan. "How is Sarah doing? I tried calling her but her son says she's working. I hope she stops by. I want to see her before I leave."

Edith remembered her aunt Florence's past. She left her daughter, Sarah, when she turned twenty. She met her uncle Luther at a family reunion. They fell madly in love and got married. Luther had a son from a previous relationship. Florence moved to New York with her husband, had a child together, and when her child turned fifteen, she worked part-time as paralegal in her husband's office.

"Well if she doesn't, you know where she lives. She would be delighted to see you," she replied.

"I may do just that. Besides I am dying to see my grandson. Sarah sends me pictures of him all the time."

"His quite a big boy," she commented, and then changed the subject. "Where is Daisy?"

"She could not make it. She had to work at the telephone company."

She was disappointed. They had so much to discuss. "I am so sorry to hear that."

"You know she's still seeing a lawyer. They are talking about marriage." Florence informed her.

"I didn't know it was getting that serious. Of course I have not talked to her for a while."

"That's what she tells me anyway," Florence added.

She stood up abruptly. "I want to see dad for a minute. I'll be right back." Edith promised.

Florence leaned back and said cautiously, "Honey I know it is none of my business, but it's been on my mind since I got here. What is wrong with John? He's been testy."

She was confused at first. "I don't understand."

"I spoke, and he pretty near bit my head off. I never seen him this way."

She remembered the confrontation her parents had earlier. "Mother and I were at odds about Thomas coming over for the Holidays. Father intervened in my behalf."

"Why not?" Florence was curious. "He appears to be a decent guy."

"I don't know what conspired after I left."

"That's why Ellen was not here to greet us," she deduced.

Edith had an afterthought. Her mother always gave the maid off during the Holidays and allowed her guest to bring covered dishes or cook whatever they chose, and kept things organized. If she was not present, who was manning the kitchen? "Who's preparing the main course?"

"Your father started but your grandmother took over. She's in the kitchens now doing her thing."

"Maybe father is in there with her."

"I just remembered, your father left a few minutes ago. He said he needed to pick up something. Unless he came in the through the garage, I have not seen him."

"Well let me go check on grandma, if you don't mind."

Florence waved toward the pantry. "Go ahead. I am going to call Sarah and see if she's home. Might drive over there this afternoon."

She went into the pantry leading to the kitchen where she discovered Grandma Bessel stuffing a sixty pound turkey.

"Grandma, when did you get in?"

"Early." She paused and focused on her grand-daughter. "Turn around, let me look at you. You're as gorgeous as ever." She wiped her hands on her apron and hugged Edith. "My, you're becoming a fine woman. I can't get over how much you've grown since last year."

"I have not changed that much," she assured her.

"How old are you now anyway?"

"Nineteen."

Bessel guessed, "Second year in college right?"

"You got it."

Bessel gestured to a chair while she resumed stuffing the turkey after she washed and dried her hands with a paper towel. "And how is college going?"

"Good."

"And this young man you been writing me about. Are you still seeing him?"

"Yes," she confessed eagerly.

"When will I get to see him?" Grandma Bessel asked.

"Aunt Bessie is introducing him to the family as we speak."

Bessie introduced Thomas to Bill Bosworth, John's younger brother and Luther, John's older brother, who was a chain smoker. Beside Luther, sitting at the card table, was his son Edward. Edward was not a drinker. He beckoned Thomas to join them in a friendly game of Black Jack. His father offered Thomas a cold beer which he declined. He confessed he was not a drinker. Edward smiled grateful knowing he was not a minority. Bessie volunteered to get him a beverage of his choice. He said a coke would be fine and she disappeared into the pantry.

Thomas took his place at the card table filling a vacant seat. Bill shuffled the deck of cards. He took a long draw from his Marlboro, and smashed it in a glass ashtray.

Bill, a doctor by profession, neglected to abide by the rules of good health. He saddled a potbelly which would eventually present a multitude of medical glitches. Luther, the lawyer, guarded his liquor, continuously refilling his glass. Thomas sensed he was a slave to his bottle. From his glassy eyes, and slurred speech, he was high. As Bill dished cards to his constituents, Edward, a tall muscular man about Thomas' age, launched an inquisition.

"Tom, you don't mind if I call you that?" Edward started in.

"That's ok."

"Where are you from?"

"Virginia. My father and I moved there after my mother died," he explained.

Bill beckoned for Edward to start the game.

"I am sorry to hear that." He paused, played his hand, and then proceeded. "Who's your father?"

"Phillip Guy. His a teacher."

"It's your turn Thomas." Luther informed him.

Thomas glanced at his hand, and plucked a card from the deck. "I haven't seen dad for several months, but we keep in touch by phone. I barely recall the last time we shared Christmas together."

Edward sensed Thomas missed his father. "You say you communicate.'

"He calls to see how I'm making out."

Bessie returned carrying a coke and a glass of ice. She placed the glass and unopened soda on a coaster. Ellen was particular about her polished furniture being stained with water rings.

She had coasters strategically placed where guest were tempted to rest a beverage.

"How did you meet my cousin?" Edward pried.

"At the library," Thomas said while opening his can and pouring it over the ice. "She agreed to showed me around since I was new in town, introduced me to her family, and we became good friends."

Again it was Edward's chance to play. "Are you serious or just friends still?" He plucked another a card from the deck.

"I like Edith a lot. And she likes me."

"Sounds like love."

"Stop dipping into that man's business," Bessie interjected.

"I hear you aunt Bessie. Just want to know this man's intentions. You know how protective I am of my cousin," Edward replied as he waited for his father to play his hand.

"I would never hurt or take advantage of her. She means a lot to me."

Bessie took a seat in a recliner near the card table. "Luther are you cheating. The way you look, can you make it through the game."

"Bessie shut up and let me concentrate," Luther fussed while placing his cards on the table and shouted, "Black Jack."

Bill gathered the cards and shuffled them again. "Want to play another game fellas?"

Edith appeared from the kitchen and approached Thomas. "Are my uncles and cousin giving you the third degree?" she asked caressing his stiff shoulders.

"Your cousin Edward is the one," Bill informed her.

"Cuss you have nothing to worry about. We are friends getting to know each other." She grabbed the necklace dangling from her neck. *Actually they were more than friends. They were a couple in love.*

Bill redistributed the cards for another game. "Edith, where is my brother?" He asked.

"I don't know. I thought he would be here."

"After this game I am going to see if I can locate him. I have a hunch where he might be."

"Bill deal me in. I want to play, if you guys don't mind," Bessie said.

"Sure. Pull up a chair."

Bessie seized a nearby chair, and accompanied the men surrounding the card table. Bill played three more games, and then dismissed himself. He intended to find his brother.

Bill parked his black Mercedes-Benz in the crowded parking lot outside the Blue Tango Night Club on Lake Street. He paced through the congested sidewalk and exchanged brief greetings with old acquaintances. He passed people smoking dope, sipping booze from brown paper bags, having a good time. *Lake Street had not changed. The capital haven for alcoholics and drug addicts. Thank God he forsake Salisbury and made a niche for himself. Thank God his father demanded and expected the best from him. Walking the dark side was not acceptable to his father.*

Bill shoved open the door leading into the dimly lit, smoke infested nightclub. The man at the door recognized him and shook his hand. "Man, how are you doing?"

"Fine and you??"

"Doing fine. Perhaps not as good as you." The man was barely five feet tall but built like a bear. His tank top shirt revealed his bulging muscles. "Your brother is at the bar."

"Thank you good buddy." Bill went to the bar and sat beside his brother who was startled by his arrival.

"Bro what the hell takes you here?"

Bill ordered himself a shot of vodka from the young bartender with a sweater secured to his waist. His brother was glassy eyed and light headed. *There was no way in hell he was going to permit him to drive home. Chances are he could barely walk let alone drive.* "I came to check on you. What are you doing here? It's Christmas, or have you forgotten." The bartender sat a drink on the bar and Bill paid him. He gulped down his drink in one swallow.

"I was pissed off with Ellen, or rather she was pissed off with me. I gave Edith permission to bring her boyfriend over for the Holidays. She caught an attitude and left."

"Left where?"

John stared at his empty glass and then glanced at his brother. John knew for several months his beloved wife was involved with his best friend, Stanly. When it started, why it happened, he cared not to entertain the thought. What she saw in him was a mystery. He was a drunkard who dwelled in a rundown shack in the boondocks, miles from civilization. It wasn't because he couldn't do better. God knows he had the resources.

He encouraged Stanly to bull-dose the shack and build a new house or place a trailer on the lot, but Stanly was determined to keep his grandmother's home. It held semimetal value he claimed. It was his refuge from city life.

He recalled the day his brother revealed his wife's secret. They were celebrating the fourth of July with friends and family. The patio was packed with guest feasting and having a good time. Guest were dancing in the backyard to soul music from an eight-track player while others gathered in small groups laughing hysterically, enjoying each other's company. Stanly helped him barbecue the meats on the gas grill.

They ran out of beer and Stanly volunteered to go to the basement and retrieve a keg from the cooler. Shortly after Stanly departed, there was a cry for potato salad. Ellen volunteered to get another batch from the refrigerator. While she was getting chilled potato salad from the refrigerator, Stanly crept up behind her and nibbled her ears. She swirled around, leaving the salad on the counter and kissed him fervently. Unbeknown to them, Bill was on his way to the parlor to get a requested tape when he cruised pass the slightly adjourn door to the kitchen. He heard a noise and casually peeped inside witnessing a forbidden scene. Stanly and his wife were locked in an insidious embrace. Stanly was grouping Ellen's exposed thighs. A few days later he called him and told him what he saw. At first he refused to believe his brother. Ellen loved him. She would never be unfaithful. They were childhood sweethearts for God's sake. Against his better judgment, he hired a private detective to spy on his wife. The detective kept him stashed with pictures of Stanly and his wife in compromising positions. Snapshots of them smooching in the park, fondling in her office, laying naked in each other's arm in tawdry hotels. The evidence was overwhelming.

"I met Edith's boyfriend. He seems like a decent fellow. Matter of fact he was there when I left." Bill started the conversation.

"Edith's a smart girl. I trust her judgment." John replied.

"Where do you think Ellen went?" Bill probed timidly.

He knew what his brother was implying. "I don't want to think about that. Let's go home.

I'm sure mother has prepared a scrumptious turkey." He stood up and dashed a tip to the bartender.

"What are you going to do?" Bill was curious.

"I don't know yet."

"Where's your car?" Bill asked.

"I didn't drive. I took a taxi."

Ellen wrapped her mink stole over her round shoulders and prepared for the journey home. Stanly was stretched out across his iron bed with a thin blanket drawn to his waist hiding his nakedness with a smile on his face.

"I better go home and clean house." She sat on the wrinkled bed and slid her small feet into her high heel shoes.

"Meaning you intend to ruin your daughter's Christmas by sending her friend on the lurch."

"You make it sound cold and heartless," she remarked.

"It is what it is."

She leaned over and kissed him briefly. Then she studied the drab and dreary excuse for a home; a decaying facade necessitating a restoration. The walls could use several coats of paint, the squeaky floors needed replacing, and the windows were lacking a good washing. The only optimistic thing in its favor was running water, and an inside toilet.

"Why don't you fix this place up? No sense you living like this," she scolded.

"As I told you and your husband, I like this place. This is where I grew up."

She snatched her pocketbook from the dresser. "I understand but the place needs renovations. What harm will that do?"

"I'll reconsider it for your sake," he promised vaguely.

"How many times have I heard that?" She opened the bedroom door. "Have a merry Christmas."

"Be kind to Thomas," he chuckled.

"Yeah," she replied sarcastically and left.

Edith gave Thomas a tour of their estate and he was impressed. The house was like a picture from a cosmopolitan magazine. He asked who decorated the house, and she credited her mother. She informed him her grandparents originally owned the house but relinquished it to her parents. After the tour, they put on their coats and went outside where she pointed out how much property they owned and where the boundaries ended. The mansion sat on ten acres of waterfront real estate.

After the tour, they relaxed in lawn chairs furnishing the screened enclosure connected to the house serving as a patio. It was freezing. Other family members were in the den watching football. From where she sat, she could hear her uncles and aunt Bessie cheering. Obviously they were enjoying themselves. Earlier her Cousin Edward told her he was going to town to connect with old buddies he had not seen for a while. He promised to be back before dinner.

Her father entered the patio through a sliding glass door. One could tell he was enumerated from his unstable shuffle, but he appeared lucid. The induced high was waning gradually. He joined them sitting around an iron table. She introduced her father to Thomas, and they exchanged handshakes.

"So you're the man in my daughter's life," he said clearly without stammering.

"Yes sir." Thomas was formal and polite. It was said good impressions go a long ways. He was already on her mother's unacceptable list. The last thing he wanted was to lose favor with her father.

"Thomas Guy, the author?" John surmised.

"Yes sir."

"Please call me John. I don't go for the sir thing," he made his status known. "Edith tells me you met at the college."

"We did."

John stared at Thomas for a moment. *There was something familiar about him. The name guy rang a bell. He favored somebody he knew. The question was who and where. His next assignment was to ask questions. His inquiring mind had to know.* "Where are you from?"

"Virginia."

"What parts?"

"Virginia Beach."

That did not trigger his memory. "Who were your parents?"

"Phillip Guy. A school teacher for many years, and now his a part-time professor at a local college in Virginia. My mother died when I was young. She was a nurse."

The name Phillip Guy sounded familiar. Where had he heard it? A collage of past faces bombarded his thoughts. Still he was unable to pin the name Phillip Guy to a mental photo. Perhaps when he sobered up, and his thoughts were vibrant, he could make the connection.

"Look, I am going to get some rest before dinner. Sleep this hangover off. Glad to meet you Thomas."

"Glad to meet you John."

"It's too cold out here for me." He shivered as he re-entered the main house, realizing he was wearing a thin sweater, not at all dressed for the weather. No wonder he was chilly. Alcohol tampered his judgment and stifled his senses.

"Father seldom gets drunk. Every now and then." She felt obligated to defend her father's behavior.

"It's Christmas. Let the man tie one on."

"Look, tomorrow my cousins, and a few friends, are having a party at the Armory. I want you to come. You've already met some of them. It will be for a couple hours. It's like an after Christmas get together." She filled him in.

"Sounds great to me."

An hour later, as the autumn sun sank into the horizon. She led Thomas into the main house only to be greeted by a host of newcomers. Sarah, Corey and Florence were standing in front of a huge oil portrait of the late Joseph Douglas Bosworth whispering.

When Corey saw her, he ceased talking to his grandma Florence, and ran to her hugging her legs, hampering her from eradicating her coat, and hanging it on a coatrack.

"Guess what cousin Edith. I got a new bike, a race car and a great big electric train set and a whole lot of other stuff." He was overjoyed with the spirit.

"You must have been a good little boy," she assumed.

"I brought my racing cars with me. They're in the garage. Mom said I couldn't play with them in here, cuss, I would be getting in the way. Come with me. I want to show you something."

Corey placed her in an awkward dilemma. Even though she loved her Nephew, she was not prepared to be his playmate. She was relieved when Thomas provided an escape.

He knelt to Corey's level. "Hey little man. Why don't you show me you're racing cars? Maybe we can race each other. What do you say?" Thomas encouraged Corey.

Corey eyeballed his mother, and she nodded her approval. That was the break he needed. Let the games begin.

"Follow me." Corey grabbed Thomas' hand and dragged him towards the garage. "Just you wait. No way can you beat me. I'm the man. My car is bad."

A small group assembled in a far corner of the foyer a few feet from Edith, Sarah and Florence. The men were engrossed in a heated discussion ignorant of their presence. Bernard, with his girlfriend clinging like a parasite, entertained the consortium with exaggerated motions of a football play. Alex, decked in his starched policeman uniform, kept interrupting clarifying how he interpreted a strategy. Her beloved cousin Eddie struggled to make a point, and her Uncle Bill attempted to dominate the debate by talking louder than everybody else. Her Uncle Luther listened to the commotion holding a can of beer. As the conversation escalated, Bernard shifted his crew to another room leaving the foyer quiet.

Her aunt Bessie wondered into the lobby, spoke briefly to those present, being it was the courteous thing to do, placed a couple of presents under the Christmas tree, and left as quickly as she appeared. The doorbell charmed and her father entered lobby from the parlor answering the door preventing anyone from doing the honor. It was her Aunt Olvera and her

Uncle Justin bearing two bags. Her father greeted Olvera with a kiss on the cheeks and Justin with a handshake followed by a pat on the back. Her grandma Bessel popped on the scene from the pantry greeting Olvera with a hug and accepting the bags they were carrying.

"What is it?" Bessel asked knowing it was her famous pumpkin and sweet potato pie.

"Oh come on Bessel, you know what I cook," she said lightly.

"Do I ever? Come on in the kitchen. I want to show you something," Bessel said with Olvera sprawling her. "I tried your sweet potato biscuit recipe. You got to see this." Together they disappeared into the pantry.

John took Justin's coat and hung it on the rack behind the door. "How was the trip coming down?"

"It was alright." He pulled a cigar from his shirt pocket and lit it. "Have you got a cold Pepsi round here? I'm thirsty as all outdoors."

"Come this way and I will fix you right up."

Florence excused herself from her daughter. "I want to see these sweet potato biscuits. Chat with your cousin."

She eased toward Sarah with her vision fixated on the portrait of her grandfather and whispered, "Grandpa loved Christmas."

"That's an understatement," Sarah said. "The extremes he went decorating the house inside and out. He celebrated the holidays in a grand fashion."

"You know, in the basement there's a huge box of gifts with different years stamped on them for each of his grandchildren. I believe it goes up to ten years. That's his way of being with us long after his gone," she said standing beside Sarah.

"I didn't know that." She was impressed.

"Grandma told me last year."

Together they strolled from the foyer into a family gathering arena where relatives and friends were assembled chatting and nibbling on appetizers strategically stationed in various sections of the room. Appetizers her aunt Florence and grandma Bessel sat up unnoticed. As the evening progressed, Florence and the other guest, wondered where her mother was. It was getting close to dinner.

While the guest waited Ellen's arrival, she fellowshipped with her cousins and family. Bernard introduced his friend to his mother, Bessie.

She could tell by her expression, she was not pleased with his choice of friends, but she was cordial and polite. Her aunt whispered, "She can't be twenty-three. Hell, she looks older than me." Bessie kept their conversation brief. She kept busy in the kitchen helping her Grandma Bessel set the dining table. Her aunt Olvera and Florence sat beside each other on the couch sharing photos of past Christmases. Sarah, Bernard and his friend, sampled the treats on display to appeaser their sugar tooth. Her father, and uncles gathered in the parlor for poker. Justin shuffled the deck and dished out the cards while he puffed his cigar. Eddie opted to join the card game ten minutes after it started.

When the opportunity came, she snuck into the garage to check on Thomas and Corey. They were sharing a stupendous moment. Thomas relished the race as much as his new found friend. There he was, flat on his belly, with Corey beside him ushering their cars to the finish line as they squeezed the control switch in hope they could accelerate their car to go faster and win the race. Playing with Corey took him back to his youth.

She was about to leave the boys to their own demise when her mother walked up behind her. At first she was startled. "Mother, where have you been? Everybody has been expecting you?"

"I went out to get a few things," she replied.

"On Christmas. What stores are open?"

"The convenient stores," she replied. "Got some drinks and snacks for afterward."

"Well since you're here, I guess we will eat."

Thomas rose to his feet dusting the dirt from his shirt. "Little man I guess we'll have to finish this after dinner."

"I'm not hungry. I want to play with you." Corey nagged.

"Thomas perhaps that would be a good idea. I see young Corey here is enjoying your company. I'll see that Edith bring you and little Corey here a plate," She said while she rubbed Corey's head. *He might be at her house, but out of her presence. He was not going to ruin her Christmas. In the garage with Corey was the perfect place for him. Sarah would understand.*

She watched as her mother gathered her wits and went to welcome and commune with her siblings and in-laws. She noticed how conveniently she isolated Thomas from the rest of the family. She was surprised she allowed him to stay. It was predestined to be a long night with food, laughter and gifts.

Ellen greeted everyone and apologized for her tardiness without offering a legit excuse. Bessel ushered the guest into a spacious dining area primed with an assortment of nourishments admits stylish engraved silver utensils, and the finest holiday china. When the visitors were seated, Ellen requested Sarah to bless the food which she did without hesitation. Afterward, John, at the opposite end of the table, between his brothers, started pacing the entrees around the table. They ate, drank and talked amongst themselves. Then John asked Edith who sat near her mother, "Where is Thomas and Corey?"

"Corey said he wanted to play with his race track and Thomas agreed to stay with him. He said he wasn't hungry." Edith explained hoping not to make a scene.

"Corey said he wasn't hungry?" Sarah heard the conversation. "He must really be enjoying himself."

"I'm going to take both of them a plate when I'm finished." Edith promised.

"Just as long as they get something to eat," Sarah expressed her concern.

"Thomas is the writer of those melodramatic books, right." Justin added while piling sweet potatoes on his plate.

"Yes, he is." Edith told him.

"I read somewhere his mother died of some kind of a blood disorder. He was young at the time. His father and his aunt moved from New York to Virginia where they finished raising him." Olvera mumbled while she chewed.

"Who made the sweet potato biscuits?" Edward wanted to know. "They are delicious."

"I did, and thank you." Bessel confessed proudly.

"Everything looks good and taste good," Bernard said as he stuffed a fork full of greens in his mouth.

"Pass me the mac and cheese. Been wanting that all day," Florence shouted elbowing her husband.

Following the feast, the gathering drifted into the sunroom where another huge tree stood in the corner flooded with presents. Someone had mysteriously transferred all the gifts to one central area when no one was watching. Florence and Bessie straighten up the kitchen while the family prepared for the next traditional event. When everybody was in the solarium socializing, Ellen and John went about distributing gifts from underneath the tree. The sound of rattling paper and oohs and gasp echoed the atmosphere as presents were opened and surprised expressions captured anxious faces.

Edith abandoned the gift giving ceremony and went to the kitchen where her aunt Bessie prepared a plate for Thomas and Corey. She took the tray of food to the garage and presented to the guys. Corey stopped playing and devoured every morsel. He pleaded for seconds but she instructed him to see his mother in the sunroom. She hinted there was a present with his name on it. Corey zipped from the garage without once looking back.

As soon as Corey left, she joined Thomas at a small desk which her father used as a work bench, and watched him nibble at his food. He seemed to be enjoying himself commenting occasionally how tasty certain things were.

"I'm surprised your mother didn't ask me to leave," he said as he drank his punch.

"She wanted to."

"If it's ok with you, after I finish this, I want to go home. I believe I have over stayed my welcome."

"Fine. We've been here most of the day anyway." She understood why Thomas wanted to leave. "I'll get our coats." She headed to the foyer.

"I'll wait here." He was determined to dodge Ellen. Her generosity was predestined to wax cold. He finished his scrumptious dinner and trashed the paper utensils. When he spun around, Alex and Bernard were behind him, prepared to leave.

"Man why didn't you cohort with the rest of the family?" Alex asked Thomas.

"The lady of the house and I are not on good terms."

Bernard understood Thomas's situation. Rumor was Ellen opposed him courting her daughter. "Uncle John likes you. That's what counts. As long as his in your corner, Ellen's disapproval doesn't matter."

If only it was that simple. John may have accepted him but his wife had the last say. What she said was law. "So you guys fixing to leave?" Thomas asked.

"Man we been here for hours. Time to leave. Besides I work tonight. I want to go home, get some shut eye before I go on patrol," Alex explained.

"Say you coming to the after Christmas party at the Armory?" Bernard asked.

"Edith mentioned it to me. I'll be there."

"Good," Bernard said, and then added, "Check you out later man. And Merry Christmas."

The men exchanged a soul man's shake. Bernard concluded by saying, "My friend is in the car. She's anxious to get home. She has to work the late night shift at the hospital."

"Take it easy guys," Thomas replied watching the men exit toward the main house leading to the front entrance.

Edith returned carrying their winter attire. Together they headed to the foyer. As they approached the front door, Thomas paused at a portrait hanging in the lobby. The man in the picture favored someone he seen before. The mysterious question was who and where. Bessel and John startled him when they crept up behind him.

John apologized for the fright. "I'm sorry man. I didn't mean to startle you."

"That's OK."

"Thomas I am glad you came." Bessel extended her hand. "I see you are fascinated with the picture of my late husband."

"His face looks familiar. Perhaps it's the photos in the magazines praising his accomplishments," Thomas remarked lightly.

"Thomas you favor someone I know. I just can't remember who," John said as he laid his hand on his shoulder.

"I thank both of you for having me over. And tell Corey I want a rematch," Thomas said as he neared the door.

"Drive safely, and take care," Bessel advised.

John opened the door. A cold breeze blew frigid air into the cozy abode. "My God it's getting colder. Looks like it's subject to snow any moment,"

"Probably too cold to snow," Bessel commented.

"Tell mother I'll be back in a few to help clean up," Edith promised.

"Baby don't worry about that. Your aunt Florence and Bessie are in charge. Enjoy your Christmas together, whatever is left." John added quickly.

Bessel remembered the gifts. "Wait here one minute. I got a little something for both of you."

John closed the door, keeping the heat inside. Before he could mumble a word, his mother returned bearing two medium size boxes and presented them to Edith.

"Don't open them now. Wait until you get to your destination. Now it isn't much but a little something from me. Merry Christmas both of you." She hugged her grand-daughter and Thomas. "Goodnight again and be safe, "Bessel repeated.

The couple stepped into the cold Christmas night holding hands. It was a Christmas Edith would cherish forever. It was a Christmas Thomas would never forget. The magic of the season drew them closer together despite the circumstances harboring to tear them apart.

The next day, Ellen, with support of Bessel, her mother-in law, prepared brunch for their sleeping guest. They had been up until two gossiping, reminiscing, playing cards and drinking. Bill kept looting the kitchen for sweet treats. His, Brother Luther, who was three quarters in the wind, accused him of eating a whole sweet potato pie, and half a gallon of ice cream. Of course he denied it. Olvera, still sporting her flowered hat, spent most of the night chatting with Ellen, her baby sister, about her children and how pleased she was with how they turned out. She thanked her for keeping an eye on her son, Alex, the policeman. Ellen confided in her, how displeased she was with her daughter dating Thomas. She said he was seven years older than she and disrespectful. Ellen updated her about their first encounter at the Cohn's jewelry store and how he persuaded Edith to elope with him to Sight and Sound for the week-end. She informed her how her daughter deceived her by insinuating she was going on vacation with sorority sisters. Olvera commented with "Sis, she's grown. We've done all we could." Of course she did not want to hear that. Justin joined his wife at the kitchen table and asked Ellen to get him a slice of pumpkin pie with a scoop of chocolate ice cream. While he spooned his desert, he relayed how troubled he was about Alex being a policeman. "I know he loves the job but it's so dangerous. God knows I tried to get him to explore other professions but his mind was bent on being a lawman. So what could I say?" He gestured loosely. "It is what it is." He finished his bedtime treat, kissed his wife on the cheek and dismissed himself. He confessed he was tired and sleepy. Olvera promised to join him soon.

Bessel asked, "Do you think we have enough?"

Ellen dismissed thoughts of the past night and concentrated on the present.

She took a quick inventory of what they prepared. It was more than enough. "We have a plenty."

She covered the prepared brunch and sat across from Bessel. Bessel started pouring her a cup of coffee.

"That's enough," she cautioned. "I want room for the cream and sugar."

Bessel placed the coffee pot on the warmer and retrieved a pitcher of fresh squeezed orange juice from the counter. She filled a tall glass with juice and placed the pitcher into the refrigerator. Then she rejoined her daughter-in-law."

"I've been wanting to talk to you about John."

She knew where Bessel was headed. She was concerned about her son playing his prospective role in the company.

"Is he taking charge? Acting like a boss?" Bessel asked.

"Mother Bessel, he's coming around. I believe he's beginning to enjoy being in charge." Ellen said. Then she reminded her, "You making him president was the push he needed."

"He visit the sister plant often enough. He's appointed good people to run it. Of course I follow-up," Bessel commented.

"If I can get Edith to join the company, it will make a world of difference. I know he would love having his daughter running the company with him." She sighed briefly. "But right now she's in love with this Thomas Guy. I'm trying my best to dissolve this affair before it gets serious."

Bessel recalled how she resented Ellen for lowering her son into marriage. Despite her reservations, they married and she was the link to keeping her son connected to the company. Her husband knew this when he appointed her a prestigious position in the Eastern Shore Plant. With that in mind, she gave her constructive advice. "If she's in love, do not interfere. I know that may be difficult because of your plans for her. But she's only known the man for three to four months. Let's see how things play out."

"I've investigated Thomas." Ellen told her. "No stray children or mistresses, clean record and a decent bank account. I believe his worth a million."

"He's a bestselling author," Bessel reminded her.

Edward, Bill, Luther and John paraded into the kitchen dressed casually, smelling of cologne. They gathered around the oblong table. Ellen and Bessel rose from their break to service them.

"Where are you guys going this morning?" Ellen interrupted the men's chatter.

Edward and Luther were in a heated discussion about a Cadillac Bill saw in the newspaper. John spoke for his contraband. "We're going car shopping at Oliphant's Chevrolet."

"Did anybody tell Justin?" Bessel wondered. "I'm sure he might want to join you fellows."

"He knows, but he and Olvera have their own plans," John said.

"Olvera said something about shopping at the Mall and Justin is going to Montgomery Wards to get a new radio for his car. Evidently the old one is on the blink, "Edward guested.

Bessel started dishing out the entrees and Ellen poured the beverages. It was predestined to be a wonderful day.

When Edith came downstairs for breakfast, it was noon. Bessel had trashed the leftovers and cleared the table but stored a covered dish in a new gadget called a microwave. She turned on the microwave for three minutes and served Edith. She filled a glass with juice and collected toast popping from the toaster placing it on a saucer with soft butter and jam. She watched Edith nibbled her meal while she sipped coffee.

"Where's mother?" Her granddaughter asked.

"In the den watching the soaps."

"Love of Life no doubt," Edith guessed. That was her favorite show. Rumor was it had been cancelled, and being replaced with The Young and Restless.

"Got any plans for today? "Bessel was curious.

"There's a party at the Armory. We are going."

"Oh that after Christmas party your cousins have every year." She remembered.

"Yeah."

"Have fun." Bessel rose to leave. "Put the plate in the sink. I'll get it later."

"Where are you going?" Edith treasured spending time with Bessel.

"Watch the soaps with your mother."

Edith consumed everything on her plate, and placed the empty dishes in the sink as instructed. She glanced at her wristwatch. It was twelve thirty. She had ample time to drive to the Salisbury Mall and pick up a dress for the party.

When she entered Hecht's Department Store, she was greeted warmly by her cousins, Cherry, who could pass as her twin, Ethel, wearing a pants suits two sizes too small, and Charlene with a purchase on the counter being rang up by the salesclerk. Ethel and Cherry hugged their cousin while Charlene reached into her wide pocketbook pulling out a credit card for the cashier. Cherry and Ethel had bags draped over their shoulders.

"Girl you came at the right time. Having a red dot sale, twenty-five percent off tagged price." Ethel was excited about the sale.

"Got terrific bargains. I'm sure you'll find something." Cherry pitched.

"I'm searching for an outfit for the party."

"I'm surprised you didn't go to Hess Apparel," Charlene remarked finishing her purchase.

"I figured I'd find what I liked her at the Mall."

Cherry volunteered her constituent's service. "Cousin, come with us. We'll help you find just what you want."

The ladies escorted Edith to a rack of outfits in the center of the store. They had her try on several dresses. She obliged the charade for a duration until she uncovered the perfect garment. Her cousins were in complete agreement with her choice. It was a cream pants outfit with a matching scarf. Next she had to locate shoes to match. High heels were taboo. They were murderous on her legs. Fashion was important, but comfort was imperative. Her cousins guided her from Hecht's to a shoe store a few shops down. They spent an hour sifting out footwear. After a heated discussion, the group settled on an eye-catching loafers appeasing Edith's peculiar taste.

As noon approached, the girls were debating on going to orange Julius for a hot dog and drink or to English's Grill for a decent meal when they spotted Olvera coming from a hat shop with a box under her arms. They went to greet her. With the exception of Edith, they had not seen her for several years.

"Aunt Olvera, it's nice seeing you." Charlene said as she went to embrace her. They were both short making it easier for them to make contact.

Cheery and Ethel took their tern hugging the short, light skinned lady. "Edith didn't tell us you were here." Cherry said glancing at her lookalike.

"I had not gotten around to it." She defended herself.

"How long are you staying?" Ethel asked standing up straight towering over Olvera.

"We are leaving New Year's Day. That is if my sister will have us," she joked.

"Mother enjoys your company," Edith assured her.

"What you got in that box?" Cherry asked knowing her weakness.

Olvera had a hat fetish. She had a hat for every occasion. She paraded her hats like her son, Alex, modeled his police uniform. That was the one thing they shared; an addiction to hats, an addiction to his uniform. "I got a hat for New Year's Eve Service."

Where's Uncle Justin?" Edith wondered. She knew Olvera depended on her husband to chauffer her abound.

"He went to Montgomery Wards to have the car repaired. Don't ask me what's wrong with it. As far as I'm concerned, it was working fine but who am I?"

"His coming back for you?" Charlene assumed.

"I hope so," she smirked. Everybody knew she did not have a driver's license. "Where you girls headed?"

"We were debating about where to eat. Cherry wants to go to Orange Julius for a hot dog and drink and Charlene and I want to go to English Grill, sit down and have a decent meal." Ethel said calmly.

"I say let's go to English Grill on me. My delayed Christmas treat." Edith spoke up. "My way of showing appreciation for helping me find an outfit for the party."

"Sounds like a winner." Charlene conceded gracefully.

"You girls go ahead and enjoy. I'm going to Sears and see if I can find a dress for church." She waved by-by as she strutted through the Mall towards Sears Roebucks.

As the girls marched toward English Grill, they taunted Edith about sleeping with Thomas.

"I know you got some of that by now girlfriend." Ethel was crude.

"What are you talking about?" Edith pretended to be ignorant of her implication.

"I can't much blame you for trying him out. I'd love to get into those pants myself." Cherry added unexpectedly.

"Come on girls. My cousin is not the type to tell. Leave her alone." Charlene came to her rescue.

She was grateful Charlene dissolved the testy teasing. Exposing her personal kinship with Thomas was not on her priority list. What they did in secret would remain private. Inquiring minds were left to wonder.

Edith paid for dinner and tipped the waitress. Her cousins ate until they were pleasantly appeased and went separate ways promising to reunite at the After Christmas Affair.

Edith went home and changed for the party. Nobody was there when she returned and no one was there when she left. She deduced her family went shopping or doing whatever gratified their fancy.

She volunteered to pick up Thomas. Hopefully he would be ready. Usually he was performing his last minute grooming ritual when she made her entrance. Today would be no exception. He finished shaving and was styling his hair when she let herself into his apartment.

She loved his suit but wondered why he neglected to wear a tie. Two buttons on his starched shirt were unfastened. At her discretion, she fastened one shirt button, hastening temptation. The less peering eyes saw, the less lurid imaginations could conjure. Thomas was her property. She refused to share him.

The Armory was packed when they arrived. Swarms of relatives and friends hailed her with hugs, pleasant smiles and salutations. They apprehended a table in the corner where her cousin Alex sat with an attractive lady, his partner. They both wore their uniform. She wondered if they were on duty or out for the evening or both.

Every table was accented with candles admits a rose centerpiece atop a crimson tablecloth and clear utensils strategically positioned on folded napkins with matching dinnerware. Covered salad dishes, and a large pitcher of ice water beside a large pitcher of ice tea marked eating sections. The place was superbly coordinated. She pondered who merited the credit.

They merged with Alex and his friend. Alex watched as they draped their coats over their chairs. Alex's friend intervened informing her they could store their coats on a rack. Being they were already seated, she declined her offer.

"This is Clair." Alex introduced his friend.

Clair was a stout lady with a pretty eyes. She had long hair which was tied with a ribbon making a ponytail. She wore wire framed glasses enhancing her round face,

Edith introduced herself and Thomas. They made small talk while listening to the bands as they waited to be served. Several hostess circled leaving breadbaskets followed by other servers strolling the aisles with a cart containing two entrees and two deserts to select. Clair, famished and bewitched by the aroma, could not resist sampling the rolls while the others practiced restraint. Minutes later, Bernard joined the consortium with his friend. He de-coated himself and his significant other before joining the assembly. He was wearing creased black slacks and a starched white shirt absent a tie. Evidently ties were banished. After surveying arriving parties, she realized no man was taxing a tie. *When did ties go out of style?*

Joseph and his fiancé joined the table, filling the last seats, completing the forum. Thomas remembered Joseph from skate-land where he almost knocked him off balance. *Or did he knock him down. He could not recollect.*

Joseph was always smiling as if he had not a care in the world. His fiancé was about his height displaying an afro hairdo with dangling, exquisite, jewels highlighting her iridescent gown. She shimmied her shawl over her exposed shoulders and rested her manicured hands on the table enticed by the ice water. When the opportunity presented itself, she whispered to Thomas Joseph's fiancé's name.

"Her name is Francis Collins and her father owns a hotel in Princess-Ann. She attends University of Maryland Eastern Shore. Studying Hotel Motel Management. Being groomed to take over her father's business."

Eddie, her favorite cousin, took to the podium. He welcomed everybody to the After Christmas Party, encouraging the guest to fellowship while the caterers scouted about. Then he quickly added, almost forgetting, "the bar was officially open," and gestured to the bar where two men dressed in black stood. He reclaimed his place at a table with Charlene, Ethel, Cherry, and a high yellow man with a nappy head. Charlene sat close to her red boned escort moving her hands as she talked. Eddie, Cherry, and Ethel did not have a companion; they were doing the single bit. Her three cousins were the committee who arranged the shindig. Ethel had a knack for decorating, Eddie was a terrific organizer, and Cherry maintained contacts with prominent local musicians.

The party was a smash. English Grill catered the bash and the Big Boys Band supplied the entertainment. After chatting and chewing, a few people took to the dance floor. Alex and Clair made their way to the bar. She tried to get Thomas to dance but he would not budge. He claimed dancing was not his thing. He preferred to watch and play it safe. He feared making a spectacle of himself. But Bernard and Joseph were relentless. After a lot of coaching, they managed to get Thomas on the dance floor when a mob lined up for the hustle. Thomas insisted he did not know how to hustle. She assured him if he watched her, he would catch on. Against his better judgment, he joined the gang. He watched every move and imitated her steps. Before he knew it, he got the jest of the dance and rocked with the music in sync with the others. When the hustle played out, he returned to his seat. Together they watched as a crowd gathered for the soul train parade. They spent the rest of the night watching her cousins and friends adlibbing and showing off their dancing skills. Periodically people stopped by to socialize realizing they were not going to participate in anymore dancing activities. They were lucky they got Thomas on the floor for one dance.

She complimented Eddie, Ethel and Cherry on pulling off an awesome bash. Charlene brought her male friend over, sitting in Alex and his friends place while they danced, and introduced him to Edith. "I want you to meet Alfred. Alfred, this his Edith and Thomas." Alfred smiled and offered a friendly hand which they accepted.

It was midnight when the last person left. She and Thomas lingered behind to assist Cherry, Eddie and Ethel clean up. Charlene left early with her new boyfriend. Thomas and Eddie gathered rubbish from the tables and stuffed it into three huge plastic barrels. While working in close together, Thomas and Eddie became acquainted on a personal level. Eddie discovered Thomas was from Virginia, his father became a part-time professor after retiring from high school teaching. His mother died when he was young and his father and aunt moved from New York to Virginia where his aunt finished raising him. He graduated from college with a BA and worked at a local television station for a short season as a reporter, but resigned after he wrote his first book which became an overnight best seller which was proceeded by three other books that did quite well. Currently he was working on another book using the Eastern Shore as the premises. Thomas learned Eddie was an only child. His mother, Ellen's sister, transferred from Salisbury Nursing Home to another Nursing Home in Philadelphia, owned by the same family, accepting a position as Director of Nursing which was an upgrade from her former position as head Charge Nurse. At the time, he was in his late teens, had just moved into his own apartment on Riverside Drive and was working at Ocean City part-time and full time at Salisbury Nursing Home as a janitor on the late night shift. His mother seldom came home for Christmas with her siblings because of her job and Ellen understood. His father's identity was a secret. His mother was quick to avoid or dismiss the subject when it arose. *He was a fatherless child.* When the kids in the neighborhood asked him about his father, he claimed he was dead. It was easier than confessing he did not know who he was.

She helped Ethel and Cherry swept the floor, washed off the tables, and salvaged decorations in boxes to be stored for future events. When all was done, the five of them dressed for the weather, said their goodbyes, got into their separate vehicles and drove off into the night. In a few days it would be New Years' Eve.

New Year's Eve, Ellen, Olvera, Bessel, Bessie and Florence congregated in the lobby styling their Sunday's best attire. They grabbed their coats, slipped into complimentary gloves primed for their grand exodus.

"Whose car are we taking?" Olvera wondered.

"We'll use my car because it's roomier. The men will probably go with John." Ellen stated.

"What are the men doing? Services will start in a few minutes and I hate being late." Bessel complained.

"Who knows?" Bessie said.

"The impression I got they were contemplating abandoning services and go to the Blue Tango." Florence added quickly.

"Well ladies, I bought this hat and I want to go to church. If the Lord should come tonight, I want to be in the right place." Olvera replied. "Besides, Justin has got to go. He's supposed to speak."

"Let me go and see what the holdup is," Bessel said leaving the foyer.

Bessel found her son, John, Justin, Bill, Luther, and Edward huddled in the patio with their coats firmly buttoned puffing out white smoke from exhaling. Apparently they were engaged in a serious discussion. They were startled by Bessel's appearance

"Do you guys realize what time it is?" Bessel scolded. "Services will start in twenty minutes," she reminded them.

"Mother we are ready." John assured her and then added, "Justin was telling us about this man he met in Montgomery Ward's when he went to have work done to his car. He said he favored me. He said after they got to talking, he said his father was Joseph Bosworth. :

Bessel was bewildered. *All the years they had been married, Joseph never mumbled a word about an outside family. She was the only woman in his life and her sons were the only children he begot. Was there a secret life she was unaware of? It couldn't be.* "His father might be Joseph Bosworth but not your father, or my husband. Perhaps he's talking about another Joseph."

"No," Justin intervened. "He was positive it was Joseph, former head of Bosworth Industries who died recently of a heart attack. And when I told him how he favored my brother-in-law, he insinuated it was possible they were brothers. He said he intended to stop by here after the holidays to see John and introduce himself."

It was another imposter trying to wiggle his way into the family fortune. Down through the decades, occasionally someone would call Joseph posing to be a distant relative or an unclaimed bastard child seeking retribution. That had to be another one of those crank cases. "Son I wouldn't let it worry me if I were you. And if he comes by, contact me immediately if I am not here. I am curious of his intentions." She quickly dismissed the allegations. "Let's leave for church. We can entertain this discussion tomorrow."

73

"What are we going to drive in?" Edward wondered.

"We'll use my station wagon," John suggested. "That way we'll have ample room for our legs." Then John turned to his mother who was about to join the ladies in the foyer. "I trust Ellen is using her Volvo."

"I believe so." Bessel remarked.

Minutes later everyone boarded their assigned vehicle and made haste to the church which was a tem minute drive. Upon arriving at Mount Olive Church, in Fruitland, they found the lot packed with vehicles. Luckily they found a parking space. Ellen, leading the way, paraded her clan into the small edifice with the seating capacity of a hundred people, greeting relatives and friend as they made path to a vacant bench to accommodate their party. They remained in their coats. The church was still warming up. Being it was twenty degrees below zero, it would be a spell before the church became comfortable.

Sarah was singing an old traditional hymn with the choir. After praise and testimonial services concluded, the pastor, a stalky elderly man with gray hair, weak eyes, and heavy mustache approached the podium. He said it was an honor to have Justin, the brother-in-law of Ellen Bosworth, in the congregation and asked him to give an opening prayer and reading of the scripture. Justin, being forewarned, gracefully assumed his place at the podium while the pastor took his seat. Justin asked the congregation to stand for opening prayer. Everyone did as instructed. He bowed his head and the members followed suit. After delivering a powerful supplication, he read palms 100 and then went back to his seat beside Edward.

The pianist commenced playing "How Great Thy Art" and Sarah ascertained that was her pitch for a solo. Her presentation was grand. The parishioners rewarded her a stupendous applaud and a standing ovation.

The pastor preceded Sarah with his message for the evening. He preached from the book of Revelations for twenty minutes with intermittent claps and praises at highlighted intervals during the sermon. He concluded preaching fifteen minutes before midnight. Then he requisitioned Justin to pray the church into the New Year. Justin, without hesitation, again resumed his spot at the podium.

Olvera was proud of her husband. He had been a lay speaker for many years. He knew the residing pastor from college and they kept in contact.

Justin bowed his head, while the congregation rose and bowed their head in reverence. He gave an eloquent and moving prayer inspiring members to cry out tributes of appreciation for God's goodness and mercy. By midnight people were shouting with hands lifted high talking in tong or weeping violently. Olvera worshipped the Lord without restraint with tears rolling down her face. The emotional calamity lasted for twenty minutes and then the congregation mellowed. It was well after midnight when Justin concluded by saying "Happy New Year."

New Year's Day after Ellen rustled up a stupendous breakfast for her lodgers, something she seldom did, permitting them to eat until stuffed, and unable to consume another morsel. Then they lined suitcases in the Foyer and said their goodbyes and assurances of reuniting again next year. Edith joined her family for their farewell ceremony in hope of mingling with her cousin Edward before he departed.

"Sis I had a wonderful time and look forward to seeing you Thanksgiving," Florence said to Ellen as she slipped into her coat. "The food was marvelous as always."

"The next time I come down, I want to go fishing. So make all the arrangements. I can't wait to get on that boat." Luther forewarned his brother.

"I hear you Bro," John said while helping his brother into his coat.

"John I'll be passing through in a couple months. What you say about getting me three dozen soft crabs. I haven't had a soft crab in months." Bill injected as he moved his suitcase close to the door.

"I'll see what I can do," John promised.

"Keep an eye on my son. Surprised he didn't come by to see us off. Guess he had to work," Olvera said to Ellen while adjusting her hat and knotting it loosely around her neck.

"He called this morning and wished us a safe journey home. He was on duty then." Justin told his wife as he stepped toward the door carrying a suitcase.

Bessel pulled her son aside and whispered in his ear, "If that man comes by, let me know. I know how gullible you can be." Then she turned to face Ellen. "Ellen, I know you're an astute level headed person. If anybody comes by claiming they are an ascendant of Joseph, do not believe them."

Justin told Ellen about his encounter with a man at Wards claiming he was John's brother. She dismissed it as a ploy to wiggle his way into the family's wealth. That was not going to happen on her clock. "Mother Bessel you have nothing to worry about."

"Edith, I am happy for you and the man in your life. Everybody needs someone to love." Florence added as she embraced her niece.

"That goes double from me," Bessie pitched in.

Each family member went about hugging and shaking hands and kissing briefly as they departed the house and went to their vehicles carrying their luggage. John and Ellen, wearing coats to stifle the bitter cold, went out to see their guest off, and assist with stacking their suitcases.

Edward, lagged behind waiting for a chance to speak with his cousin alone. "Cousin, I love you. You know that. And I see you love Thomas. He appears to be smitten by you. I want you to be happy and careful." He hugged her. "Enjoy your life."

"Why didn't you come to the After Christmas party?" Edith was curious.

"Edith I am not the same. I gave my life to Christ a few months ago. Yes, I still have a long ways to go but I am working on it. I'm like sis, Sarah, a newborn."

"Well, you were never a worldly person. And I am happy for you." She hugged him.

"Take care cuss."

"I will."

He left.

Minutes later her parents returned, hung their coats on the rack and went into the kitchen where they sat at the table. Ellen volunteered to pour her husband a cup of black coffee. Edith got a handful of chocolate cookies from the cookie jar, a special treat left from her grandmother Bessel. Ellen asked Edith if she had any plans for the rest of the day, and she told her no. She said she intended to stay home and watch football with her father. Since she started dating Thomas, she seldom spent time with her dad, and felt guilty. New Year's Day was an ideal time to remedy that.

John was pleased to spend time with his only child. Secretly he missed their quality moments together. Before she became a college student and fell hopelessly in love, they attended the Wicomico Theater beside the

County Library twice a month; a place showing movies produced by people of color. He relished action films and Edith enjoyed them equally as well. At least that is what he chose to believe. They concluded their evenings by gorging on pizza or greasy hamburgers with hot, salty fries and large drinks from a fast food joint. On other occasions they visited Cherokee Bowling lanes where Edith beat him unmercifully no matter how desperately he tried. He wondered where she achieved her bowling skills. It certainly wasn't him even though he taught her how to play the game. Apparently she inherited it from her mother who was a terrific bowler when she was in high school. His wife and her father were in a bowling league until he moved to Wilmington to help establish a sister plant. Shortly after he left, she stopped bowling totally.

While Edith and John sat on the couch in the family room watching the football game, sharing a bowl of popcorn, Ellen sat in the corner reading a novel written by Jackie Collins. She was content having her daughter home. All day she neglected mentioning his name, which was unusual. She was beginning to wonder if she could breathe without him. An insane but soothing thought crossed her mind as she gazed at a printed page. *Perhaps it was over. Maybe her precious daughter came to her senses, and realized it was best to back off. Maybe she realized her education, and career was more important than a superficial romance which may not lead anywhere. Maybe Thomas wanted space so he could sew his wild oats someplace else. Perhaps there was another love interest in his life; a new heroin on the scene.*

Who was she fooling? Yes, the idea was refreshing, but the reality was Edith was committed to Thomas. The look in her eyes when she mentioned his name, the way she clung to him when they were together. She seldom left his side. She was always there for him. Her daughter was in a relationship for the long haul. If only there was a way she could separate them until she got her degree at least. Deep down she knew there was nothing she could do. Edith wanted Thomas, and she feared Thomas wanted her. Yet there had to be a way. She could not give up. She had to terminate that relationship. The down side was, Edith might hate her afterward. She might never forgive her for ruining what she thought was the best thing in her life. She might lose her. But it was a chance worth taking.

It was eight when the game ended, and Edith retired for the evening. She was tired. It had been a long, quiet, day. John watched the after game commentaries.

It was nine o'clock when the doorbell rang. Ellen wondered who it was that time of night. She feared it was Thomas. She laid her book on a coffee stand, and went to answer the door. If it was Thomas, she would send him back out in the cold where he belonged.

When she opened the door, she was greeted by a man that favored her husband. It was the man Justin informed her about. The man he met at the repair garage who claimed he was possibly the brother of her husband. The imposter Bessel warned to be leery of.

His timing was impeccable. A stranger appears at one's door New Year's Day baring God only knows what. *Why didn't he have the decency to make a daytime appearance?*

"May I help you?" Ellen managed to say.

"My name is Phillip Guy. I'm sorry bothering you this time of night, but my car stalled a block from here. I was wondering if I could use your phone to call a tow truck, and a taxi."

John walked into the foyer. He recognized the man standing in the doorway. "Phillip, is that you!"

"John Bosworth!"

"Man come in."

Phillip stepped inside the cozy foyer. "It's a beautiful place you have," he said taking in the scene. Phillip paused, staring at the oil painting of Joseph Bosworth, but said nothing.

Ellen closed the door. "The phone is over there." She gestured to the receiver."

"What happened to your car?" John was curious.

"Man, I don't know. I think it's the alternator. Just got it out of the shop a few days ago." Phillip telephoned the towing company giving directions to his vehicle. The dispatcher promised someone would be there within sixty minutes.

"What did they say?" John asked.

"Tow truck be here in an hour." Phillip excused himself, and called a taxi. A heavy voice said a taxi was on route.

"Come in and have something hot," John urged. "Which would you prefer, coffee, or hot chocolate. I know it's freezing outside." He waved him into the kitchen with Ellen trailing.

"I wouldn't mind a cup of coffee."

"I'll get it," Ellen volunteered. She left the coffee pot plugged in. All she had to do was pour it into a cup. "Do you want sugar and cream?"

"Black."

"John do you want some coffee?" She asked.

"No, I'm fine."

"The last time I saw you, we were in college. And I was watching over you per Joseph's request. He was adamant about you taking over the company. I presume you granted his wish before—

"Yes, I am president of the company. I didn't have a choice after his death." John rudely interrupted.

"I read about his death. I am so sorry to hear that." Phillip was sympathetic.

Ellen placed the steaming coffee before Phillip resting a spoon on a paper napkin. "I remember your face," she said. Many years ago Joseph, and Phillip were in the parlor talking when she came in bearing an affidavit for a signature.

"I have been here with Joseph awhile back. We met in passing. You thought we were business associates, and he never told you different." Phillip sipped his coffee.

"Honey, I think you better brace yourself. There's something we have to tell you." John started slowly.

Reluctantly she joined the men. "OK."

"When Justin told us earlier about a man he met at Montgomery Wards who claimed to be my brother, he was talking about Phillip. Mother does not know, and neither does anyone else in the family." John paused for a few seconds.

"I'm listening. "Her heart pounded. She was afraid of what she might hear.

"My father got a thirteen year old girl pregnant before he married mother. It was brought to Grandpa Douglas's attention by the girl's parents. He paid the girl's parents a good amount of money seeing their daughter left town. I saw a check written out to Melisa Guy for five hundred dollars laying on grandfather's desk when I was eighteen, a few weeks before I went to college. I asked him who Melisa Guy was. He sat me down, and told me the story, but made me promise not to tell mother, or my brothers, which I agreed to. He said that was our secret. Unbeknown to me, before I started college, my father contacted Phillip, and told him to watch over me. Phillip was in graduate school when I started college. That was when you saw Phillip. That was also when my father summoned him here and told him he was his father. I told father when I returned home for spring break, there was a boy at school who looked exactly like me, but he dismissed my curiosity by saying we all have lookalikes. It never registered that Phillip, the guy who favored me was my brother. Phillip was Melissa's son. When I was getting ready to graduate from college, my father told me the guy I favored in college was my brother. We kept in touch through mail. Not as much as I should have. Phillip went his way pursuing his career as a teacher, and I came home to run the family business with my father. The bottom line, is, we are brothers."

Ellen was confused. "Why didn't your father, and grandpa, want the rest of the family to know?"

"Grandpa and father feared my brothers would tell mother. And daddy did not want mother to know about his outside son. He feared she might divorce him or cause trouble for Melisa and Phillip," John explained. "Mother was jealous of father,"

She knew Bessel would give Joseph a dirty look, or hit him on the shoulder if she caught him admiring another woman. She was certainly jealous. "I am aware of that," she commented.

"How long have you been in town?" John asked.

"A couple days. I came to see my son." Phillip said, enjoying the black coffee.

"I didn't know you had a son. I know your wife died." John added.

"My wife died of a blood disorder. I thought it was cancer at first." He took another sip. "She had a peculiar strain of sickle- cell anemia."

"Sorry to hear that." John apologized. "Why didn't you tell me you had a son?"

"It happened so fast. I hardly had enough time to collect my thoughts. We met, fell in love, got married, had a child, and then she became sick, and I spend the rest of my life caring for her. I watched her grow weaker everyday while our child grew up. Finally I had to solicit outside help. And then she died, and I had to pick up the pieces, and start a new life with my son. Thank God I had my sister there. She stayed with us when we moved from New York to Virginia. She was a God send. I don't know what I would have done without her."

"You had a rough past." Ellen sympathized.

"The reason why I wanted to see you John, is my son has moved into the area, and I am concerned about him."

"Concerned," John echoed.

"He's been calling me complaining about pain in his limbs, and shortness of breath. I told him to contact a doctor, but he's afraid."

"Afraid of what?" She was curious.

"My son knows his mother died of sickle-cell. He also know that it's hereditary. He's a carrier."

"But he doesn't have it." John assumed.

"He has to have routine blood test. I hope that he doesn't. That's why I am here. I am going to the doctor with him at his next visit, and we will find out what's going on."

"If there is anything I can do to help, please let me know." John volunteered.

"Yes there is. I understand my son has been seeing a young girl by the name of Edith. He never told me her last name."

"What is your son's name?" John was curious.

"You've heard of him. His a famous author, Thomas Guy. He's written several books. A matter of fact, that's why he's here. He's working on another book as we speak."

John looked at Ellen, and Ellen jumped to her feet. "Thomas Guy is your son!" She was in shock. It was not possible.

"You two looked alarmed. What's going on?"

John took a stab at explaining the situation. "Phillip, I don't know how to tell you this, but my daughter Edith is the young lady your son has been seeing."

"That's impossible. It can't be." He was alarmed.

Ellen paced about nervously. "I'm afraid John is right. My daughter, and your son are involved.

"Well." Phillip was temporarily at lost for works. Then he finally managed to say, "You have to break it up. This cannot be. First of all they are first cousins. But we cannot expose that because of your mother finding out about me."

"You're right about that." John agreed. "I don't want mother's memory of father tarnished.

"And then there is the thing about his health. If my son has acquired the disease, which I pray not, he will die a slow painful death, and I don't want your daughter to go through that. She is eighteen or nineteen right?"

"Yes." Ellen whispered.

"I know this is hard for both of you, but I beg of you, discourage your daughter from seeing my son. They will not have a happy future together."

Suddenly Ellen's world changed drastically. For a long time she wanted desperately to terminate her daughter's relationship. Finally she had the ammunition to accomplish her wish. Now it was irrelevant.

Knowing her daughter loved her first cousin was rough enough, but there was a possibility her cousin, her boyfriend, was facing a debilitating death; a death that would destroy her. In her heart she feared they consummated their friendship. Breaking up would be arduous for both parties. Yet she had to spare her daughter the pain, and suffering of watching the handsome man she loved dwindle from a healthy person to an invalid depending on her support and care. It was tough for Phillip watching his wife die a slow death unable to help. He was older, and stronger and wiser. Would she have the strength to tackle each degenerative stage? There was only one thing to do. However, she would wait until the report came back. She would grant them a few weeks together.

The animosity and distain evaporated. Pity and sorrow took preeminence. Star crossed lovers were battling two invisible foes not of their making. They were first cousins, a product of a seed sewn in the wrong place, and an impending death sentence, a product of natures' unjust act. What was once an affair striving to burst into a beautiful flower, was now stagnant, waiting to wither like autumn leaves.

The second week in January, Edith informed her mother about her plans to take the Cape May Ferry to Atlantic City with Thomas celebrating of his twenty-seventh birthday. She expected a vehement denial. She was flabbergasted when she simply said "Ok." without rebuke. It was an unprecedented response. Evidently trouble was brewing at the plant, and she lacked the vigor to combat her. At the moment, Thomas was not on her priority list. Her mother kissed her forehead briefly, a habit neglected since her courtship.

The drive to the ferry was quiet. Thomas kept staring at the highway and resting his trembling hands on her knees. He did not seem like his cheerful self. His thoughts were a thousands of miles away. She anticipated he was thinking about his mother. She died on his birthday.

Unbeknown to Edith, during the past few days, his future was uncertain. He kept remembering a surprise visit from his father.

A few days before Christmas, His father, Phillip, showed up at his doorstep. They had communicated via a phone every other week. His father was concerned about his health and how he was doing in general. He told him everything was fine and he met this wonderful girl. His father was pleased hearing good news. But the week before Christmas, when his father called, he had bad news. He informed him he was experiencing sharp pains and shortness of breath. At once his daddy strongly suggested he see a doctor. He said it was probably nothing serious, but it would be wise to have it checked out. Days later he scheduled an appointment with a local doctor who requisitioned papers from his family physician in Virginia.

"How long has this been going on young man?" Dr. Pernell, a young, black man with a well-manicured afro and skinny frame hovered over him with a statoscope listening to his chest and back while he coughed when asked. He probed a flashlight into his eyes and down his throat searching for signs of infection. Then he squeezed his sides and pressed his stomach asking if he felt any pain. He told him he was fine. "Well your lungs are clear and there is no extension. I want you to have some blood work. Meanwhile, I will wait until your primary doctor fax me your medical records, and then we can go from there. I want you to fast for twelve hours before you have blood work." Dr. Purnell sent him to the receptionist, a black lady with a heavy Jamaican accent, who handed him a lab slip with a card bearing his next appointment.

His father accompanied him at his follow-up appointment. At first he thought it coincidental but realized his primary physician contacted his father insisting he be present at his next visit.

He had a sinking feeling in his stomach. The report was not going to be good. He was thankful his father was there. Together they walked into the dimly lit parlor already populated with people gazing aimlessly in space or pretending to read outdated magazines. He signed in and found a seat adjacent to his father near the entrance.

"After this Dad, let's go to lunch, on me. I usually go to Johnny & Sammy's. It's a nice eatery. Food is great."

Phillip grabbed his hand. He was trembling. "Thomas, it's going to be fine. You must believe that."

They talked briefly about the progress of his new book before burring their face in the antiquated pamphlets. An hour later they were escorted by a young black nurse to a brightly lit examining booth with wooden chairs and a paper protected slab which he used as a resting bemch awaiting the doctor's arrival. Dr. Purnell entered wearing a grim expression. He leaned against the paneled wall and thumbed through papers.

"You're Thomas's father I gather," He assumed. He previously spoke to Thomas' primary physician, and he alerted him Thomas' father would be at the next visit. He had no objections. Evidently his father was aware of his condition.

"I am," Phillip replied.

"I'm glad you're here." He paused for a moment, assessing the report. "From the blood test, it appears Mr. Thomas, you have sickle-cell anemia; A very aggressive type. I know you've had routine checkups because your mother had the disease, and it showed negative, but this time, unfortunately, it appears positive. If you do nothing, from my speculation, you have about nine to twelve months." Then he reiterated quickly to relieve the impact. "Nowadays we have methods to delay progression, but you will have to leave from here. John Hopkins is the place you will have to go. They are equipped with pioneer drugs and state of the art treatments that may arrest this disease. Hopkins has proven to be successful."

All he heard was nine to twelve months. He was predestined to die like his mother. A once feisty Iris lady full of energy reduced to a quivering excuse of a failing feeble minded soul yearning for hope; a second chance which God never granted. Now he was plagued with the same curse. He would be reduced to a hollowing excuse of a man depending on others for his care. Visions of his mother lying in bed, a skeleton frame with bulging eyes, sunken in jaws, unable to speak, just gazing into space, a vegetable, taunted him. He blocked out his alternative treatment, a cure, a second chance.

Phillip knew he was devastated and incoherent. He spoke in his behalf. "Is it possible the disease could be forced into remission?"

"There have been cases where that has happened. I know of clents, like your son, who went through treatment and they lived for many years. They were expected to live for a few months and it turned into five to ten years. Some are still alive today. Now keep in mind the treatments are continuous and there is no guarantee." Dr. Purnell sat in a chair beside Phillip and said, "Thomas is young and I know he would be a terrific candidate for the treatment."

"Of course we will try it."

"I am going to make arrangements for Thomas to be admitted into John Hopkins. It may be a six to eight weeks wait or less. Depends on their availability."

"Will he have to stay there the entire time during treatment or what?"

"He will be there for a few weeks observing his responds to the treatment. After that, depends on his status, and response to treatment."

"Thank you doctor." Phillip shook his hand. Thomas was still in shock.

Phillip patted his son's knee indicating time to leave. He stood up and followed his father out of the room. Phillip placed his hand on his shoulder for support and guidance. They paused at the receptionist who promised Phillip she would call him when she heard from John Hopkins.

When they were snug inside Thomas' car with him in the passenger seat, and his father the designated driver, his father broke the silence.

"Thomas, I know what you're thinking but this is a new time. Medicine has come a long ways since your mother."

He could not hear the words. Everything was muffled and distorted. *Nine to twelve months. That's what the doctor said; a life sentence.*

Phillip punched his son's arm as he paused at a stop light jerking him back to reality. "Where is this restaurant?"

He refocused realizing they were on thirteen going towards downtown Salisbury. The restaurant was fifty feet away on the right. He pointed to Johnny & Sammy's. "Over there."

Phillip slowed down and pulled into the lot. Finally he had his son's undivided attention. He turned off the ignition. It was beginning to snow. He turned off the radio that was playing quietly in the background.

"Thomas, the Doctor, and I, want you to go to John Hopkins for treatment. There is a good chance we can beat this. I have already agreed to it." Phillip brought him up to speed.

"He said nine to twelve months," Thomas repeated.

"And he said John Hopkins has been treating people with sickle-cell for years and have proven to be successful. This is our chance of fighting this thing and I want you to take it. The worst scenario is it will give you another five to ten years. So what do you say?"

He thought for a few minutes. He would have to leave Edith. That was going to be hard. He loved her and treasured what they shared. At the same token, if he had the treatment, and it did not work, he had no intentions of dragging her through what his mother put his father through. It would not be fair. She was young with a long life ahead. She would find someone else. He did not want her to wait on him to recover. And then he thought about his book. He was more than half done.

"When does the doctor want me to go to John Hopkins?"

"They'll call us with the arrangements. It may be a while."

Maybe he had enough time to finish his book and mail it to the publisher. He had to get started immediately.

Before Thomas realized it, they had boarded the Cape May Lewis Ferry parking platform, unfastened their seatbelts, left the car in the garage and ascended steep stairs leading to the cruiser. Edith gave him a quick tour of the Ferry pointing out the food commissary, where they purchased two cups of coffee and pastries for breakfast. The bar had a few people entertaining the bartender while drinking beer or sipping cocktails. The small bathrooms were apparently occupied by elderly people taking a lavatory break before the ship disembarked. The arcade area was vacant since it was a school day and there were few if any children aboard. The upper deck was furnished with lounge chairs and benches with people looking at the scenery below from the balcony snuggled in winter coats to block out the frigid January breeze. The middle deck was decorated with comfortable sofas and tables were people could eat and socialize and peep out of the glass windows. The lower deck had plush sofas and chairs with few windows to gaze out of. It was a place people could relax with little distractions. Edith selected a table on the middle deck to rest and enjoy their breakfast treat.

Edith did not pressure Thomas to talk on the trip over. Months ago he had told her his mother died on his birthday; a day he would never forget. The day he stopped believing in God. That was why she planned a trip, a miniature getaway. Something to get his mind off his mother. She was careful not to mention birthday when she told him she had something special planned. She simply said she wanted to show him another side of the Easter Shore. A place he could use in his book.

"This is a nice place," Thomas said as he sipped his hot, steaming coffee.

"Have you ever been to a casino?" Edith quizzed.

"No. My aunt has. I have seen shows about it on television."

She reached out and grabbed his hands across the table. "Today we are going to have fun gambling, eating and take in a show."

"Can all this be done in one day?" Thomas wondered.

"It will be close, but I believe we can do it."

"I hope you know what you're talking about."

"What do you think of the ferry?" Edith asked.

Thomas glanced around, taking everything in, watching people as they passed. "It's nice. I like it."

They nibbled at their food as they made small talk and poked fun at the passengers as they went about their affairs. Even though words were coming out of his mouth and he pretended to be interested in what Edith had to say, his mind was fixated on his future. Yes, the doctor believed the treatment would be beneficial but there was no iron clad contract promising that. What if the treatment failed? Where would that leave him? Back to nine to twelve months.

He studied Edith's endearing smile. She deserved better. She was young, beautiful, full of life and tender. He could not, would not subject her to a life of uncertainty. He would have to terminate their relationship. They had grown so close in the last few months. She was his soul mate, his lifeline. Living without her would be futile. Yet at the same token he would not subject her to watching him die a painful debilitating death. She deserved better. He had to release her to live a life without him. He would proceed and have the treatment. Even if the treatment was successful, he might live for another five to ten years but that was not enough for Edith. That was not enough for him. He wanted to live a long life with her. He wanted to marry her, give her children, and be a father and eventually a grandfather. He wanted to be a husband, a friend, a lifelong companion. It would not be fair for him to allow her to think they could have a life together knowing it would be short, leaving her alone to mourn his death and having to collect the fragments. Besides, they had only known each other for a few months. She would get over him. Time could mend a broken heart. His chief concern had to be Edith. He had to protect her from the sorrow of his terminal illness. The question was, when and how would he end their affair.

A couple hours later, they drove from the ferry onto New Jersey soil. From there Edith drove them to the Trump Casino in Atlantic City where a Valley Attendant parked their car for them while they entered the humongous casino with hundreds of slot machines ringing and chiming simultaneously. Anxious gamblers sat on stools pulling bars repeatedly in hope of winning the grand prize losing coins by the bundle. Crowds encircled card tables, roulette wheels, crap shooting tables, gigantic wheel of Fortune wheels and various other games of chance hosted by men or women in dark suits. Every twenty minutes a loud bell resonated indicating someone hit the jackpot.

Edith sat at a slot machine with Thomas beside her. She opened her pocketbook and dished out a hand full of quarters and handed some to Thomas.

"What am I supposed to do with this?" Obviously he was green to the sport.

"You see that coin slot over there. Put the quarters in there. Then select how much you want to bet by pushing this button." She showed him. "And then pull the bar and pray for a miracle."

"Ok. Here we go." Thomas did as instructed. The machine lit up like a light bulb. He selected his betting amount and pulled the bar. The machine made a weird sound as it rotated several times and stopped. Nothing happened. He did not have three sevens in a row.

Edith filled her machine with coins and started pulling the bar. No luck for her either. They commenced pulling the slot bar in sync many times. After the eight pull some coins fell in the container below the screen. Thomas asked Edith what he was supposed to do next. She instructed him to remove the coins he won, put them back into the machine, and keep playing until he had nothing to gamble with. That was simple enough.

They stayed at the triple seven slot machine for an hour before running out of money. Edith ran out first and she watched as Thomas played until he lost his last coin. He was relaxed and enjoying the new experience. It was ashamed he couldn't win. They went to three other slot machines testing their luck. They were facing a losing streak. But it was fun and rewarding.

Thomas felt brave and tried his chance with the roulette wheel. He remembered how they played it on a television show. He used his money instead of Edith's even though it was her treat.

He purchased chips from the host and put them on his favorite number seven. After everyone had placed their bet, the young lady spanned the wheel. The ball bounced about erratically and landed on seven. His co-players gave him a victory cheer. The lady collected all the chips from the board, and gave Thomas three times the amount of chips he bet, and asked if he wanted to play again. Thomas said no. She traded in the pile of chips for three chips on another color, and instructed him to take it to the cashier to collect his newfound riches. Edith showed him where to go. When he handed the chips to the cashier, she handed him three brand new hundred dollar bills. Thomas was ecstatic. His luck had changed. He was on a winning street. But he had no intentions of challenging fate. It was time to stop and venture onto the next event.

Ironically Edith suggested they check out the buffet. It was getting late and she was starved.

The restaurant was crammed with customers piling their plates with more food than they could possibly eat. They waited twenty minutes to pay for their food and beverage before they were released to explore and partake of the goodies laid out for their choosing.

There was so much to select from, she was tentative where to start. Thomas put a dish in her hand and led her to the vegetable bar. She forked on a stalk of broccoli and a scoop of sweet potato fluff. She wanted room for the meat. He planted two scoops of mashed potatoes crowned with brown gravy with string beans in his plate. Then they went to the meat entrees. Edith saw nothing to her fancy. Thomas grabbed slices of barbecued spareribs. Next they toured the seafood section. There she partook a helping of steamed shrimp and a slab of golden fried trout. Thomas was allergic to seafood. They both pronged a soft yeast roll, exited the food court, and located a place to sit where they could enjoy their meal. A waitress asked them what they wanted to drink and brought it to them. Thomas went back for seconds and asked her if she wanted anything. She bid for apple pie alamode to appease her sweet tooth.

To conclude their delightful evening, they visited the Theater. "Hello Dolly" was the play being featured. It was presented by amateurs who did a fabulous job. The show lasted approximately ninety minutes with no intermission. Edith thought this was unorthodox. Every play she attended had an intermission. Then she remembered the schedule posted outside the theater. The next performance was scheduled thirty minutes later. The actors had little time to recuperate before they were back on stage entertaining another audience. Bartenders patrolled offering cocktails and Thomas opted for a virgin martini to quench his dry throat.

Late that afternoon they boarded the Ferry. It was dark and snowing. A significant accumulation cast a white shadow on the landscape creating a winter postcard. After parking the vehicle, they climbed the steep stairs to the middle deck where they found a comfortable chair made for two and snuggled as the ship made its way back to Delaware. When Thomas entered his apartment, he found his father sitting on the couch flippimg through the newspaper and listening to the radio. Edith was surprised discovering a stranger convalescing on the couch. Silently she urged Thomas to introduce his guest.

"Edith this is my father. Father this is Edith Bosworth, the girl I have been seeing."

Edith offered her hand. "Glad to meet you"

Philip laid his paper aside and accepted her gesture. "You're as pretty as my son said you were."

"Thank you," Edith said smiling. Finally she had the privilege to meet an important member in Thomas's family. Oddly enough he favored her father.

Thomas removed his coat. "How long have you been here?"

"A few hours."

"Look, it is getting late and I have early classes in the morning. I am going to call it an evening and go home. Give you quality time with your father." Edith put her arms around Thomas's waste and kissed him tenderly.

"Please don't leave on my account. I can make myself scarce. Give you two privacy."

"No. I really must leave. We've put in a long day." She told Phillip. Then she focused on Thomas. "I trust you enjoyed the day and you have pleasant memories."

"I had a good time." He pulled her close and kissed her again.

"I'll see you tomorrow." She said while pacing to the door. She was baffled how much Phillip favored her father. It was spooky.

"Love you, and thanks again." Thomas echoed as she opened the door and left.

When Edith was gone, Philip started in. "You know she has to be told about your illness."

Thomas sat at the kitchen table. "All day I could not help but think about that. How to breakup with her?" A nervous sensation tortured his stomach. He felt uneasy.

"There are ways to do that. Tell her the truth or –

"She must never know I have sickle-cell or may be dying. I want to spare her that." He lowered his head. "She's too young to deal with something this devastating."

"Do what you think is best. "Phillip was tempted to reveal he knew his girlfriend's parents but decided otherwise. He had to respect John's wishes. Being they were brothers was a secret.

All that mattered was seeing Thomas through treatment. It was probable they would never see each other again after the breakup. He ascertained from the gleam in his son's eyes he was deeply involved with Edith. It was the identical gleam he witnessed in his wife's eyes before they fell hopelessly in love and married.

Chapter Nine

Phillip got off the phone with Ellen. He alerted her about the doctor's visit and informed her he meet her daughter. *No wonder his son was head over heels in love. Saying she was attractive and charming was an injustice. She was like a rose from heaven.*

He mentioned his son was considering terminating his relationship with her daughter but had reservation of how Edith would react. His son thought it was best for her to start a new life.

Ellen thanked Phillip for the update. She knew what had to be done. Losing Thomas would annihilate both of them. Yet she had to intervene. The problem was would Edith believe her. Would she assume it was a ploy to keep them a part? She knew how much she disliked Thomas. She never had a nice thing to say about him. That was before she saw his father and heard of his uncertain future. Now things were different. She actually felt sorry for Thomas. She understood how Edith could fall aimlessly in love with him. He was a good man. Unfortunately it took an act of God to bring her to her senses. For months she had been blinded by bitterness and mistrust. As far as she was concerned, he was an opportunist, a rude young man waiting for the chance to steal her daughter's innocence. Perhaps she was wrong on all accounts, and now the moment arrived to rectify her past actions; to clean-up her unsubstantiated accusations.

Her mind was set. In a few days, she would have a frank chat with Edith, bring things into perspective. Once the truth was out, she would be a supporting crutch; a shoulder to cry upon. She would inspire her to venture onward without Thomas. Something Thomas sought. Chances are she would drown herself in her studies. Anything to help her get over Thomas was welcomed. It was imperative she was absent when he went for treatment. One thing they both were in agreement about was protecting Edith.

John walked into her office carrying a vanilla folder. "I want you to look at these designs and tell me what you think?" He flopped the folder on her clustered desk.

Ellen flipped through the folder and studied the contents before she spoke. "It looks fine."

"Good. I want to start production in a few weeks."

Ellen changed the subject. "Phillip called. Thomas was diagnosed with sickle-cell."

John collapsed in a nearby-seat. "I feared that."

"He said the doctor thinks he would be a good candidate for advanced treatment at John Hopkins. It may give him five to ten years."

John was relieved. "That's good news."

"He said Thomas wants to brake off with Edith. He doesn't want her around him when he goes through treatment. He wants to spare her the pain. He wants her to start a new life without him." She brought him up to speed.

"You know that will devastate Edith. She really loves Thomas," John reminded her.

"She's young. She will survive with support from us."

John took a deep breath. "If that's what Thomas wants, we have no say. We must respect his wishes."

"I will do my best to break the news to her gentility," Ellen stood up and went to the couch in the corner of her office, a place she napped during her lunch break following a hectic morning.

Knowing his wife, John knew she had an agenda. "Ellen what are you going to do?"

"I am going to tell Ellen before Thomas does. It would be better coming from me. She may not believe me considering our rumpled relationship over the past few months. That's where you come in."

"To confirm what you tell her," he guessed.

"Precisely."

John meditated on Ellen's actions. Despite their difference of opinion concerning Thomas, She loved her daughter and desired nothing but the best for her. He feared what she might tell Edith. Against better judgment, he told her the whole story. Family secrets had been unveiled. A young man's future was hanging in the balance. His wife, the mother of his only child, could crush the lives of many people if the secret got out. He prayed she would make the correct decision; a decision that would keep the family constant. Even though his father was dead, he feared his past sin might be resurrected. That would devastate his mother.

"What are you going to tell her?" He had to know her intentions. He hoped she would only address the illness. There was no reason for Edith to know anything else.

Before Ellen answered him, the phone rang, and the office door sprang open. An excited employee dressed in white rushed in. "There's been an accident. Joe passed out, we think he's having a heart attack. We called the ambulance."

John dashed out of the office behind the employee leaving Ellen calmly instructing another panicking staff person on what to do. "Is he conscious?" She paused for a response. "So he didn't hit his head." She paused again. "Good, just stay near him. Josh and John are on their way. Send someone outside to direct the ambulance to the site." Ellen headed out the door thinking loudly. *Of all they days, our nurse calls in sick. Why couldn't this have happened yesterday?*

Ellen ran down a long corridor, through a battery of doors passing several offices before she reached the production line where the incident occurred. When she arrived on the scene, the old man Joe who had been in their employee for many years was being rolled out on a stretcher by two paramedics drilling him on his condition. Joe kept complaining about chest pains as sweet accumulated on his forehead. He was ash black and breathing heavy. Joe was in his early fifties and appeared to be in good shape; certainly not a heart attack candidate. His co-workers knew he ran a mile every day, provided the weather permitted and worked out in the gym at least three times a week. While his peers gorged out on fired chicken, pig feet and other high cholesterol fatty foods, his diet was strictly vegetables and poultry. It was strange how things happened. Joe was the last person expected to have a heart attack.

John went to his wife's side when he saw her walking from the accident sight. He just encouraged the employees to return to their post.

"He looked bad." Ellen commented approaching her husband.

A siren blasted and lights flashed as the ambulance raced toward the hospital.

"I hope it's not too bad. Joe is a good man. I don't want anything to happen to him."

"I agree with you." Ellen responded.

John took his wife's hand. He looked into her baby blue eyes remembering why he married her. He drew her close to him and kissed her lips tenderly. "Let's go to lunch. I am hungry for a big juicy steak."

Ellen felt guilty. How could she be unfaithful? John seldom showed affection. Something she had not seen for ages. Usually he treated her like a colleague, not a wife. Business was the closing topic before retiring for the evening and the opening headline at the breakfast table. They coexisted like foreigners sharing the same abode, forsaking the covenant of matrimony. His medical condition forced her into the arms of another man.

They left the scene holding hands and climbed into John's truck. Ponderosa Steak House was a twenty minute commute from the Industrial Park. Traffic was light for the lunch hour and the lights worked in their favor. When they rode into the crowded parking lot, they had to ride around several times before they located a parking space. Business was booming. Half of Salisbury shared John's craving for a luscious steak with all the trimmings.

They had to wait for fifteen minutes before the host led them to a table. Ellen took liberty of the opened salad bar granting John permission to order in her behalf. He knew her favorite foods. They had a pleasant meal discussing Philip and his crisis. When John questioned her about what she intended to tell Edith, she changed the subject. She simply said, "I don't know yet" and moved onto another topic.

Ellen had difficulty remembering the last time they went out together. It might had been eight to ten months. Even though she would not admit it, she valued their private outings. Memories of their childhood courtship which lead to their marriage penetrated her thoughts. As her daughter clung to Thomas, she once clung to John. His mother, even if she desired to, could not separate them. She knew Bessel saw her as an opportunist trying to wiggle her way into the family's business. She knew Bessel was displeased when Joseph appointed her a prestigious position at Bosworth in hope of inspiring his son to follow in his footsteps. Joseph knew John wanted no part of Bosworth, but if she was there, he would stay connected to the company. She was the magnet that kept him in place. She remembered when they were teenagers, they would go to the plant to see their parents. She would visit her father who was shop foreman at the time. He would give her a tour of the plant, tell her about the general operation from the beginning to the final product. John would get the same tour from his father. But where she took interest in what her father said, John took it lightly. He could care less about Bosworth Industries. Yet his father would not give up. His two other sons enlisted a career outside of Bosworth. John was his last straw. He had no choice. He was the elected one.

When they weren't at the plant bugging their parents, they did what most young kids did in a small town. They socialized on street corners, partied at friend's homes when their parents were away, experimented with cigarettes and alcohol, praying their parents would not find out. They had a lot of fun in those good old days despite the consequences of their actions.

She recalled the spanking of her life when her father smelled liquor on her breath after a date with John. He grounded her for three weeks. The only time she saw him was in school. She hated that with a passion. What seemed like eternity came to an end and they resumed courting. John never mentioned how his parents disciplined him for boozing. Whatever it was, John never drank another drop until he was twenty-one.

They finished their meal, tipped the waitress, and made haste to the office. Lunch was a call for feminine attention. He expected her to pacify his manly urges. A small chapter in their exotic life. Stamina was the one thing John lacked. Once upon a time, they could make love for twenty to forty minutes. In the last few years of their marriage, things changed. The frequency and longevity of their love making sessions dwindled due to the side effects of medicine; medicine for his hypertension.

Each day he withheld the pleasure of his body, she hungered for the touch of a man. She necessitated handling and satisfaction. Stanly was the link; the man filling the void; her medicine of choice, her addiction. He titillated her sexual drives making her vulnerable. Where her husband fell short, his friend sufficed. But that night, John was anxious and ready to oblige. She saw lust in his eyes indicating he was anxious to go home, tear off his clothes, gently slide her sensitive naked body on top of the bed, spread her long legs, and straddle himself between them shoving his monstrous erection inside her pulsating flesh. He would ravish her body. Five minutes later he would roll on his back exhausted, sweating as if he ran a marathon. He would not request her services again for weeks. *Thank heaven she had a man in the wings; A man she could depend on in time of need. A man she was falling for.*

The second week in January, Ellen summoned Edith into the parlor. John was working late at the office on a special project of his demise. The maid concluded her winter cleaning pocketing a bonus check for a job well done. They were alone with no looming distractions. She gestured Edith to sit beside her on the couch.

"I know you love Thomas, "she started slowly.

Edith panicked. She figured her mother devised a plot to separate them. "Mother no matter what you say I will stop seeing him."

"I understand that. If you noticed, I have not protested against you being with him lately." She reminded her.

Edith realized she received no static when she relayed her and Thomas had plans for the evening. It was if she did not care. "Yes, now you mentioned it, you have not contested ort being together lately."

"There's a reason." She ran her fingers through her hair. A flash back of a ten year old Edith flashed before her. Now she was nineteen, and in college, dating a man of her dreams.

Edith's fingers trembled and her stomach fluttered. "What is it mother?" She managed to say fearing what she might hear.

She took in a deep breath and then sighed slowly. "A few weeks ago your father and I had a visitor. Someone he had not seen for years. We got to talking and some very important facts came out."

"Who was the person?" Edith was curious.

"It was Thomas' father."

Edith remembered seeing Thomas' father at his apartment. "I met his father in his apartment. He introduced us."

"Apparently your father and Thomas' father went to college together."

"It is a small world," She remarked. Then remembered how much Thomas's father favored her father. "You know Thomas's dad and my father favor," she commented.

"That's another story," Ellen said, and then continued. "As your father and Phillip reminisced, some unexpected information was revealed. Information you're entitled to know. Information I am afraid to tell you."

Edith's mind began to wonder in a thousand directions. *Could Thomas's father be dying and he wanted to spend his final days with his son. Perhaps a close relative had been killed or injured in an accident. But it had been a week or more. If it was anything of that magnitude, Thomas would have told her. For the life of her, she had no idea what it could be.* "Mom what is it?" She had to know the truth.

"What I'm about to tell you will change your life." And then she went on to say, "Circumstances will change your whole outlook."

"Whatever it is, I can handle it." Edith sounded confident."

"OK." Ellen took a deep breath and said, "This is what Philip told your father."

Chapter Ten

"Mother I don't believe you. It can't possibly be true. This must be a ploy to break us up." Edith shouted in denial.

"I knew you wouldn't believe me." She looked into her daughter's teary eyes and said, "You can ask his father. He will confirm what I have told you."

The shocking news shattered her life. Her thoughts and emotions were locked in limbo. Her sixth sense, her intuition relayed her mother was sincere. What she spoke was true. *She had to face facts and deal with reality. There was no avoidance; no ignoring. Too many hints supported her acquisitions. His weird behaviors for the past few days were questionable. At times she felt he wanted to tell her something but was afraid. After what her mother said, she understood why. Where would he begin? What could he say? He wanted to spare her the shock. All the pieces were coming together like a jigsaw puzzle. Everything made sense. Their future, their romance was suspended in balance. She could only imagine the turmoil he was undergoing. Surely he was fretful of her acceptance and sorrow. The last thing he wanted was to hurt her. That was why he procrastinated.*

"Mother I need alone time. I am going for a walk." Edith went into the foyer to grab her coat from the rack with her mother steps behind her.

"Honey I had to tell you. I know how much you love Thomas." Ellen said as Edith slipped into her coat and gloves.

"Mother you did the right thing. The truth had to come out." Edith hugged her mother and left the house.

Ellen watched through a window as Edith walked into the backyard to the river. It was a place her daughter went when she was troubled. It was her secret place, a refuge of solitary confinement.

Tears slid down Edith's redden face as the fierce January wind pressed against her cheeks. If only she could change things, but that was impossible. Fait landed its fatal Ax. She listened to winter sounds praying for a solution, but there was nothing. Birds could not soar away the torment, the wind could not sweep away the pain, nor the falling snow bury the harsh pending decisions.

The frozen river behind her house brought tranquility after the storm. For an hour she stood watching fallen snow blanket the river providing a false since of security. For months she skated high with a man she loved not knowing one day it would crack.

"Come on baby. Let's go inside." It was John, in his trench coat, leather gloves and fur hat.

Edith faced her father. He was her rock in time of trouble. Knowing he was there, gave her strength to face tomorrow. "Daddy I thought you were at work."

"Ellen told me her intentions earlier. So I came home for you. You don't have to go through this alone. I am here and so is your mother." He pulled his daughter close.

"I can't believe this. In the short time we have known each other, we have grown so close. I hate the idea of-

"Let's not think about that now. You need time to adjust to what you have just heard."

"You're right. I must figure out my next move."

"How long have you been out here?" John wondered.

"About an hour or so," Edith confessed.

"Let's go inside and we can discuss this."

"Ok."

Edith and John walked slowly back to the house. The once tiny flakes transformed into big, cotton ball drops littering their coats as they approached the mansion leaving behind footprints. Images of a twelve year old Edith having a snow ball fight with other kids in the neighborhood brought a smile to John's stern face. If only he possessed the power to change events, his daughter would not be facing her predicament.

Ellen called Phillip informing him she told her daughter about his son. At last his son's illness was out. He was spared the arduous task of confronting his girlfriend. Now he could ponder on getting the treatment he required to remain alive. Her timing was perfect. John Hopkins t moved up his admission date.

"So Edith knows?" Thomas asked as he poured coffee in his father's cup.

"Her mother told her."

"I should have been the one to tell her. But I am glad Ellen did." Thomas sat across from his father at the kitchen table. "You know Ellen was not too keen about me dating her daughter from the start." He updated his father on the hostile relationship shared between him and Edith's mother. "She's probably glad our affair is over."

"I did not know this. I did not get that impression when we met."

"So you told her about my illness?"

"Yes I told her and John. I told you John and I have a history together. We knew each other from college."

The phone rang again. Thomas answered it. It was Edith. She wanted to see him. He knew what was on her mind. In a few hours, it would be over, provided that was what she wanted. There was the possibility she would stay despite the prognosis. But he figured her mother convinced her to leave and moved on with her life. In a way, he hoped she had. Edith was too young to be with a man that was unable to provide her a future. All he had was hope for another five to ten years, and that was no guarantee.

Anticipating the couple needed privacy, time to discuss their plans, Philip grabbed his coat and said he was going to the Wicomico Theater. There was a movie playing he wanted to see. He promised he would return if Thomas wanted to talk.

Sixty minutes after Phillip left, Edith walked into the apartment. Thomas finished typing another chapter. He grabbed Edith's coat and rested it across the couch. He was about to kiss her when she pushed him away. Kissing Thomas would only complicate matters. She had to keep a clear head.

"Ok, what's on your mind?"

Edith sat on the couch. Thomas sat beside her. She scooted down. She had to keep distance between them. "Thomas, I talked to my mother. She told me about you."

"Yes, I got that impression from your actions."

"Thomas this is not easy for me. We've shared good times together, and I do not want them to stop. I like being with you."

"What are you saying?" *Could it be she still desired to be with him despite his illness?*

"Considering what I know, I believe it best if we split." Edith grabbed his hands. "Please don't hate me. But it would be best this way. Give you time to do what you must. And time for me to get another life."

Thomas looked into her teary eyes. Her heart was breaking. He was helpless. There was nothing he could say to ease the pain. "I know you're right. I wish there was another way, but there is none." He sighed deeply and said, "Sometimes life is so damn unfair!"

"After tonight I will not bother you or call." Edith promised.

Thomas took a deep breath. "I see the pain in your eyes and I will not cause you anymore suffering by prolonging what is predestined."

"The sooner we end this affair, the better for both of us." Edith stood, preparing to leave. She grabbed her coat.

"Edith," Thomas said, still on the couch. "I enjoyed our short time together. And I will always love you no matter what."

"Sometimes love is not enough." She slipped into her coat. "I wish it did not have to end." She took in a deep breath and added, "Take our good times and put it into your book."

"I will." He replied.

"I'm going to leave while I can without crying." Tears were building up in her eyes.

Thomas started to stand. "Let me walk-

"Stay here." Edith said sternly. "I need space." She beckoned him to sit back down.

"I will never forget you." Thomas managed to say while Edith walked out of his apartment.

After Edith left, Thomas bowed his head and sobbed. *It was over. The months they shared, the activities they celebrated, their intimate moments together were lost forever. Why did good experiences parish with the fading leaves. First his mother was ripped away from him when he needed her the most. Now a woman he loved was erased from a chapter in his life. Thank God his father appeared on the scene when he did. Again he would be his support and strength in his most vulnerable hour.*

When his father did return around midnight, he was working on the last chapter. Phillip could tell by the deathly quietness and his red eyes, the breakup took a toll on his son. He waited until Thomas closed his typewriter before he spoke.

"I gather that it's over." Phillip snatched a cold Pepsi from the freezer and busted the cap.

"I am afraid so," Thomas remarked and then added, "We have to check into John Hopkins in a few days." He grabbed the remote control from the coffee table and turned on the television. Johnny Carson was on. "I did not realize it was so late."

"Yes it is pretty late." Philip said.

"Dad you've been gone for some time." Thomas reminded him.

"It was a long movie. Three hours I believe."

"I hope you enjoyed it." Thomas started sweeping the floor. He could not sit back and relax. He had to keep busy. His thoughts kept replaying his last conversation with Edith.

Phillip seized his son's elbow. "Thomas, my son, you will get over Edith and she will get over you. Each day will get easier and easier."

His father always knew what to say. "I know."

Phillip changed the subject while sinking into a recliner and elevating the foot rest. "How's the book coming? You've been diligently working on it."

"Still revising and inserting chapters. I want it perfect when I submit it." He swept around the furniture making sure he got every piece of litter.

"I know your publisher has been harassing you. I heard some of the messages on your answering machine."

"I pray this book does as well as the others." Thomas commented.

Philip sipped his drink. "I'm sure it will be fine. If it's anything like your last book, it will be another best seller."

Thomas cleaned his apartment while his father watched the late show. When he finished, his father was asleep holding an empty can. He removed the can from Phillip, covered him with a thin blanket from his closet, switched off the television and turned off the lamp leaving him in darkness. When he awakened, it would be morning. The sun would be rising in the horizon, when Phillip retired to the guest bed. At ten thirty, the smell of black coffee and fried bacon would beckon him into the kitchen. He would scuffle into the small bathroom, brush his teeth, gargle with a capsule full of Listerine, wash his hands and then join his son for breakfast. By then it was almost ten. *Thank God he was on a sabbatical for several months. He did not have a clock to click or a boss to appease. After he consumed his continental breakfast, he would return to his sleeping cot and sleep for another three to four hours. Officially his day did not start until late noon.*

Seven days hence, Thomas was admitted into John Hopkins Hospital in Baltimore Maryland. An orderly in a green smock, gave him a bag for his clothes and a gown to wear. His father reclined in a bedside chair observing his son undress, slip into a skimpy gown and then crawl underneath a thin sheets resting his curly head on a soft pillow.

"I'll take these clothes with me." Philip promised.

"What are you going to do?" Thomas wondered if he was going to commute back and forth from his apartment or stay at a hotel.

"I am going to stay at the hotel down the street."

"Ok."

"Son I believe everything will be fine. You have to believe the same."

"I wish I had your faith daddy." Again he remembered his mother and how she suffered. "I hope the doctors can help me."

A tall, muscular African doctor in a white coat with a statoscope dangling from is thick neck, entered the room, leaving the door open, and came to his bedside holding a clip board. He acknowledged Phillip. "You must be his father."

"I am."

"Gentlemen let me tell you the game plan. We are going to run a multitude of blood test checking for various abnormalities. Then we are going to administer a series of injections and intravenous medicines. We will monitor your reaction to our treatments. If your response is favorable, which I believe it will be, we will release you and schedule routine visits at our clinic for follow-up checks and routine injections when necessary."

"How effective is this care?" Thomas was curious.

"We've had decent results. Matter of fact we have been doing it for ten years or more. You have nothing to worry about."

Thomas' worry lessen. The butterflies in his stomach went away. *The doctor was optimistic. Perhaps all was not lost. Maybe he could be cured of his illness.* "There is a good chance I may over conquer this disease?"

"Sir I cannot promise the disease will go into remission. You may always have sickle-cell but we have a way to slow down the progressing and extend your life. We have people on our records who are forty years old living a normal life after our treatment." The doctor replied as he wrote something on the sheet fastened to his clip board. "The nurse will be in to draw blood. You have three more doctors attending your case beside me. You will see them periodically. We will start treatment tomorrow. Today we will be running test. Mister Guy, you can stay here while orderlies transport Thomas to different departments for more examinations."

"Thank you."

"Gentlemen, have a good day." He shook Thomas and Phillip's hand and left, closing the door.

A phlebotomist, a middle-aged woman with silver gray hair, carrying a small container, came in to draw blood. She managed to fill three test tubes from one needle puncture which he barely felt. A nurse, crowning a hat identifying her position, followed holding a bag primed with a clear substances, hooked it onto a rod mounted the bed. She hand him stretch out his arm, scrubbed a small area with alcohol, spotted a healthy vein and assaulted it with a needle. Bingo. She accomplished her mission. She connected the needle to a bag, taped it in place, instructed him to relax his arm and left. His room was like grand central station with people patrolling in and out. A young lady, in her early twenties, in a blue outfit, made herself comfortable on the corner of his bed and commenced asking a hundred personal questions, documenting his answer.

Philip, realizing his son was going to be occupied for a while, decided to tour the little shop they passed while in route to their destination. A caffeine withdraw took possession of his faculties. "Thomas, I am going to get some coffee. Would you like anything?"

"No dad. I am fine."

The lady asked him if he was allergic to any type of medicine."

"No mam." He said watching his father leave him alone with his friendly interrogator. The interview lasted twenty minutes.

"Are you married?"

Thomas wondered where that question came from. Was it pertinent to his health? Still he answered. "No." *Could the young, white girl with curly red hair secured with a bow, be flirting?*

Jessica smiled. She withheld documenting his response.

Chapter Eleven

Life without Thomas was lonely. They shared so many memorable moments together in the last few months. Circumstances brought them together and circumstances separated them. She had to bury their past and continue. She was tempted to call but declined. She drove by his apartment, hoping to get a glimpse of his car, but it was gone. She drew the conclusion he left town. That was probably the best move.

She concentrated on her studies withdrawing from the social scene. Her cousins tried breaking her free from her seclusion. She told them what her mother said about Thomas. Sarah prayed for her over the telephone. Edith's faith was stagnate. She blamed God for everything. She stopped praying. Ethel, Cherry and Charlene approached her in the Student Union cafeteria. She was eating lunch. They coaxed her to join them at the Ecclesia Night Club. She refused their invitation. But they were persistent.

"Look, it's been weeks. Get over Thomas, move on." Cherry strongly encouraged her. "Hang out with us."

"You know I don't do night clubs." Edith reminded her.

"You don't have to drink. Just sit there and chat with us. We know you're a college girl." Ethel added quickly.

Edith realized they were not accepting no for an answer. "OK. I'll meet you there at eight. But I am letting you know, I'll only be there for a few hours. You got that."

"Yes cousin, we got that." Charlene said hugging her.

"What are they serving today?" Ethel asked. Her stomach was growling.

"Go check it out for yourself." Edith suggested. She knew Ethel enjoyed eating.

Ethel made her way to the food bar. Cherry and Charlene remain seated socializing with their beloved cousin. They knew she was at a bad place, and they wanted to perk her up. There was no better cure for a fallen affair than spending time with people who loved her, sympathized with her and understood her situation. Charlene requested Edith's approval to allow her new friend to tag along, the high yellow guy who accompanied her at the after Christmas shindig. Edith gave her consent.

"His a nice guy. Very quiet." Charlene filled her in.

Cherry added. "He'll probably spend all night sipping two beers. Never seen him drunk or even tipsy."

Edith remembered Alfred from the party.

Charlene regurgitated how she met Alfred. "We met at the club. Ethel hooked us up. Cherry you remember that night. You were there."

Cherry corrected her. "No cousin, I was not there. That was the night you and Ethel went out without me. I was home sick with the flue. Remember?"

"That's right." She waved her hand. "Anyway we started dating and that's the whole story."

"What does he do for a living?" Edith asked.

"His a paralegal." Charlene brought her up to speed. "Works with a lawyer on the plaza. Buying a three room rancher on Jersey Road. Nice place with lots of land. Never been married, no children. Perfect catch."

"Happy for you Charlene."

As promised, Edith kept her engagement at the Ecclesia. She pulled into the already crowded parking lot searching for a familiar vehicle, one belonging to her cousins. They usually carpooled. A shiny Ford Maverick was parked close to the entrance. It was Ethel's automobile. Charlene probably accompanied Alfred, her new love interest. She parked beside Ethel's vehicles and headed into the Night Club. A man at the door asked for her driver's license, checking her age. He handed her license back and beckoned for her to enter.

The place was packed. Yet it was still early. Barely nine o'clock. She scanned the joint for a familiar face. There was Charlene sitting beside Alfred who was sipping an alcoholic beverage, probably a beer. She moved cautiously through the dimly lit room towards Charlene, making sure not to bump into someone or stumble and fall. The tables were in close proximity. When Charlene spotted her, she waved for her to join them.

"Where is the gang?" Edith asked, resting her coat on the back of the chair and sitting her large pocketbook on the floor.

"Around here somewhere." Charlene assured her. "Alfred you know my cousin Edith."

Alfred extended his hand and Edith accepted it gracefully. "I remember you from the after Christmas party. You and your friend."

"Thomas." Just saying his name made her sad.

Alfred replied. "Charlene told me your family owns that big plant in the Industrial Park."

Edith nodded and whispered, "Yes we do."

Alfred was impressed by Edith's appearance. She looked like Cherry. They could be identical twins. "You favor your cousin Cherry."

"Yes we do favor," Edith agreed.

Charlene glanced at her watch. "It's almost nine. Didn't realize it was that late."

"How long have you two been here?" Edith asked.

"About twenty minutes I'd say." She took hold of Alfred's fingers. "You know I take for granted how much Cherry and Edith favor. When you grow up together, you don't notice things like that."

"There they are." Edith saw Ethel and Cherry coming in their direction. "Over here." Edith yelled attracting their attention.

"I'm sorry to hold yawl up." Cherry apologized for the both of them. "We went to the mall to pick up a pair of shoes Ethel had on layaway and we were in the bathroom trying them on. She couldn't wait until she got home."

Charlene glanced at Ethel's feet. "Are those the ones you're wearing?"

"Yes." Ethel rested her leather coat across a chair and modeled her shoes. "They only cost thirty three dollars."

"I like that. Think I am going to get myself a pair. Where did you get them?"

"Hecht's."

"I should have known." Charlene remarked. She knew Ethel's favorite store was Hecht's. She purchased all her clothes there.

The girls spent the evening joking about their childhood. Alfred excused himself from their fellowship when he spotted his buddies grouping around the bar. It was his chance to escape. Charlene, realizing he felt uncomfortable, encouraged him to connect with his friends giving her the opportunity to be wild. She had to behave and be ladylike when he was present. They just started dating and she feared giving him the wrong impression. Besides, she knew he did not want to hear a bunch of cackling ladies bashing men.

Ethel ordered her favorite drink, a screwdriver with a straw. Charlene and Cherry ordered margaritas. Edith ordered a virgin pinna colada. Charlene relaxed and said whatever crossed her mind. Alfred was enjoying the company of his friends.

Bernard, with his girlfriend gripping his arm, mysteriously appeared from nowhere. "Hey cousins. I didn't expect to see you here on a Thursday night." Then he realized Edith was present sipping a drink. "And I certainly didn't expect to see you. And what's this you're drinking?"

"Nonalcoholic," she assured him.

"How did you gals get her here? My innocent cousin."

Ethel jumped in. "Are you insinuating we are a bad influence?"

"Well!" Bernard teased.

A song came across the intercom his friend apparently liked. "Bernard, let's dance. That's my song."

"Sure baby."

His friend dragged him away from his relatives to the dance floor.

"She's got that man hooked by the nose." Cherry said.

"He doesn't seem to care." Ethel reminded her.

"I can't cling to a man like that. Got to give him air." Charlene added.

"And where do you get off inviting Alfred to join us tonight. Sounds like you keeping him on a leach to me." Cherry pointed out.

"Yeah but where is he now. Over there chatting with the fellas."

"Only because you wanted to act ignorant and didn't want him to see you." Cherry guessed.

"You got that right." Charlene laughed.

Ethel recognized Joseph, as he approached the bar and yelled out, "Hey Joseph, come here!"

"Girl don't be all loud embarrassing me. Act like you got some home training." Charlene scolded.

"Oh hush up. I haven't seen Joseph in a long while. Wonder where his fiancé is?" Ethel stood up so Joseph could see her.

Joseph came over and hugged Ethel. He was glad to see her. "What's going on cousin?"

"Nothing much." She pulled out a chair for Joseph to sit.

"Charlene, Cherry." He paused when he saw Edith sitting at the table. "Edith that can't be you."

Nightclubs were not Edith's scene. She felt out of her element. "Just decided to hang with my cousins. Take a break from studies."

"I hear that."

"Where's the lady to be?" Ethel asked.

"Working. Just came by for a drink and hang with the boys before I tie the knot."

"Have you picked a date?" Edith was curious.

"March twelve. Still working out final arrangements. You'll get an invitation, all of you." He promised.

It was midnight before they left. Edith enjoyed the company of her cousins and forgot about her curfew. For a few hours, she forgot about Thomas. Her cousins's plan was effective. When she got home at twelve thirty, she was surprised her mother was not up to greet her. She went to her bedroom and slipped into her pajamas. It had been a long day. She needed her rest. Tomorrow she would face three quarterly exams. Exams she should have studied for instead of parading to the Ecclesia. Yet she felt confident she would ace the test. She memorized notes from lectures and text readings.

Two weeks later, Edith missed her period. She panicked. Immediately pregnancy jarred her thoughts. *No way could she be pregnant. Yet there were times she was unprotected. Especially in the beginning. How could she be so careless? Maybe she was jumping to conclusions. One missed period did not necessarily mean she was pregnant. Other test had to be taken. Test to confirm her suspicions.*

She went to the pharmacy and purchased a pregnancy test. She had to know. Her reputation was on trial. Her education was in jeopardy. The test proved positive. That was all she needed. What was she going to do?

She couldn't tell her mother. She couldn't tell her father. She couldn't tell anyone. There was no telling how her mother would react. Especially since she reminded her thousands of times how important her education was. How she wanted her to assist her father with running Bosworth Industries. Constantly she discouraged her from getting pregnant. Her motto was, romance and motherhood ranked second to her role in the company. That was her mother's golden rule. Bosworth took preeminence over everything else.

She had to keep her pregnancy a secret. But the semester just commenced. What was she going to do? She would leave town. Go someplace far away from her parents. There she would decide what action to take. Still there was a minute chance the assessment was erroneous. She had to make an appointment with her doctor.

Peevishly she squirmed in the examination room. What was taking the doctor so long? She glanced at her silver watch. It had been fifteen minutes since the nurse left. All she needed was confirmation. She was tempted to walk out. The place was cold. Why was examining rooms always cold? Maybe it had something to do with keeping bacteria down.

The doctor walked in holding a chart. She was an elderly woman in her early sixties. She brushed her bangs back from her forehead and sat on a stool across from Edith, crossing her plump legs. "Well Mrs. Bosworth you are eight weeks pregnant. Congratulations." The lady smiled and took her shaking hands.

Congratulation was not the word she sought to hear. Sorry would have been welcomed.

"Thank you doctor," she said forcing a smile. The last thing she wanted was to give her physician the impression she was dissatisfied with the results. "You said eight weeks, almost two months."

"That's correct."

"I didn't think I was that far along." Edith began calculating in her mind when the conception may have happened. *It had to be sometime during their trip to Lancaster. Oddly enough, perhaps the first times they consummated their relationship, taking it to the next level. Was it possible she conceived on the day she lost her innocence? Was it possible she was pregnant by the first man she slept with? Well it didn't matter when, where or how it happened. She was pregnant and she had to take action. Time was not a luxury. Soon she would start showing.*

She vowed blindly to retain her appointment. She left the office in a daze. It was if she was floating through the pages of a book. As she drove down route thirteen towards her home, she entertained her options. Her mother could never know. At least not at the present. Her father could not be told even though he would be understanding, supportive and forgiving. But he would also be disappointed and hurt; hurt because she allowed herself to get into that predicament. It was her responsibility to spare him that hurt. If she had the baby, she would call her parents together and announce they were grandparents. It would be hard for her mother to scold and ridicule her with her holding the next generation of Bosworth in her arms. And then there was the thought of having an abortion. If she aborted the baby, no-one would know. She would leave town for a few weeks and come back void of life, ready to resume her education and take her place in the company. Her mother's wishes would finally be fulfilled. Her father would be thrilled to have her run the company with him. So many times he told her, one day baby, this will all be yours.

She had the family company looming in her future, and now his child growing inside of her. The child of a man she worshipped and thought would be a part of her life forever. Then it struck her like a bolt of lightning. She knew what to do.

She would strike a pact with her professors to challenge her classes. It would be hard, but she was confident she could make it happen. After she passed her contested exams gratifying her requirements for that semester, she would leave town. She would move to New York. *Her cousin Edward stayed there. Maybe he could locate her a place to stay.* Quickly she dismissed the thought of aborting Thomas' child. Despite circumstances, she still esteemed Thomas. From that love, a child was conceived. She would have the baby. Yet it was imperative she vacate the eastern shore where her mother could condemn her, her cousins could reprimand her, and her friends could gossip about her.

At first, Edith was apprehensive about challenging her class. There was always the chance, somebody would not comply. Nevertheless she took the gamble. She had nothing to lose. She explained to each instructor, personal matters were pressing her to leave college immediately. "I was wondering if I could challenge the class."

"You realize if you don't pass the exam, you've lost everything." A young professor with a thick beard and curly hair said as he reared back in his leather chair smoking a pipe.

"I know." Edith waited patiently for an answer.

He leaned forward, emptied his pipe into a silver ashtray resting on the edge of his desk. "Alright. I'll have a test ready for you in two weeks. Meet me here in my office three weeks from today."

"Thank you sir. I appreciate this."

Her history teacher was the last one on her list. Unanimously all her instructors honored her request. For the next three weeks, Edith spent every wakening moment studying. She skipped breakfast and seldom ate lunch. When she wasn't cooped up in her bedroom studying, she was at the library, in a booth behind closed doors. No matter what it took, she was determined to pass every challenged class. There was no other option, if she wanted her plan to succeed. She had to get as far from Salisbury as soon as possible, before people started asking questions. Questions she wanted to avoid. Time was running out. The hour glass was low.

She took each exam as scheduled. The night before she received the results, she prayed to a God of whom she disbelieved, asking for a miracle of which she was not worthy. Three days later, a letter arrived from all her teachers confirming she passed with a B. A satisfactory mark would have sufficed but a B would look good on her transcript.

Her cousin Edward made arrangements for her to reside in an apartment fifty miles from his house. Edward knew the owner of the complex. They were good friends and had been for many years. When he told him he had a relative needing housing, he was eager to help.

"I have an apartment, fully furnished. The lady that was staying there died. She had no family. I sold all her personal affects but kept the furnisher. So, if she doesn't have a problem with living in an apartment of a deceased person, she is certainly welcomed to it." Steven, a pot belly Jewish man in a tea shirt, sitting behind a huge oak desk, drinking black coffee, said to Edward.

"Like I said it may be a few months. I don't think it's going to be a long term deal." Edward cautioned as he walked to the front door of the main office where his friend presided three days a week.

"When can I be expecting her," Steven was curious.

Edward turned to face him before departing into the frigid morning. The place was like an oven. No wonder Steven wore a tea shirt. It must had been at least ninety some degrees or more. "Man why is it so hot in here?" Sweat accumulated on his forehead.

"I've got men working on the furnace. My patrons were complaining about no heat this morning. That's why I am here. Evidently they fixed the problem." Steven explained.

"Edith, that's my cousin's name. She has not given me an exact date but it should be soon."

Edith never told Edward why she wanted to move and he never asked. She feared if he kept tabs on her, her secret would be exposed. She would discourage him from impromptu visits. She intended to keep her pregnancy a secret for as long as possible.

After everything was set, she started packing, preparing for her getaway. Naturally her mother sensed she was plotting something. When she entered her room late one evening, she found suitcases in the floor and clothes strung across the bed. Ellen anticipated she was moving.

"What's all this?" She asked, not really wanting to know.

"I am moving out," she said tossing dresses onto the clustered bed.

"Why now. School is still in session." Ellen added solemnly.

"I challenged all my classes and passed." Edith informed her.

"I gather you're leaving because of Thomas," she stated slowly.

Edith paused. "I need to get away from here. Time to gather my thoughts, sort things out, and move forward." She explained as best she could.

"I understand. And I won't stop you. "Ellen promised.

"I'm leaving tomorrow."

"Are you taking your car?" Ellen asked.

"No. I won't need it where I'm going." She continued packing.

Ellen bowed her head sorrowfully and left her alone. She was losing her daughter. Tomorrow she would abandon her home and venture off into the real world without her protection. If only she could convince her to stay, but that was unfeasible. Her mind was made-up. She had approached a cross road. It was her getting off season. She feared she made a drastic decision when she revealed Thomas's secret. It was a heavy burden to carry. But she did what she thought was best. A decision she would live with for the rest of her life. Repentance was not an option. There was no going back.

The next day, Edith walked downstairs carrying her suitcases. Her parents waited in the lobby. They volunteered to drive her to the bus station. Ellen told John about Edith leaving that night before they retired. Ellen knew Edward secured her daughter a place to stay but she never questioned where.

If Edith didn't want her to know her whereabouts, then so be it. She would honor her wishes. She owed her that much. When she was ready to come back home, she would. She was entitled to time and space to sort things out.

It was a short ride from their house to the Bus Station. They waited impatiently inside the greyhound bus station. A few people were scattered about sitting close to their luggage, looking aimlessly in space, or chatting with the person who came to see them off. Her parents were silent as they sat sandwiching their daughter. Neither of them wanted her to leave. But it was her decision and they had to respect that.

An announcement bombarded the intercom announcing the arrival of the Bus bound for Manhattan New York. John grabbed her suitcases heading toward the Ramp. Ellen grabbed her daughter hugging her before she caught up with her father.

"Baby I love you. Remember that." Ellen struggled to keep from crying but failed. She was losing her daughter. Her heart was breaking.

Edith brushed the tears from her mother's face. "Mom, despite all that has happened in the past few months, we shared wonderful moments together. Right now I want to remember them. I'm sorry we have to depart like this."

Ellen held her shoulders and looked into her sad face. "Regardless of what transpired between us, never forget, I did what I did because I Love you. And you have been a good child." She paused for a moment and continued, "You're my jewel. I want to thank you here and now for the happiness and joy you have given me and your father."

"Mother I know."

Ellen continued in an even tone. "I know you feel empty and void. But remember your father and me will always be here for you. As long as we live, you will never be alone. "Ellen assured her.

Edith was about to cry. She had to break the moment. She took her mother's hand and together they walked to the bus where her father was standing near the driver as he stuffed suitcases into the storing compartment.

"Well honey this it." John hugged his daughter and kissed her forehead. "Call us when you can."

"I will," she lied.

"If you need anything, please let us know," Ellen injected.

Edith boarded the bus and located a seat near the window. She waved to her parents when the vehicle disembarked and headed towards its ultimate stop. As the greyhound pulled onto the main highway, Edith experienced butterflies in her stomach. *Something terrible was predestined to happen. What, she did not know.*

Chapter Twelve

Edward met Edith at the Grand Central Greyhound Bus Station in Manhattan. He grabbed her luggage and tucked it in the trunk of his Cadillac. They drove from the crowded bus station to her apartment on the Westside. It was a lovely fenced in three story residential complex with a private pool which was covered for the season and an immense contemporary lobby leading to the front desk. A stout bald man wearing wire framed glasses hung to his nostrils, sat on a stool watching football on a twelve inch Television. He peered over his spectacles as Edith and Edward approached. He pulled a key from a desk drawer handing it to Edward as he went pass. Edward thanked the man leading Edith down a long well lit corridor. They stopped at A333. Edward presented her the key sanctioning her to unlock her new domain. Anxiously she unbolted the door and touched the switch.

The place was fantastic. It was completely furnished. She sprinted from chamber to chamber inspecting the decor and the furniture. She slid back the drapes hiding a bay window only to discover a fabulous view of the city streets. The place was divine.

"This is perfect. Thank you cousin." She hugged and kissed his cheeks.

"I thought you would like it." He put her luggage in the master bedroom shutting the door for privacy.

"How much will this cost?"

"Your father leased the place for a year."

Edith panicked. *So her father knew where she lived. Edward promise not to tell a soul. He reneged on his promise.* "You assured—"

"He doesn't know where you are. When my father told him you were moving out, he volunteered to pay the rent. Yes, he knew you had enough money in your personal account to pay for the apartment but he was determined to help. He wants you to use your money for daily living expenses. My father did not tell him where you were moving to. Uncle John did not ask and my father did not volunteer any information."

"How much does mother know?" Edith was curious.

"Only that you're in New York. Where, she does not have a clue. And no, she hasn't called Dad enquiring about you. As long as you're safe and well provided for, she is content."

Edith breathed a little easier. *Her mother relinquished opposing her departure. She practically offered her blessing. Her location was* undisclosed. *Maybe no one would seek her out. She had to believe that.*

Edward made himself comfortable in a recliner beside a book shelf. "I know you want your privacy and all but I need a favor."

Edith was inquisitive. "What's that?"

"A friend of mine is in town for a few days. I was wondering if you could show him around the city. I would do it myself but I am pretty busy this time of year. Besides, I believe he would enjoy your company better."

Immediately Edith knew her cousin's intents. *The matchmaker. Thomas was absent from the scene. She needed a companion. Didn't he realize she wasn't prepared to launch into another relationship?* Besides, unbeknown to him, she was pregnant. "I don't think that would be a good idea." *She had to wiggle her way from the commitment.* "You're a native. I don't know New York that well."

"You've spent many summer vacations here. You know this place like the back of your hand." He reminded her quickly. "Besides." He paused shifting about nervously. *What if his cousin flatly denied him? His friend would be greatly disappointed.* "His only here for a few weeks. He needs a guide; A friend." He pleaded his case.

"A few weeks." She echoed. *He did set her up in a fabulous apartment, fully furnished. What was a few weeks? A favor for a favor. That was the least she could do to show her appreciation. She owed him as much.*

Edward took the repeat as a yes. "I'll bring him by tomorrow." He stood abruptly. *He had to leave before she changed her mind.* "I'm going to leave. Let you relax and enjoy your new home."

Edith hugged him before he left. "Thanks cousin. The perfect hideaway." Once again she scoped out the decorations and amenities.

Obviously the previous owner had good taste, the talents of an interior designer. It looked like a page from a Home & Garden magazine. And it was all hers. It was her home. A place to lay her head. She touched her belly. The realization of why she was there rushed back. It was a place she could have her baby in secret.

Her first night in a new place was blissful. Gorgeous house plants strategically positioned in corners highlighting its surroundings, the fresh scented bed linen caressing her face when she laid across her bed swayed her to sleep initiating images of parading amiss a field crammed with lifelike floral floats as she drifted off.

Late the next day, Edward introduced Edith to his best friend from college, Daniel Collins. Daniel was a short, thin framed man cursed with a jagged smile but blessed with sparkling white teeth. He offered his hand in friendship and she accepted. In an odd way, she found his jagged grin charming. Ascertaining from awkward gestures and timid movements, he was somewhat apprehensive. That was understandable considering they just met. *She wondered how he pictured her through those hazel eyes. Was she pretty or some old hag he couldn't wait to escape?*

She ushered her callers into the dining area, bypassing the organized lounge. Early that morning, she rushed to a grocery store a block from her residence, grabbed a few items, rushed home and conjured up a quick, simple meal. She filled Daniel and Edward's plate with spaghetti. A large salad bowl garnished with cheese sprinkles rested in the center to be shared. Upon returning the pot of spaghetti to the stove, she retrieved hot garlic bread from the oven, transferred it into a baskets with prongs near a pitcher of ice tea with pieces of lemon surfacing the top. Edward assumed the honors of praying over the meal before they dug in.

Edward began the conversation as he poured tea into a glass. "Daniel lives in Chicago. His a magazine journalist. His here for a few days doing a story on Bill Cosby. But his heart is in acting. That is his destiny."

Edith dissected her meatballs. "How long have you been a journalist?"

"Evvvver since college." He stammered. "M-m-m-my first Job." Daniel managed to say while shoving noodles into his mouth. *It was delicious. It was stupendous.* "This is good."

"Thank you." Edith accepted the compliment.

"This is Daniel's first visit to the Big Apple." Edward continued stuffing food into his face as he talked. "That's where you come in."

"Well Daniel. What do you want to see?"

"I don't know." Daniel whispered. *Edith was an attractive young lady. His heart pounded in his chest pumping zealous adrenaline throughout his body. A warm, comforting emotion overpowered him. She could carry him anywhere. Being in her attendance delighted him even though they just met. Perhaps the old cliché was true. Love at first sight. She was speaking to him but he was at lost for words.*

Edith could hardly hear him. Retracting Daniel from being timid would be a challenge. Yet she was confident, it could be achieved in no time. She just had to get him to relax. "Do you like plays?"

He took a swallow of tea to clear his throat. "Yeah."

"If you don't have anything on your agenda, perhaps we could go see a play tomorrow evening."

Daniel dabbed his mouth with a paper napkin. He had an interview scheduled with Bill Cosby at his pen house apartment. That would take a few hours. After that, his plate was empty. Slowly he informed Edith about his engagement with Bill Cosby, wary not to stutter, stressing he would be free afterward.

"That sounds wonderful." Edward keyed in. "Have you ever been to a Broadway play?"

"No." Daniel said. "Too busy."

"That magazine company keeps you busy I'm sure, sending you all around the country interviewing celebrities from all walks of life." Edward added.

Edith searched her wardrobe for the perfect dress to wear to the theater. She was tempted to contact her cousin Cherry for advice but soon realized that was an unwise. She would inquire where she was, why she left and a battery of probing questions she choose not to entertain. She would trust her own taste. She pulled out a satin blue gown with a matching shawl. That would do fine. She spent the morning styling her hair. *If only she knew a good beautician in the area. But there was no time to scout the neighborhood for a hairdresser Hopefully Daniel would be impressed by her looks. She couldn't possibly embarrass him.*

Late that evening, she slid into a bathtub consumed with bubbles and started scrubbing her itching back with an extender. While relaxing in the tub filled with a variety of scented shampoos, she wondered how Daniel's interview went with Bill Cosby. Rumor was he was a pleasant, cordial man who welcomed reporters with opened arms. Well, he had been at his trade for years. Surely he could handle Mr. Cosby and get a sensational story for his boss.

It was six thirty when Daniel came calling. There he stood in the corridor, flashing his uneven smile, modeling a black suit harmonized with a dark tie over a starched white shirt wearing black shoes completing the outfit. He was carrying a dozzen yellow roses, a gratitude offering. A familiar aftershave scent lingered from his clothes; a smell reminding her of Thomas. Daniel reeked of old spice, a fragrance she would never forget.

Edith beckoned Daniel into her cozy apartment, taking the roses. "They're beautiful." She immediately placed them into an empty vase on a bookshelf.

She was gorgeous. He wanted to kiss her but it was too soon. This was their first date. He had to be a gentleman. "I'm glad you like them."

Daniel was handsome. But he was not Thomas. Despite his looks, her heart still belong to Thomas. Yet that had to change. Thomas was her past. And then she realized she was carrying his child. That only complicated her life. "How did you get here?" Edith asked.

"I rented a car for the evening. I didn't want to catch the subway. I want this to be a special occasion." He explained. "Of course you will be the driver. That is if you don't mind."

"No problem." Edith put on her shawl and coat. How is the weather?"

"Brisk." Daniel too was wearing a trench coat which he left opened modeling his suit.

"We're going to see Applause at the Palace Theater starring Ann Bancroft." She grabbed her purse resting on the couch.

"Here's the keys." He retrieved them from his coat pocket and presented them to Edith.

Together they exited the apartment. Edith asked him where he was staying while he was in the city as they walked down the long corridors leading to the parking lot.

"I am staying in the hotel across the street from you."

Daniel had rented a white Cadillac for the event. The ride from the apartment complex to the Palace was a forty-five minute drive. Traffic was hectic but Edith had no trouble maneuvering through the bumper to bumper streets to her destination. It was a far cry from riding on the Eastern Shore. It was like wondering through a maze with a ton of unexpected barriers.

Daniel and Edith entered the Palace holding hands in friendship. The place was crowded.

They purchased tickets from a booth and was quickly ushered to their seat. The show would be starting momentarily. The usher handed Daniel a program and went to greet another approaching guest.

Daniel enjoyed the play but Edith was disappointed. As they drove to a restaurant for a late dinner, they critiqued the actor's performance, the story line, the music and costumes. Edith expected more from the actors, and the costume lacked something, what, she was unsure. Daniel though the actors did a stupendous job and the costumes were fabulous. They came in agreement about the music and the choreography. Edith thought the story line was weak but Daniel insisted it was strong and moving.

They dined at an elegant restaurant in Manhattan. Being the place was packed, they had to wait an hour before being were served. Despite the lousy service, the food was divine. Daniel paid for the meal. Since Edith purchased tickets for the play, that was the least he could do. When he saw the bill, he figured Edith got the better end of the deal. It was almost two hundred dollars. But then they did order lavish appetizers, entrees, and drinks to conciliate their exquisite taste buds.

Edith fulfilled her commitment with her cousin Edward by taking Daniel on deluxe tours of New York. Her first stop was the Statue of liberty, where Daniel snapped a heap of pictures for his album. They took in a shows at Radio City Music Hall, explored the Empire State Building and attended a sightseeing guide of The World Trade Center.

Each day they spent together, they warmed up to each other and enjoyed being together. It was nothing for Daniel to come over to her apartment for a homemade meal. It was nothing for her to address his doorstep with a tape for them to watch as they shared a bowl of popcorn.

Soon the time for Daniel to leave and return to Chicago drew near. Edith could tell by the look in his eyes, he dreaded leaving her. Even though she fought from admitting it, she did not want him to leave. He became a good distraction in her life. Her cousin's magic was working. She could feel herself falling for Daniel. And then she remembered the baby growing inside her.

She could not get involved with another man. At least not yet.

The two weeks they shared, were wonderful. Many times she caught Daniel gazing into her eyes, yearning to kiss her, to embrace her, but she never encouraged him. Unresolved passion alienated them, a friendly liaison was necessary. Yet Daniel sought more. Casual association was not enough.

It was a sorrowful day when Edith accompanied Daniel to the airport seeing him safely off. She figured she owed him for easing her raw sentiments concerning Thomas. He was a pleasant interference. A temporary relief.

"Thank you for a wonderful time," Daniel said cruising through the gate with a knapsack straddling his shoulders.

"Thank you for the company," She replied watching him hustle onto the embankment platform.

"I'll call you when I get to Chicago." Daniel yelled back as anxious passengers shoved him aboard an idling plane.

A taxi dropped her off at her residency. Opening the doors to a well lite but empty flat felt bizarre. Daniel would not be accompanying her for one of her fantastic meals. Meals she enjoyed creating for him. He was her greatest customer. Tomorrow she would sleep late. There was no reason to rise early. No plans to treat Daniel to lunch in an unexplored heaven in Manhattan. No plans to take the subway to the Bronx and go sightseeing on a crowded bus with rowdy tourist vacationing. Even though she refused to admit it, she was lonely. She missed Daniel. Daniel gave her that warm fuzzy feeling she experienced when she was with Thomas. That unsolicited thought forced her to retire early. She had to forget about Thomas. He was a chapter once lived but was over. If only there was no baby; a baby responsible for her leaving her family.

As promised, Daniel called after he settled in his one bedroom abode in Chicago. She was in a deep sleep when the princess phone by her bed rang. He let her know he was home safely and was about to edit his story on Bill Cosby. She asked him about the weather which he reported was windy and cool. An average day in Chicago for the middle of February. It struck him then, it was Valentine's Day. He should have gotten her some flowers but it was too late. Nevertheless he wished her a happy Valentine's Day.

Edith also had forgotten the Holiday. As she hung up the phone enabling Daniel to edit his column, she wondered what Thomas was doing on that special day. If they were together, he would shower her with exquisite flowers and boxes of chocolates. He treasured celebrating holidays. They both did.

There she was thinking about Thomas. Her mind needed refurbishing. *Past connections were finished. They could not be resurrected. They had to be buried and sealed in a vault. But there was a remnant. A life force circling inside. An inequity string that looped them together. If she remained celibate, reserved her purity, none of this would be happening. She could have made a clean but painful getaway. If she failed knelling to her flesh, but persisted loyalty to her spirit, she would not be the victim of her impending condition. Perhaps it was a mistake, perhaps it was a blessing. Once it was over, she could move forward. She could come out of hiding.*

Chapter Thirteen

Philip Guy sipped a cup of black coffee. He was in the lobby outside of Thomas's room. His son had been in John Hopkins for almost five weeks. A gray shadow painted his face. His nights were spent tossing and turning in agony. Nurses kept him sedated with pain killers. Meals were left untouched. Often he expressed the desire to go home. Anything to abandon the torture. Treatments were stagnant. Administered vaccines were ineffective. Hope was vanishing. Death was predestined. But he refused to surrender. He forfeited his precious wife. Now the same diabolical blood ailment sought to claim his beloved son. Well, he would not surrender. The war was on. A battle fumed in his mind. Faith was his ammunition. Prayer was his strategy. He shut his eyes and communed with the God his mother worshipped; the God he learned about in Sunday school. Where else could he turn? Every alternative avenue had been exhausted. The doctors did their best but it was not good enough. Now the hour arrived to expect a miracle. He was still meditating when the African doctor in charge of Thomas' treatment startled him by pulling up a chair across from him.

"Mr. Guy it appears your son is responding gradually to the injections." He smiled when he saw Phillip gasp releaved. "He's still in the woods." He cautioned. "Some patients respond quicker than others. Thomas is one of those slow acting clients. We want to keep him here for a few more weeks and see what happens. Give the injections time to work."

"Of course."

"I know his in pain and wants to go home. I tried to explain it's taking longer for the medicine to react than we expected."

"I'll talk to him." Phillip knew his son was restless and anxious to leave. He had threatened to stop treatment. Apparently the pain was getting the best of him. But he could not give up. He had to be strong.

"Thank you sir." He extended his huge hands.

Phillip shook his hands. "Thank you –"

"Call be Doctor Adam."

"Doctor Adam. I appreciate what you're doing."

Thomas studied a wall calendar. Four weeks had disappeared into eternity. It was Valentine's Day. What a way to spend the holidays. Here he was captive in a monstrous hospital being probed with needles, intravenous cocktails draining into his body, and lousy food to appease his pinching appetite. All the doctors said, "It takes a while for the treatment to kick in. Be patient."

How much patients could one man endure? But then what choice did he have. Either he stay and live or leave and die. Mutely he implored the God whom he was skeptical of, to heal his body.

A young lady wearing a blue smock, whom he became to know of as Jessica, came in bearing a small boutique of wild flowers she purchased at the Junior Board Café. Jessica made it her priority to check on him daily. Obviously she was attracted to him. The flowers confirmed her intentions.

Jessica deduced from the interview, he was single, unattached and available. She violated company policies by fraternizing with the guest. But she did not care. Thomas was handsome, charming, and intelligent. He possessed all the attributes of a perfect boyfriend and maybe future husband provided the treatment proved successful.

"Happy valentine's Day." Jessica said sitting beside Thomas.

"You didn't have to do that. I am sure a girl as pretty as you, have plans for a festive day like this." Thomas commented.

"Thomas, I told you there is no one. I work, go home to an empty house and watch television. "She sounded as homey as she looked.

Thomas adjusted himself in the bed. Pain penetrated his body. "I find that hard to believe."

Jessica immediately realized he was uncomfortable. "Do you need something for pain?"

"No, I'll be fine." He lied. The last thing he wanted was a nurse jabbing him with another needle.

Jessica noticed he had not touched his food. "Want something else to eat?"

"No." He nodded.

"I can get you something from the Junior Board." She volunteered. "Tell me what you like?"

"Look, you've done more than enough. Bringing me these flowers."

"That was nothing."

Jessica was cute but very young and certainly innocent. Naive like Edith. Hell she was probably her age or perhaps younger. He had to be careful. Despite her generosity and her company, he could not encourage her. Any word or action could be interpreted wrongly. Romantic magnetism between them was void. His breakoff with Edith was fresh. Unresolved emotions were still boiling in his heart. There was no space in his life for her. Especially not now. He had to set the record straight. "Jessica," he started. "I appreciate your visitations and friendly gestures but please don't read anything into it." He had told her that before.

"I know you're ill and not interested in me romantically. But please let me be a friend. I don't hold you responsible for my feelings. I don't expect you to retort. Humor me with your hospitality." Jessica selected her words gracefully. But her conversation was far from her heart. Whenever she was near Thomas, a fuzzy sensation tickled her stomach.

Without realizing it, he grabbed and squeezed her tiny hands "As long as you know that. And thanks again for the flowers."

It took all her energy to restrain from kissing Thomas. She pretended to glance at her watch and fabricated a flimsy departure excuse. She was getting weak and she refused to weep before him. "Listen, I have work to do. I'll see you tomorrow." She left the room closing the door and commenced sobbing quietly. Thomas was in a bad place. His condition was in question.

As soon as Jessica left the scene, Phillip entered the cool room finding his son watching television. He could tell by the frown on his face he was in pain. "Son I have good news." He sat in his usual bedside chair.

"Daddy what is it?" He managed to say turning to face him.

"I talked to Doctor Adam. He said the treatment is working slowly. He wants to keep you here for a few more weeks."

Thomas thought for a few minutes. *How could the regiment be working when he was in more pain now than he was when he was admitted. Was the increased discomfort level an indicator the treatment was progressing? He wanted to go home. Anything to escape the suffering. Now his doctor was offering a tray of hope. What did he have to lose?* "OK."

Jessica read Thomas' medical records daily, praying for improvement. Her prayers were answered. His blood results proved favorable. Treatment was kicking in. His abnormal blood cell configurations were dwindling. Thomas was sleeping better at night and required fewer pain pills.

That ashy tan that once blanketed his face disappeared. His appetite increased. His father often snuck out and brought him a juicey hamburger with hot salty fries and a large milkshake which he devoured in no time. He was on the road to recovery and she was pleased. Now the thing she feared the most stalked her like a bad dream. Soon Thomas would leavethe hospital and she would never see him again. A man she met and fallen in love with would be gone. The bed where he slept would be stripped, washed, and prepared for another constituent. Nothing would be left except the memories of a fantasy that never materialized. So many times she traveled that road. Thomas was one of many. A price to pay for falling in love with unattainable men.

Chapter Fourteen

Edith located another gynecologist through the yellow pages. As the baby grew, she wanted to make sure everything was fine. The doctor's office was about three blocks from her apartment. That was convenient. At least in walking distance. It was on the third floor of an old towering office complex building which serviced residency for insurance companies, lawyers and doctors.

When Edith entered the small waiting area, she was greeted by an oriental woman sitting behind a glass window scribbling on a clip board which she gave to her with instructions to write her name and the time of her appointment. She knew the reception by name and spoke cordially "Good morning Stefani." It was her second visit. Edith signed in and found a seat away from the entrance. She wanted to avoid a draft from people coming in. There was another woman, about her age but of Mexican descent, sitting quietly engaged in a crossword puzzle. Edith collected a magazine from a nearby rack and fumbled aimlessly through it abiding her time. *Why didn't the doctor have a television attached to the wall? Anything to pass the time.*

Twenty minutes later, a young black nurse summoned her into the back. She escorted her into a small room where she weighed her, took her height, led her into another room with a bench protected with paper and had her sit on it while she took her vital signs followed by her blood pressure. She wrote her findings on a chart and left it on a counter for the doctor to review when she came in.

Her doctor was a short Pilipino woman with straight black hair and small hands. She immediately went for the chart without acknowledging

Edith. After glancing over the information she focused on her patient. "I see you about five months pregnant. Just beginning to show I see."

"I guess so."

"Everything looks ok from your sonogram. How do you feel?" The doctor was curious.

"A little nauseated from time to time."

"That's a part of the territory I am afraid." The doctor smiled revealing her gleaming white teeth. "I want to see you in two months."

As she walked back to her apartment, she thought about what her mother said. Could Thomas's genes have an impact on her child? Of course it was too early to tell. According to her doctor, the child's development was on course and blood drawn from the fetus tested normal. Yet she couldn't stop worrying. There was always a chance something could go wrong.

After she arrived at her apartment and settled down, she decided to call Edward. In a few weeks her pregnancy would become obvious. She could not keep it from him any longer. He had to be told. Before she had the opportunity to prepare herself a snack, Edward was knocking on her door. She waved him inside her apartment smelling of fried hotdogs and onions sprinkled with garlic and sharp cheese. She made Edward a sandwich and offered him a cold Pepsi. Together they sat at the kitchen table nibbling their snack.

"What did you have to tell me?" Edward asked while chewing his delicious hotdog.

"I'm pregnant. That's why I left home. I didn't want anyone to know." She confessed.

Edward laughed lightly. "I knew you were picking up weight. I never thought this."

"I suppose you're disappointed in me." Edith felt guilty and ashamed. *Edward always held her in high esteem. Now his sanctified cousin was the not the saint he alleged her to be.* "I should have told you from the start."

"Don't worry about me. What about the father. Does he know?" Edward assumed Thomas was the father; the man she loved.

Edith was not at liberty to reveal the conversation she had with her mother. That was something exclusive between them. But she could expose the outcome. "Thomas and I separated. Some things happened and we thought it best if we went our different ways." It grieved her to convey even that portion.

Edward knew his aunt Ellen opposed Edith's courtship with Thomas. Perhaps she devised a scheme to separate them. It all made sense. "Aunt Ellen –"

Edith jumped to her defense. "Not this time. Circumstances worked in her favor but she was not the culprit."

"I gather you're not going to tell Thomas about his child," Edward assumed.

"I am going to wait until the child is born and then I will decide what I'm going to do."

Even though Edward was against her decision, he kept silent and offered his support. "If there is anything I can do, please let me know."

"Promise me you won't tell mom or dad," she pleaded.

"You know I won't but they will find out eventually. How long can you keep this a secret?"

Edith knew Edward spoke the truth. Soon the baby would be born and he would play a central role in the family. Her father would elect him or her as the future heir to his dynasty. His entire life would be mapped out from the day he took his first breath to the day he died. That was the price one had to pay for being born into wealth. Sometimes she wondered if that was more of a curse than a blessing. Her mother dictating whom she should marry and her father waiting impatiently for her to take her place in the company so he could retire and live a common man's life.

Daniel made a surprise visit one late evening in April carrying a dozen roses and a box of chocolates. Edith was glad to see him. Spending long days watching soap operas, reading magazines and eating alone was no fun. She welcomed the company of another person. Edward seldom visited due to the long hours he spent in his office.

Daniel was not shocked by her big belly and swollen feet. Edward notified him about her pregnancy shortly after Edith told him. That was why he was there. He did not want her to go through it along. He wanted to be there for support and guidance.

"What takes you here?" Edith asked taking the roses and disposing of them into a vase.

"I'm working on several stories here for the magazine. I'm going to be here for a long spell. I got an apartment in this building so I could be close to you. I hope I'm not being too forward," Daniel said while making himself comfortable on the leather sofa.

Normally she was hesitant to encourage Daniel but she was so glad to see him, she dispatched her guard. She plumped down on the sofa beside him and propped her feet on a stool. Her back was aching terribly. "As you can see I'm pregnant."

"Your cousin told me. And that's why I'm here."

Edith looked into his gentle eyes. "I appreciate that."

"I hear you're a good typist." Daniel looked away. He felt his heart growing towards her. He had to simmer down. He knew she would not respond to passion.

"I do sixty-eight to seventy words a minute on the average." She boasted.

"Would you be my secretary? I will pay you handsomely."

Edith reared back hoping to relieve the cramp in her back and said, "Since you're here to help me, let's say it's a fair exchange. You take care of me, I work for you."

"Sounds good to me."

Daniel had breakfast prepared every morning Edith came to the kitchen and a pillow for her back when she relaxed on the couch clicking through channels on the floor model television searching for the local news. He served her lunch on a collapsible table pre-empting her from walking no more than necessary. In the evening, he filled her bathtub making sure her bathing accessories were within reach. If the weather was pleasant, they would stroll through the park feeding the pigeons along the path.

Three times a week he would interview a celebrity with his miniature tape recorder backed by notes he scribbled in a composition tablet. Other times he went to Broadway Plays and evaluated the performance for his column. Afterward he rushed to his apartment, wrote his articles in long hand and distributed his texts to Edith to type and stuff into a vanilla folder to be delivered to his Boss the following day.

Each day Edith grew bigger and more miserable. She could feel the baby moving inside of her. Her breast expanded formulating milk for the infant. It became difficult getting out of and into bed. Daniel tucked her in bed at night and pulled her to her feet enabling her to stand in the morning. No one told her the challenges a woman faced when she became pregnant. She graved for things that weren't in her vocabulary; such as kosher pickles and chocolate ice cream. She horded chocolate chip cookies, and cinnamon buns, and drank a large glass of cold milk to wash them down. The more she ate, the more she wanted.

The fact that Daniel was a great cook, only made matters worse. He was always concocting something bizarre and tasty. One night it might be succulent southern fried chicken, garlic mashed potatoes and glazed carrots with lemon pie for dessert. Another time he might have spaghetti sauce seasoned with sausage, ground beef, yellow bell peppers, diced garlic, and a finely chopped sweet onion over pasta noodles. Garlic bread and a colorful garden salad completed the meal. He put his culinary skill to work.

The more tine they spent together, the harder Daniel fell for her. It was arduous denying his true feelings. He was there in the morning when she awakened and the last person she saw at before falling asleep. When there was nothing on the tube to satisfy their fancy, they resorted to board games like Chinese checkers and chess. Edith became a whiz at Chinese checkers and Daniel was a pro at chess.

Occasionally Edward came over to a free meal when he could find time amidst his hectic work endeavors. They would cap off the evening with a friendly game of rummy, Edward's sport of choice. Daniel filled a pitcher with finely crushed ice submerged in various fruit juices combined creating a healthy virgin cocktail. As an encore, he would have a plate of petite apple turnovers as an after dinner treat.

"These are delicious," Edward would say evenly.

"Daniel is quite a chef." Edith complimented.

"I can see that."

When Edith felt up to it, the three of them would go to a late night movie. The crowd was less then. They avoided the hustle and bustle of people staggering in the dark searching for a seat, stepping on your toes in the process. Usually at that hour, the theater was almost empty with the exception of a handful of patrons waiting eagerly for the screen to descend and the program to start following a battery of promotions.

After the show, they would crawl into Edward's Cadillac Deville and head for a twenty-four hour restaurant where they ordered a light meal and spent hours drinking coffee or sipping a cold beverage spiked with caffeine while they chatted.

"How much longer do you have cousin?" Edward would ask.

"Three more months," she said while rubbing her big stomach.

"I can imagine you'll be relieved when it's over."

"I am so grateful Daniel came back to watch over me." She reached out and clutched his warm hands. "I'm glad you told him about my pregnancy, otherwise, he would not be here." She thanked her cousin.

"I had reservations at first. I know how private you are. I took a gamble and it seemed to work out for all of us."

Daniel was confused. "What do you mean all of us?"

"Well. I wanted someone to be with her during this period. I certainly could not be there. You know how busy I am. I took a chance you might be able to swing things with your boss, allowing you to work on this end for a few months instead of Chicago," he explained.

Daniel smirked. "That impromptu visit with my Boss might have been the icing on the cake."

Edward lifted up his hands. "OK. Your Boss and I are friends. She was returning a favor. I hope you don't hate me for my meddling in your career."

Hate him. He was doing him a favor. There was nothing he wanted more then to spend time with Edith. So she was pregnant. So what. That did not stop him from loving her even though she did not love him. Perhaps in due season all of that would change. "I don't begrudge what you did. You answered a silent prayer."

As the time grew closer, Daniel wondered what Edith's intentions were after she had the child. For a while he was afraid to ask her anything concerning her pregnancy. But finally he could no longer restraint his curiosity. He had to know.

She was stretched out on her back with two pillows under her head, doing a crossword puzzle. He finished scrubbing her bathtub and closed the door. *There she was, as beautiful as ever, belly bulging out like a balloon ready to pop any moment. The moment was then. It could not be delayed. He had to know her plans. Was she going to raise the child alone or return to the baby's father and try to start a new life?* He cleared his throat as he sat on the bed facing her.

"Edith looked up from her book. "What's on your mind?"

Daniel stammered. Something he had not done for months. Something he done when he was nervous or felt intimidated. Something he done when he first met Edith. "I- I- I wa-wa-was wondering w-w-w-w-what yo-yo-you're going to do after you have the baby?"

Edith was silent. The truth being she was uncertain. Then she managed to say, "I may stay here for a while."

Daniel mustered up enough courage to ask the ten thousand dollar question that had been probing his mind for weeks. "What about the baby's father. Are you going to tell him or what?"

Again Edith was silent. *Was it wise to tell Thomas he was a father? Was it feasible considering the position stagnating them. What advice would her father give? What would her mother suggest? She was not in this alone. Daniel was there for support and guidance. She could trust and depend on him even though she knew it was wrong to fill his mind with false hope. She could never love him like she loved Thomas.* "I don't think I am going to tell him," she whispered. "It's over between us."

Before he realized it, the words slipped out. "I'll be the baby's father."

Edith was not startled by his proposal. "Daniel I would be honored to have you as my baby's father. But there are conditions."

Daniel braced himself for what she was about to say. "Ok, let's hear it."

"As much as I love having you here and being in your company, I do not love you. Please don't read any more into our relationship than what it is," she cautioned him. Then she focused on his question. "I believe you would make a good father image for my child. And even if the child's natural father should appear on the scene, I still want you to play an important role in his life. You're a good man." She took his sweaty hands. "I appreciate everything you have done and continue to do for me. Unfortunately I can't yield your zeal for my affection."

Daniel was hurt by her confession. *If she allowed herself to be vulnerable, she could fall for him. They could be an ideal couple. They could be there for each other; a never broken chain; A love to sustain all trials and tribulation life toiled at them. If she lowered her guard and permitted him to be her lover, her companion, her soul mate, the circle would be complete. If only she learned to love him as much as he loved her, his life would be whole. The pain of being alone would be abolished. It was dubious that was going to occur. Still there was hope.* "Thank you for letting me be the baby's father."

Edith gasped a short breath. The baby kicked inside her. "His getting restless."

"You think it's going to be a boy?" Daniel asked.

"I just said that. I don't want to know until it happens." Edith guided Daniel's hands to her stomach. "Can you feel that?"

Daniel smiled as he looked into Edith's eyes. "Yes. His an active little fellow."

The next day Daniel presented Edith with his composition book crammed with notes for his editorial column. He had interviewed two celebrities that week; an upcoming black actress on Broadway and a female novelist with a book climbing the best seller list. Edith glanced at the draft while she sipped her coffee, turning off the morning newscast so she could concentrate. Daniel was at the front door, with his hands on the door knob when the phone rang.

"Would you get that for me please?" Edith was comfortable in her recliner with her feet elevated. It was good to get off her feet and relax. *Carrying a child took a toll on her body. She prayed her delivery date would be soon.*

Daniel answered the phone which was resting on a desk in a corner of the room. A place Edith set up for her office when doing her secretarial duties. "It's your cousin. He said he'll be over to see you this evening. He wants to know if you need anything special from the super market."

"Tell him I'm fine."

"She said she's fine." Daniel listened to Edward and replied. "I rented a car and I'm on my way to Washington DC. My Boss wants me to interview the Vice President. I should be back late tonight or early tomorrow morning." Daniel waited for Edward's brief response, then hung up.

"Be careful." Edith warned as Daniel opened the door to leave.

"I'll call you when I reach my destination." Daniel promised.

Chapter Fifteen

Ellen headed home from the plant. It was getting dark. She turned her lights on. Traffic was light. She had put in long hours at the office. The union was asking for more money and benefits. Her husband would certainly oppose their request. He increased everyone's pay by seventy-five cent per hour plus and enrolled them into a better but cheaper health plan with low out-of-pocket deductible for prescription and doctor visits. What more could they want.

She decided to stop at Super Giant to get some food for breakfast. When she left home that morning, they were almost out of eggs and bacon. She meant to leave a note for the maid to pick up some stuff before she left but forgot about it. It wouldn't take long to get what she needed and be back in her car. She parked in front of Super Giant and went inside the store. It was vacant with the exception of a few stranglers lurking about like her. She went to the breakfast section, grabbed a cartoon of eggs and a pack of bacon and went to the casher. She handed him a twenty dollar bill and he handed her change, bagged her merchandise and gave it to her. Ellen got back into her car and started it. She pulled back onto the road.

She looked into her rear view mirror. A black car had been following her ever since she left the plant. Maybe she was imagining things. Maybe she was being paranoid. Just in case, she did an illegal U turn and acted as if she was headed back toward the plant. The car was still behind her. She could not make out who it was because it was dark and he kept a distinct distance from her. Then she recalled that same dark car had been trailing her for the last couple days. At first she didn't pay it any attention. People who worked at the plant lived near her. They travelled the same route. But this was strange. Here it was, almost nine thirty and this man was pursuing her. Her heart pounded in her chest. She had to get home. God only knew why a lunatic was stalking her or what his intention was. She did another illegal turn headed towards her home. She pressed the accelerator hoping to lose her stalker but he stayed dead on her trail. There was no easing up. Finally her house was in view. Thank God she had a garage. As she approached her house, she pushed the remote control which was in the ashtray elevating the garage door. She pulled into her garage and lowered the door. She knew her husband was home. He parked in front of the house.

When she went inside, she was shaking. The idea of someone taunting her was nerve racking. There was no telling what he had in mind. He might have thought she had money and planned to rob her. She jumped out of her car and ran inside the house.

She found John sitting at the kitchen table eating a bun and sipping coffee. He noticed she was upset and nervous. "You look like you saw a ghost."

She collapsed into a chair realizing she had left her package in the car." Somebody has been following me for the last few days."

"Let's call the police," John suggested immediately.

"I can't prove anything yet. I want to be certain before I bring the authorities in on this."

"What are you going to do?" John appeared to be concerned.

"If he follows me tomorrow, I'll call the police."

"Are you sure?" John asked.

"Yes." Ellen said calming herself down. "I won't be staying late at the plant anymore. I'll come home with you."

"I think that's wise. "John changed the subject. "You had a telephone call."

"Who?"

"Stanly. He said something about dropping by."

Again her nerves were jangled. *What was he thinking, calling her at home? Was he out of his mind?* "What did he want?"

"I don't know. I didn't ask."

She relaxed for a few minutes watching John finish his snack. Then she went to the refrigerator to get a soda. "I guess it's about that necklace I ordered."

John leaned back in the chair patting his stomach. "I think you should contact the police. I would feel better if you did."

"If he follows me tomorrow I will." She snapped the cap on the coke can. "But there's nothing she can do until a crime has been committed. I'll have to be careful." She added.

The phone rang.

"Who could that be?" John wondered.

"I'll get that." She went to the wall and picked up the receiver. "John I left a package in the car. Would you get that for me please?"

"Sure." John left the room.

"Hello."

Stanly was calling from inside his store. "Darling I want to see you tonight. Can you get away?"

"You told John you were coming by here," she reminded him.

"Well he answered the phone. I had to say something." Stanly closed his cash register drawer. "Is he still there?"

"He went to the garage to get something for me."

"Can you meet me at the Statesman's Motel in Salisbury?" Stanly asked.

"See what I can do."

"Who was that?" John asked entering the kitchen carrying a little brown bag.

"My father." Ellen hung up the phone.

"I haven't seen him since he retired. What is he doing with himself these days?" John always liked Ellen's father. He was smart and had a great rapport with the people at the plant. His father could depend on him to set things straight whenever an up-evil was brewing.

"He's having trouble with his back and he was wondering if I could drive over there, spend the night, and take him to the doctor in the morning."

"That's in Laurel Delaware. What are you going to do?"

"I guess I'm going to have to drive up there, spend the night, take him to the doctor and come back in the morning." Ellen said.

"What about your pursuer?" John asked calmly.

"I'll stay in the car until I get to my destination. I'll call Dad when I get there and have him meet me at the front door."

"I can go with you." John removed the eggs and bacon from the bag and put them in the refrigerator. "It's not safe for you to be on the road alone at night. Especially if you think somebody is following you."

"You stay near the phone. If I am being followed once I leave here, you come looking for me." Ellen suggested. "Besides, they will need you at the plant tomorrow. We have more trouble with the union. They have additional demands. My secretary will bring you up to speed when you get there."

"It's times like these when I wish your father was still working. He was a pro at handling grievances and stuff like that."

"I'm going to go upstairs, grab a change of clothes and be on my way."

John watched Ellen leave the room. Then he snatched the phone off the hook and dialed a series of numbers hastily. A rusty voice echoed across the line. "Hello."

"You've got to be more discrete. She suspects she's being followed." He whispered.

"Ok sir."

"Talk later," The phone went to a steady buzz.

An hour later Ellen came downstairs sporting an overnight duffle bag. She passed a folder to her husband who was sitting in the foyer pretending to read a magazine.

"Here are some documents needing your signature."

"I'll look at them later." John rose to his feet and kissed her briefly on the lips. "Give your father my love, and be careful."

"I've already called daddy and told him to be watching out for my coming."

"I still don't feel comfortable with you being out there knowing you're being stalked."

"I'll be fine. I still have that pistol you left in the glove compartment." She reminded him.

"Alright. Go ahead and I will be watching from outside for your stalker."

"Do that."

Ellen exited the house through the side entrance leading to the garage. She slid her night bag into the backseat and scooted under the steering wheel. Hesitantly she ignited the car, remotely signaled the garage door to rise, and carefully backed out. When she was safely out of on the street, the door went back down. She witnessed her husband standing in the doorway watching her cautiously. A few blocks from her house, she checked her rear mirror, seeking her stalker. No one was trailing her. She took a deep breath. A load was lifted from her. She turned on her radio. Contemporary music soothed her nerves. Occasionally she glanced at her rearview mirror. Her trailer was gone. No sight of him. Traffic was light.

To think she took chances with her life to be with a man. A man that wasn't her husband. What kind of fool was she? He had nothing to offer except physical pleasure. Perhaps the old cliché was true. Sex with a worthless man was better than a good natured guy. He could please her in ways John couldn't even come close to. And then a thought shot through her mind. Maybe her husband was having her followed. Maybe he suspected she was cheating on him. No. That was not possible. She was always discreet. Immediately she buried the thought into the back of her mind.

In a few months, John would be out of town attending a business convention in Chicago with Edward. They would have two wonderful weeks together to frolic in a pool, dine at expensive restaurants, and make love beneath satin sheets in a hideaway about ten mile from Ocean City; A little resort few people knew existed.

Ellen thought it wise to park down the street from the motel, in a parking lot behind a store. She seized her night bag and walked to the Statesman Hotel which wasn't too far from where she ditched her transportation. She had to be inconspicuous.

On the opposite side of the street, in a dark sedan, sat an elderly man smoking a cigar observing every move. He scooted deep in his seat retrieving a camera. He snapped a shot as Ellen enter the Statesman Motel. He waited five minutes, giving her ample time to enter. Then he slung his camera in the floor and stamped his cigar in the ashtray. Slowly he approached the motel.

"Do you know what room Stanly Cross is in?" Ellen asked the desk clerk on duty.

"158. He's expecting you."

"How do I get there?" She asked.

"Down the hall on your right. Can't miss it."

She walked down the dimly lit corridor, reading each number until she found 158. She knocked lightly and the door opened.

"Come in," Stanly said shutting the door behind her.

"I hope I wasn't too long. I got here as quickly as I could." She tossed her luggage on the bed.

"Timing is perfect." Stanly pulled her close to his excited body and started kissing her harshly.

At that precise moment, the chubby elderly man entered the lobby and leaned on the counter. He pulled out a picture of Ellen and showed it to the clerk. "Have you seen that lady tonight?"

"Yes sir."

"Where did she go?" The man asked.

"Sir I'm afraid I am not a liberty to tell you that." The clerk was defensive.

The man pulled out a hundred dollar bill from his shirt pocket and presented it to him. "It's very important."

"She's in a room 158."

"Thank you sir."

"I hope I don't get in trouble for this," The clerk muffled his worry.

"It's our secret," the man said evacuating the building.

Chapter Sixteen

Jessica rolled Thomas to a Cadillac in front of the hospital, and assisted him into the passenger seat. She would miss Thomas. He was handsome, charismatic, and quit a gentlemen. Touching his firm muscles during the transfer made her fantasize him embracing her. His shaven face, sparkling eyes and juicy lips intrigued her. She forgot she was working and kissed him on the lips before shutting the door.

"Thanks Jessica." Thomas was not startled. He foreseen she would do something unorthodox. She had fallen for him.

"Call me." Jessica said rolling the wheelchair into the lobby turning to wave as Thomas's father drove off the premises. *She would miss Thomas. He was a reason for coming to work. Now she needed another prospect.*

Thomas glanced at the back of a photo with Jessica's name and phone number scribbled on it. When he turned it over, there was the face of his personal aide, Jessica Longfellow. His admirer.

"What are you going to do now?" Phillip asked.

"Would it be wrong to see Edith?" He could not stop thinking about her since he was discharged. He missed being with her. He missed her silly laughter and endearing smile. He had never felt about any woman the way he felt about her.

He was scheduled for a follow-up appointment in six weeks. They had to monitor the progress of the treatment. They were hopeful it would drastically slow down the progression of the disease. Some members of his medical team believed the injections might force the disease into remission. At his next visit, the doctors would have the answer to the effectiveness of the treatment. They all agreed it was working but he still had a long way to do.

"Son, you heard what the doctor said."

"They want to make sure the disease is stagnate." Thomas repeated.

"I understand from John, Edith has left town. So you won't have to worry about running into her." Phillip updated him.

"Where is she?" Thomas asked.

"He did not know exactly. According to him, she wanted time to herself." Phillip explained.

Thomas figured it was difficult being in the same town where the man she loved stayed without running into him. She needed to get over him. Time to start fresh. The more he thought about it, he knew she was right. Even if he got a good report, he was still predestined to die pre-maturely. If they married and had children, he would be dead before the children were grown leaving her the responsibility of raising their children alone. "She made a wise move," Thomas managed to say.

"So you're not going to try and contact her?" Phillip had to ask.

"I don't think so."

Phillip squeezed his son's hand. "Your head is in the right place."

Phillip changed the subject. "I received a call from your publisher. Apparently you sent your manuscript off before you went into the hospital. It was published and my understanding is, it's selling like hot cakes."

Thomas forgot about the book. He was concerned about his health. The book required extensive editing and possibly revisions yet he submitted it. His was under pressure to meet a deadline. By right it should have been rejected. It was not his best work. And now his father reported it was selling like hot cakes. Was that possible?

He instructed his father to pull into the parking lot of a nearby mall. He had to see his book on the shelf. With his father beside him, they Entered Westminster Mall. For nine o'clock in the morning, the place was busy. Stores opened their doors for customers. Phillip pointed to the Nobel Bookstore. A young, blond lady slid back the railings ushering them inside. He saw his novel on a bestselling rack. He pulled a copy from the shelf and handed it to the clerk behind the cash register.

"Is that all you want?" she asked.

"Yes mam."

Phillip reached in his pocket and paid the lady with a twenty dollar bill. He left his wallet in the car. The lady gave Phillip change. She stuck the book into a paper bag and handed it to him. Then she realized the picture on the back of the book was the man standing in front of her.

"You're Thomas Guy. You wrote this book." She was elated. *Wow, Thomas Guy was in her store.* "I'm a fan of yours. I have read all of your books." She picked up a copy which she had been reading and handed it to him. "Would you sign this for me?"

"Sure." He took her pen and scribbled his signature on the last page.

"Thank you." *Not only was he famous but as handsome as hell. If only she could run her fingers through his curly hair and place her arms around his broad shoulders.*

Chapter Seventeen

Edith strolled through the Mall with Daniel, halting at a bookstore to purchase literature for her leisure. She spied a stack of books under Thomas Guy's picture poster. Her heart skipped several beats. Raw emotions rushed into play.

Daniel noticed her mood alteration. "What's wrong?" He asked.

"I'll tell you later." She purchased a copy.

Her back ached, and she had to get home soon. She was in pain. Outside the Mall, she had Daniel hail a taxi. Getting off her feet, and relaxing in the rear seat of a cab, brought relief.

Being pregnant was miserable. Bending to put on shoes, was a task. She bought maternity attire replacing her regular clothes, and wore open-end slippers for her swollen feet. She felt like a blimp. Nausea was a daily condition.

Daniel prepared a simple dinner. He placed ingredients for homemade chicken soup in a crock pot before leaving for the mall. While Edith relaxed in her recliner, reading the novel she purchased, he made three grilled cheese sandwiches. That would be more than enough. He wasn't that hungry. He might eat one with a cup of soup.

He brought Edith a steaming bowl of soup with two sandwiches cut in half on a saucer. To drink, he gave her a large glass of ice tea. He joined her with a cup of soup, and half of a sandwich. He placed his food on a tray, and sampled his soup. It was perfect. He watched Edith devour her meal, and pushed her aluminum table aside. The she resumed reading her book.

"Have you got enough?" Daniel asked.

"I'm fine."

After he finished his snack, he placed the dirty dishes into the sink, rinsed the plates thoroughly, and stuffed them into the dishwasher. He turned on the machine listening for a click.

"Daniel, if you don't mind, bring me some more tea." Edith yelled from the living room.

He retrieved a glass from the cabinet, poured tea into it, and brought it to Edith. He was greeted by a young lady near the brink of crying with the book resting on her belly. Something upset her. Concerned he asked, "What's wrong?"

Edith took a deep breath, and focused on Daniel standing bewildered.

"I'm going to tell you something I have told nobody. Not even Edward."

"OK." Daniel eased into a chair embracing himself for the news.

"The man who wrote this book is the father of my baby."

Daniel remembered the name from the poster. "Thomas Guy."

"Yes," She answered. "My mother opposed our courting for various reasons. She thought he was too old, a shark seeking the fruits of my family's wealth, a cow taking advantage of a young girl's innocence, she simply detested him on all levels." She explained.

"This man has written several best sellers. I have seen him on the Mike Douglas show promoting his books. I don't think he needed your family's money," Daniel commented.

"I think she realized that." Edith continued. "Anyway we continued seeing each other. I fell in love with him. And then my mother had a talk with me. She had discovered something about Thomas she felt I should know. At first, when she told me, I didn't believe her. I thought it was a ploy she invented to separate us. But she insisted it was true."

"What was it?"

Edith told Daniel what her mother deliberated to her. He was shocked by her revelation.

"Did you ask Thomas about this?"

"No, I did not. But I could tell from his non-verbal behavior when I suggested we stop seeing each other, it was true. I saw pain and fear in his eyes. I knew I was doing the right thing." Edith brushed the tears from her eyes.

"Knowing this secret, doesn't it make you wonder about the baby? He or she could--"

"I don't want to entertain what might be. As far as I know, the child is healthy. I have to believe that." She began to hyperventilate.

"I didn't mean to upset you. Just relax and breathe slowly." He instructed her.

Edith laid her head back and took in several deep breathes. A few minutes later, she relaxed, and simmered down. "Promise me you won't tell Edward. He knows we separated but he doesn't know why. No one does except me, and now you."

"I won't tell a soul," Daniel promised.

"This book is part of our story. The two leading characters are based on me, and him."

"May I read it after you finish?" Daniel asked.

"Sure."

Daniel knew he couldn't compete with Thomas for Edith's affection. No man could pacify the hunger. Though they were miles apart, and foreboding circumstances dividing them, she lodged feelings for him. Feelings she refused to terminate. All he could do was wait. Perhaps one day she would lean to trust and love him.

Chapter Eighteen

Stanly lit a cigarette, and Ellen slipped into her high heels. They were lodging at the Sandcastle Motel in Rehoboth. Unbeknown to Stanly, she made reservations at the Dickens Parlor Theater for the evening.

Stanly moved awkwardly modeling a black suit with matching shoes. She persuaded him to dress formally for a special outing. His wardrobe consisted of jeans and plaid shirts. She snuck a suit in the closet when he was unloading their luggage.

She removed the cigarette from Stanly, and crushed it an ashtray. "This is a smoke free establishment—

"I hear you Lady. Just be thankful, I am wearing this monkey suit." He was about to retrieve a cigarette from a pack in his pocket when she kissed him.

"Let's go, and you can smoke in the car," she assured him.

"Where are we going anyway?" Stanly was curious.

"A place you will enjoy. Promise." She grabbed her purse as they prepared to leave.

A Chubby man with a cigar was sitting in a red Maverick seven spaces from a white Cadillac Ellen rented. He observed Stanly getting into the driver's seat with Ellen beside him. He waited until Stanly swirled about to leave before snapping a picture.

In the days building to that occasion, Ellen noticed Stanly treated her differently. In the past, he summoned her for a quickie, and then sent her back to her husband. But during the last few months, their sexual encounters dwindled, and their personal moments increased. They talked, watched television and enjoyed each other's company. She sensed he was falling for her. Strangely enough, she felt herself falling for him.

As they drove to their destination, she gave directions and snuggled close to him. Stanly puffed, blowing smoke out the window.

"You know we've been seeing each other for a couple years. But tonight I feel closer to you than I ever did. I wake up in the morning thinking about you. I don't want to share you." Stanly confessed.

"I feel the same. I love being with you," she admitted. It felt strange making confessions.

"Regardless of how I feel, I won't ruin your marriage. You're John's wife," he told her as he rethought his behavior. *John had been a good friends for years, and now he was sleeping with his friend's wife. What kind of friend was he? John would be devastated if he knew the truth. He would never forgive him. He couldn't blame him. Perhaps it was time to end the affair.*

"I could divorce John," she suggested. "Then we could be together. *What was she saying? What was she thinking? She could never divorce her husband. He had something she treasured. Bosworth was her baby.*

"You talk like a fool. You know John would never divorce you. He needs you." He pointed out. "He loves you, and maybe deep down, you love him. You're the brains behind Bosworth. Together you're a team."

She knew he spoke the truth. *She played an intricate role in John's life on multiple levels. She was a good wife, a mother to his child, and a business partner.* "I know you're right." *Bosworth meant everything to her. Bessel was right, she wanted to control Bosworth Industries.*

"Maybe we should end this affair, even though I don't want to," Stanly said quietly as he took another puff from his cigarette.

She knew that would be the wise thing to do. John certainly deserved her loyalty, but she was not ready to end the affair. She liked what they shared. "Maybe in the future," she mumbled loud enough for Stanly to hear.

Realizing the conversation was getting too serious, Stanly changed the topic. "John eluded something about a yacht."

She lifted her headleaning back in the passenger's seat. "He bought it a couple weeks ago. He said he bought it for family gatherings, but you know how John is. Always buying things he don't need."

"I'd like to see it. Have you seen it yet?" Stanly asked.

"I've seen it from a distance," she said.

"What do you think?"

"I like it."

Stanly came to a stop light. "Where do I go from here?"

"Make a right at the stop sign about twenty yards ahead."

Stanly drove to the Stop Sign, and turned right as instructed. "Where are we going?"

"We're almost there. Keep driving."

They drove into the crowded lot of Dickens Parlor Dinner Theater. Men decked in suits, and women in gowns or fancy dresses lined up at the entrance. With Ellen at his side, they joined the ingoing precession. Once inside the dinner theater with booths surrounding a huge stage, they were escorted to a booth for two. A waitress came by with silverware wrapped in a cloth napkin and two glasses of ice water. Soft music played in the background. After everyone was seated and door were closed, a young boy in a white tuxedo directed people to the food bar by sections. There was so much to choose from, Stanly did not know where to start. Everything looked scrumptious. Ellen knew what she desired. She had been there with John. She choose corn on the cob, fried chicken, spinach and mac and cheese. Stanly tried to get a scoop of everything but soon realized his plate couldn't accommodate it. Finally he surrendered his greediness, and joined her. Another young man wearing a white uniform asked what they preferred to drink. He was trolleying a card of beverages. Stanly selected a beer, and she took an ice tea. They enjoyed their meal, and was nipping their desert when the play began. The show was Annie. A local production of a Broadway Play.

Musicals were not Stanly's fancy. He preferred a contrived mystery with unforeseen twist. Being with Ellen made the evening a success. He drank until he was light headed and had to be escorted to the car. She drove back to the Motel. That night he rested his head on her breast and slept until late morning.

When Stanly returned to his bungalow, he found a note tagged on his front door. Ellen dropped him off and headed to Salisbury. She had to dispose of the rental. The note read. "Stanly I want you to see my yacht. Give me a call."

Anxiously he returned his call. He never been on a yacht before. It would be a treat. He entered the dark, dusty bungalow. He needed to sweep the floors and wipe down the walls. Cleaning a house was foreign to him. Tomorrow he would solicit his associate to janitor his dwelling for fifty dollars. She would jump at the opportunity to make extra cash.

He picked up the old rotary phone beside his couch and telephone John. "John. I got your message."

John was sitting on his patio eating a bowl of peanuts. "Where have you been?" He asked.

"Took a short vacation," Stanly replied. "You said you were going to a convention. When did you get back?"

"Yesterday," John informed him.

"I know you've been looking at yachts. What made you decide to buy one? "Stanly was curious.

John leaned back in his chair and tossed a nut into his mouth. "You know I've been thinking about it for a while. So I got up one morning and bought one. You know how impulsive I can be."

Impulsive was John's middle name. As long as he knew him, John always did things at the spur of a moment. He spotted a truck on a dealership's lot and purchased it on the spot. He bought his fishing boat after seeing an advertisement in the newspaper. He never procrastinated when it came to buying what he desired. What he saw, he got. No questions asked. "When can I see it?"

"What are you doing now?" John asked.

"Nothing really."

"I'm on my way over."

"I can meet you somewhere. You don't have to drive way down here." Stanly informed him.

"Stay put."

John collected him from his house and drove him to a pier in Ocean City where his newly bought yacht was docked.

The yacht was huge. It was three tiers high and appeared to be the length and depth of a football field, with a fenced in fishing platform. Stanly equated it to a miniature cruise ship.

"Wow, man this is beautiful!" he exclaimed.

"You like it?" John was thrilled showing of his yacht.

"I love it," Stanly said walking around the boat examining the exterior.

"Come on, let me show you the inside."

John took him aboard and gave him a grand tour of the ship. They descended steep stairs to the bowels of the ship which was separated in two sections. One side was where the equipment and machinery to operate the ship was kept. The other side was the bedroom quarters. In that layout was three spacious bedrooms with king size beds draped with bold bedding, contemporary dressing ensemble, and expensive oil paintings accenting the purple walls. Opposite the sectioned boudoirs were two monstrous restrooms with step-down tubs hidden by petition. From there John took him to the middle deck with its bar and lounge amenities. Off in a far corner of the ship was a pool table and a jukebox. Across from the pool table was a small room serving as a theater with several rows and a big pull down screen. In rear of the theater was a booth with a projector. Between the Bar and Theater were comfortable luxurious chairs and oval tables close to the walls. In the middle of ship was a dining area and beside the bar was a kitchen hidden by double doors. The upper deck was exposed to the elements. A place where guest could relax in beach recliners while watching the ocean or walk down to a lower fenced in section where they could fish. Above the fishing platform was the enclosed captain's galley with its sailing apparatus. The yacht was like a house boat but big enough to accommodate a small army of guest.

John took him to the bar and prepared a drink. "Name your poison."

"Vodka over rocks."

John poured his drink over crushed ice and sat in before him. "There you are."

"Has Ellen seen this?" Stanly wondered.

"She has seen it but not been aboard yet."

"I'm sure she'll like this." He was impressed by what he saw.

"This weekend I plan taking this ship ashore. Me and Ellen. I want you to tag along." John rendered his intentions.

He was shocked but grateful. "Count me in."

Ellen wondered why her husband beckoned Stanly to accompany them on their yacht excursion. Personally she had no desire to have anything to do with the ship. It was not her focus of interest. She preferred being at the plant making corporate decisions. When John invited her to cruise on the yacht out with him and Stanly, she was quick to decline.

She closed her desk drawer and reached John a folder. "I can't join you fellows this weekend. I have work to do here."

John accepted the folder. "The business is fine. They don't need you. You're just making excuses."

Ellen scratched her head. "Look. That yacht is your pride and joy. Not mind." She reminded him. "Why don't you call your brothers and mother to tag along? I am sure they would enjoy it."

"I want you and only you." He left the folder in a chair and went over to her and caressed her stiff shoulders. "Please join us. Besides, Stanly will probably spend most of his time drinking. He won't be much company. I want you there with me." He kissed her neck. "Please say yes."

She meditated for a moment. *Why was he so abstinent about her accompanying him on the yacht? Did he really miss her companionship that much? Or he wanted to show off his new toy. And who better to brag about his newly acquired prize with than his wife. He figured she would be flabbergasted by the pleasantries. Secretly she was dying to see what it looked like. She had never been aboard the ship.* Against her decree, she yielded his request. "OK. I will come." She consented.

When she boarded the liner, she was impressed by the layout. The bedchambers were equipped with built in bureaus, matching nightstands and spacious walk-end closet. A vanity set with an oval mirror was carefully placed between the dressers where she could sit and apply cosmetics. The bathrooms with their step down tubs was an extravagance she could hardly wait to enjoy. The bar and recreational area was Stanly and her husband's playground, not hers. But the closed off cinema was intriguing. She imagined siting in the quiet auditorium watching her favorite Love Story play out on the big screen while nibbling popcorn. She couldn't wait to stretch in the plush lounge chairs and meditate as the ship voyaged the sea. The cafeteria reminded her of expensive restaurants were you were escorted to a table by a hostess and served by a waiter wearing black pants and a white shirt. She halted at the upper deck and reared back in a recliner. It was a calm evening. Squealing birds flocked a cloudy sky spreading their wings like angels sent from God.

Stanly trotted to the tavern with John beside him. He ordered his favorite drink. John went to the bar and prepared two drinks. Both men gathered at a barrel-shaped table with a high-back chairs and discussed their day.

"How's things at the store?" John opened the conversation pouring his beer into a glass.

"It couldn't be better," Stanly replied.

"Glad to hear that."

Stanly gulped his liquor. "Got any plans to open up another plant."

"Mother and Ellen are considering that. You know about the plant in Wilmington." John mentioned.

"Oh yes. It's been in the Daily Times."

John realized Stanly kaput his drink. "Would you like another?"

"If you don't mind."

John grabbed a bottle off the shelf and presented to Stanly. "There you go."

"Are you trying to get me drunk?" Stanly laughed lightly as he refilled his glass.

"Not really. Just want you to enjoy yourself. I'm sure you will be sober by Monday. He knew Stanly was a weekend drunkard but an upright citizen during the workweek. If he drank during the week, it was done in moderation. He never allowed himself to become overly intoxicated.

"You know how I roll do you." Stanly remarked.

"Listen. I'm going to go to the kitchen and hustle us a few steaks. How do you like your steak?" John asked.

"Don't you have a chef on duty?" Stanly wondered why a wealthy man would bother with something mundane as cooking.

"No. Not this weekend. I am the chef and captain. The only people on this ship is us three."

Stanly panicked. "If you're the captain, whose navigating this yacht."

"Auto Pilot. Don't worry old friend. You're in good hands." John turned on a large television set mounted behind the bar and walked through double doors leading to the kitchen. He yelled to Stanly, "Watch the game and tell me what's happening."

"I want my steak well done." Stanly answered his former question. "And I will."

He watched a college Basket Ball game. A commercial interrupted as players dribbled down the court warding off their opponents hoping to score. Before he knew it, he emptied the bottle and dozed off into a dreamless nap. He was awakened by the smell of food. There before him was a well done steak, a garden salad and baked potato. Ellen greeted him with a pleasant smile.

"Hope you had a good nap," she said.

He sat up straight and scratched his head. His neck was cramped from sleeping with his head back and mouth wide open. It was dark from the stripped windows. "What time is it?"

"Almost nine-thirty," she informed him.

"I must have slept—

"Almost an hours," John interjected as his joined his wife and friend at the table carrying his tray of goodies.

Ellen stuck a piece of steak into her mouth. "Honey this is good."

"Thank you." John accepted her compliment.

Stanly started with his potato which he drowned in butter and sprinkled with salt and pepper. "Chef extraordinaire."

"I can cook a little something or other."

All in the Family was playing on the television. A show Ellen detested but her male cohorts enjoyed. The men laughed as the characters took turns insulting each other as they reeled through the dilemma.

They concluded their evening with a friendly game of Rummy where Stanly reined champion. He was tipsy when bedtime arrived and John assisted him descending the steps using the rails for support. Ellen followed close behind.

He was sluggish when John laid him across the bed. He was out cold when John removed his shoes and covered him with the comforter.

John closed the door and turned off the light. Tomorrow Stanly would have a headache. When he caught up with his wife, she had slipped into a flimsy nightgown and crawled into bed. Several pillows were propped to her head and back while she read Thomas Guy's latest book.

"When did you get that book?" John asked while he stood in front of a mirror unbuttoning his shirt.

"Just picked it up a few days ago."

He wiggled from his shirt and tossed it into a hamper which was conveniently located in a corner of the room. "Is it any good?"

"Like his other work. Terrific story teller."

He unbuckled his pants allowing them to drop to his ankles. "His father is proud of him. I can't blame him." He stepped from his trousers and tossed them into the hamper.

"I feel sorry for Phillip. I wonder how he and Thomas are doing." She repositioned her body. "Have you heard from him?" She was curious.

"Not a word."

John sat on a corner of the bed and removed his shoes and stockings. "When I get home, I will call him. I'm curious, myself. I hope things work out for Thomas."

"All of his books are dedicated to his mother who died when he was a young boy, and his father who always stood in the gap." Ellen flipped to another page.

John shoved his shoes containing his socks underneath the bed. He flipped back the thin sheet under the comforter and joined his wife wearing his briefs and a tee-shirt. "Do you like the yacht?"

Ellen closed her book with her finger securing her page. "I like it. But I like my home better."

"Is that all you're going to say." John was offended.

"Baby things like this don't faze me. As long as you're happy, I'm pleased." She touched his hand. "It's a great getaway and an entertainment fortress for the family. I am certain your mother and brothers will love it."

"Bill and Luther can't wait to see it." John said on a lighter tone.

"I'm sure they can't."

John rolled to his side and shut his eyes. It had been a busy day. He was tired and yearned for sleep. Ellen continued reading the book.

Stanly awaken before Ellen and John. He had a headache. He went into the spacious bathroom with a shower and step-down tub. He sat on the commode and discharged the meal from the day before. Then he took a quick shower and dressed in his blue jeans and plaid shirt. He climbed to the top deck and leaned against the balcony as he stared across the ocean. It was a tranquil and peaceful morning. He wondered where they were. Off in the distance was land. He glanced at his watch. It read nine o'clock. The husband and wife team were probably in bed striving for a few hours of sleep before addressing the challenges of another day.

He marveled what John proposed for the day. Where were they going to go? What new activity awaited them? He preferred fishing and drinking;

a great combination for fun at sea. But he was sure, Ellen had another agenda.

If John wasn't aboard, they would cruise for hours soothing in each other's arms. He felt awkward cruising with his mistress and her husband. He felt guilty coveting with his best friend's wife.

Ellen was a terrific actress. Pretending they were friends on a casual outing came easy for her. She barely blinked an eye or leaked any indication they were having an affair. The question was how long she could maintain the mascaraed before cracking. Everybody was subject to a slipup. He hoped he could play his role. So far he was doing a terrific job. He was able to cohort with John as if nothing was going on. Living a lie was routine.

What he and Ellen shared was special. At the same token, his friendship with John was important. He membered when John forgave him for violating Stella. He remembered the pack they made; a pack he reneged. If John knew he was sleeping with his wife, there was no telling what he might do.

Stanly decided to raid the bar for a screwdriver; a breakfast start-up nourishment. Orange juice and vodka over crushed ice was the perfect way to start the day, as well as the perfect remedy for a dry throat. As he mixed his alcoholic concoction, he glanced at his feet realizing he stepped on something. Bending his stiff back, he reached down retrieving a wallet size photo. When he turned it over, his heart thumped in his stomach. The bar counter braced his fall from the shock. It was him and Ellen embracing in the doorway of his house. He put the photo in his rear pocket. Taking his drink, he paced the lounge. Slowly he sank into a chair resting his drink on a table and gazed through a window.

John knew about their tawdry affair. Perhaps the description tawdry was inappropriate. In the beginning it was crude but it blossomed into a wonderful affair. He treasured their moments together. He was hurt when she left him for her husband. He looked forward to being with her. Strangely enough, he hated sharing her. Yet she was not his. She belonged to another. Despite his feelings, guilt prevailed.

Sipping his screw-driver, he wondered how long John knew. Better yet, what was his intentions? Was the yacht trip a part of his ploy for revenge? He remembered how angry John became when he seduced Stella. He cut him off until he agreed to stop drugging and taking advantage of innocent girls. This was far worse than that. If he knew he drugged his wife, he would kill him. But when the drugs wore off, and he stopped summoning her; she still came. She had fallen for him. At least that was what he choose to believe. Even though they shared a terrific sex life, it was rapidly becoming insignificant. Sex was a small part of what they shared. He too accidently fallen in love: A love that was forbidden. A love with a consequence. He feared what the punishment might be. Only God knew what was rambling in John's mind.

It was imperative he alerted Ellen. She had to know their affair had been exposed. Her husband, his friend, knew about their secret rendezvouses. They had to decide what action to take. They had to get off that ship before John did something crazy. He didn't care what John did to him but he could not fathom the thought of him hurting Ellen. Despite everything, she was a good, decent person. He had to find a way to get her alone, far away from John. He had to take caution making sure John never discovered what he found. Together they could diffuse a potentially explosive situation. The million dollar question was what.

He finished his drink and went back to the upper deck. He saw John in the captain's galley stirring the ship to an outlet where other yachts were docked. He was wearing a cap, a polo shirt and black shorts. He crept up behind him, not quit knowing what to say. His hands were trembling and his legs were wobbly. In all his life, he never feared anyone or anything like his impending confrontation with John.

"I didn't see you when I was up here earlier," he managed to say.

"Just got up." John turned the wheel to the right. His destination was still several miles in the distance.

"Where are we going?" Stanly asked afraid of the answer.

"I'm going to dock at the North Carolina port for a few minutes. Get some fishing gear and then head back to the shore." John explained.

"I thought you had fishing gear below," he said evenly.

"I left it in the other boat at the house. I intended to bring it along, but forgot." John confessed.

Stanly paced about trying not to be suspicious. "How much longer before we dock?"

"I'd say about twenty minutes."

"I see." He paced about looking at his feet. He was afraid to look into John's face.

"Say, check on Ellen for me. Tell her if she wants to go shopping, she better get up. When I left she was still in bed." John turned the steering wheel toward the fast approaching shore.

Why would he ask him to check on his wife? If he suspected they were having an affair, why would he trust him within a foot of her? Could he be setting him up? It seemed odd. "Man I don't want to disturb her. She might not be presentable," he protested.

"The door is locked. You will have to knock. Trust me she won't let you in until she's decent." John assured him.

"Still man, I don't feel comfortable—

"Stanly I trust you. Please do this for me." John urged. "Besides, when we dock, we're going to have breakfast at a restaurant within walking distance."

Reluctantly he paced to Ellen's bedroom suite. Each step taken, he could hear his heart pounding. His hands began to sweat and his breathing labored. It was the longest walk of his life. When he entered her sleeping chamber, Ellen was stationed at her vanity combing her hair. She was dressed in a three piece pants outfit. He came in and stood behind her.

She saw his refection. From the expression on his face, she ascertained he was troubled.

At once she confronted him laying her comb on the counter. "Stan, what's wrong with you."

"He know about us," he blurted out.

"What are you talking about?" She was caught off guard and confused.

He explained eyeing the adjoined door. Fearing John might appear any moment. "John knows about us."

"That's not possible," she insisted.

He pulled the photo from his pocket and presented it to her.

"Where did you get this?" She asked.

"I found it behind the bar. It was in the floor and I picked it up. He knows." He shook his head in disbelief. "He knows."

Ellen was speechless. Her face turned ashy gray. *Her husband hired someone to follow her. That was the man who followed her home. Evidently from that picture, someone had been trailing her for a long while. Her husband was no fool. He knew about those imaginary late night work schedule. He knew about their affair for a while but said or did nothing.* "OH God, what are we going to do?" She handed the picture back to Stanly.

"John is getting ready to dock in a few minutes. First thing, we have to get off this yacht,"

He suggested. "Then perhaps we can think of what to do next."

"Yes he did mention getting some fishing gear, having breakfast at a restaurant and allowing me an hour to shop before we head back to the shore."

"You don't think he plans on killing us." His mind thought the worse.

"No. John is not a violent man. He might ruin your business." Ellen generated a possibility.

He prayed it would be that simple. Deep down Stanly suspected something far worse. "I hope you're right."

Ellen thought for a few minutes. "You said you found the picture in the floor. It probably fell out of his wallet. Chances are he doesn't realize it's missing. Let's forget about the picture and go along with the schedule."

"I've got a plan. When you go shopping, don't get back on the ship. Fabricate an excuse to stay off the yacht. "He advised Ellen.

"We are in this together." Ellen reminded him. "I will not abandon you."

"I'm afraid for you." Stanly sat on the bed. His hands trembled and butterflies paraded in his stomach.

Ellen stood up and sat beside Stanly. "Since he knows, perhaps we need to come clean. Besides, I'm tired of sneaking around. John and I share a house and a child. Our marriage has been dead for months. We might share intimate moments together every now and then but they are far between. We're together because of the business. If it wasn't for that, we would be divorced."

"All of what you say may be fine and dandy but it still doesn't make me feel any better. I have betrayed a good friend. I fell in love with his wife. I deserve whatever happens to me. But I want you to reconcile with your husband. What we had is over." He gave his summation discourse hoping to clear his conscious.

John walked into the bedroom. Ellen rose to her feet. Stanly remain seated with his head hung low.

"What's wrong with him?" John asked.

"Hangover from last night I guess." Ellen lied hoping he believed her. After all he was a drunk.

"He was fine a few minutes ago."

Stanly stood up and said, "I'll be fine. Just got a headache all of a sudden." He changed the subject. "Have we docked yet?"

"Just did. Are you all ready to depart?" John asked.

"Let's go." Ellen grabbed her pocketbook and led the men to the deck where she exited the yacht and marched down a boardwalk leading to the shoreline. John guided them to an elegant restaurant where they had breakfast and watched the morning news on a television mounted from the sealing. When they finished their meal, Ellen went shopping for souvenirs in the stores near the dock. John took Stanly to a sports boutique where they purchased fishing poles and live bait. Then they went back on the boat.

John challenged Stanly to a game of pool. John was anxious to break in the new table. Stanly found it difficult to concentrate. His mind kept returning to the picture in his pocket.

Ellen claimed he was a nonviolent man. But he knew John since he was little boy. He knew his ugly side. He seen him beat up boys within an inch of their life. He seen his wrath and it was not a pretty sight. He was waiting for him to release his wrath.

Even though he wasn't trying, he beat John. His friend was a lousy pool constituent. He challenged him for a rematch but he declined. He wanted John to react resolving the anticipation. Waiting was as debilitating as the pending punishment. Why didn't he beat the hell out of him and call it a day. Instead John choose to be snug and calm. Acting as though nothing was wrong.

It was almost three in the evening. Ellen had not returned from her shopping spree. Stanly began to worry. Had John paid someone to ambush her? Did he kill her and left her body to be found by the authorities.

John noticed Stanly was tense and uneasy.

John left Stanly on the deck drinking his usual concoction while he went into the kitchen to prepare four fried hotdogs with fired onions and French fries. He served Stanly on the deck and stretched out in a recliner adjacent to him. He had eaten his hotdog in the kitchen.

"What takes you so jumpy Stan?" John asked.

Stanly could not pretend any longer. The truth had to come out. He turned to John, resting his plate beside him. He reached in his pocket and handed the picture to John. "I found this in the bar floor this morning."

Before John had the chance to look at it, Ellen appeared from nowhere on the deck carrying a bag. "Honey would you take this to the bedroom for me. I am pooped."

John stuck the picture in his pocket and grabbed his wife's shopping bags. He excused himself leaving the deck. Ellen plumped down in John's recliner taking the plate of food he prepared for Stanly and started eating.

"These hotdogs are delicious." Ellen realized she had taken Stanly's plate and not her husband's. "I'm sorry. I thought--

"Your timing was terrible." Stanly remarked.

"What are you talking about?" Ellen inquired.

"Just gave him the picture. I couldn't take the suspense of waiting. But he didn't look at it. He put it into his pocket," he said.

"What did you do that for?" Ellen was shocked. Then she relaxed and said calmly. "I got to thinking while I was out there. John knew about us for a while. If he hasn't done or said anything by now, then chances are he never will. But now you've changed the whole scheme of things."

"See if you can get the picture from him," he urged.

"I can't without raising suspicion." Ellen mellowed and resumed eating her hotdog. "He'll forget about it." She felt confident. "I find things in his pocket he forgot was there all the time."

"I hope you're right."

Shortly before dusk, John insisted he join him on the fishing platform. They spent hours fishing as the boat drifted in the middle of nowhere. As usual he drank until he was enumerated and had to be carried to his room and tucked into bed. Not once did John mention the picture.

John took the fish they caught and put them in a large bag covered with ice and stored them in the freezer for later. He returned to the Captain's pit and set the boat on auto pilot. Late Sunday afternoon, they would be back on the shore.

Ellen could not sleep. It had been a trying day. Stanly showing her the picture and then giving the picture to her husband. Luckily for them, he did not get the opportunity to see the snap shot. He changed pants before he went fishing and she found the picture in his pocket. She took the picture and shredded it into a hundred little pieces before tossing it overboard.

She walked into the dark theater and turned on the light. She wanted to check out the set-up. She was surprised to find her husband sitting in the dark. "What takes you here?" She asked.

"I couldn't sleep. I was getting ready to look at some slides of the family. "He pointed to the carousel projector beside him. He touched a remote and a screen disembarked from the ceiling. "Join me."

"Why not." Ellen found a seat beside her husband.

John pushed another switch and the room darkened. A clear square appeared on the screen. A few minutes later, it began revolving. Pictures of Edith when she was a baby appeared followed by a collage of photos of the family at various functions. And then the pictures became personal. Shots of Ellen and Stanly at various places. They were at his house holding hands, kissing and lying in bed. Snap shots of her going into the Statesman Motel. Pictures of her and him making out in her office. As the slideshow continued, the pictures became more graphic and sensual.

Ellen was shocked and speechless. Her heart pounded in her throat. She had to escape. She stumbled to the exit bumping into chairs. The lights came on.

"They say what you do in the dark will come out in the light." John echoed.

She dashed from the theater, rushed down the steep steps almost tripping, went to their bedroom, slammed the door shut, slung herself across the bed and wept violently. Her husband set her up. The cruise was a ploy, his way of getting even. She never dreamed he could be that cunning. He bamboozled her.

When Stanly awakened that morning, John was sitting on the edge of his bed. "You saw the picture." The words slipped out.

The reckoning hour had arrived. He witnessed the furry in his friend's eyes. He was fuming. He trembled with terror. His heart was about to bust. Tears filled his eyes. John had been a dear friend all his life. How could he betray him? What devil stole charge of his life?

"I watched you rape innocent girls for years until I could not stomach it any longer. I hated you for what you did to Stella but I forgave you and rekindled our friendship. I was closer to you than I was to my own brothers." John raged quietly.

"John I'm sorry." Stanly apologized.

"Please tell me you didn't drug my wife. Please tell me you didn't brainwash her." John's anger grew as his heart hardened.

"In the beginning, I wanted her." Stanly whispered. "I drugged her once. I knew it was wrong. I knew you had trouble satisfying her—

John grabbed his neck and started chocking him. "You son-of-a –bitch. I ought to kill you right here and now."

"She came to me willingly," Stanly managed to say between the gagging. "We fell in love."

John released his grip. "When did you fall in love?"

"I don't know when. It just happened. We kept getting together. She made me feel important. We enjoyed being with each other." Stanly confessed.

"I will never forgive you for what you did. My heart is filled with hatred and disgust toward you. You violated another woman I love. Sure we had problems and maybe I wasn't as affectionate as I was in the beginning but I love and will always love my wife. You had no right to use my wife as your whore." He punched his face three times.

"Man I'm sorry." Blood dripped from his busted lips. His eyes puffed up from the fatal blows.

"Get up and come with me." John ordered.

"Where are we going?"

"To meet your maker."

Stanly discerned John's ulterior motive. His eyes were blood red. His blood pressure was rampant. He was crazy. The men tussled like wild dogs. Stanly battled for his life. They plummeted to the floor with John landing on top punching and swearing at the top of his voice. John became a lunatic. Stanly strained pushing him away but he harnessed the strength of ten men. Out of desperation, Stanly managed to snatch a brass lamp from his nightstand and clobbered John in the forehead. He fell backward releasing his death grip enabling Stanly to escape and charge through the open door. But John quickly regained conscious and lagged close behind. Stanly raced up the steps like a panther. He heard John puffing as he struggled to capture his prey. He sought restitution. Justice for the lies and deception. Stanly struggled to the top deck. He saw John lurch toward him and the fight was on. They exchanged bloody punches and brutal blows in the abdomen. Suddenly the tables turned. John kicked Stanly in the groin causing him to collapse to his knees and bellow like a wounded animal. Then he hoisted Stanly to his feet and initiated beating him unmercifully until he stumbled backward against the balcony and fell overboard.

Chapter Nineteen

Thomas packed his luggage. He would miss Salisbury. Video of the day he met Edith replayed in his mind. She was his tour guide, his friend, and his lover. Now she was gone forever.

The reason she left him was more catastrophic than he imagined. It was more than his terminal illness. Ellen exposed a family secret. Whether she did it out of love or selfish gain, he would never know. She never approved of their relationship. At last her wish was fulfilled.

The doctor had given him a good report, but it carried no weight. The treatment was successful. He was going to live. Yet Living without Edith was futile. Happiness was a folly. If only their life transpired like the characters in his book. Despite the trial and tribulations blocking their path, they conquered their pitfalls and lived happily ever after; a fairytale romance pasted in the pages of the Lower Eastern Shore.

"How did you find out what Ellen told Edith?" Thomas asked.

"John called me." Phillip reported his story. "Before Edith left town, John asked Ellen what she told her daughter resulting in her leaving. She confessed she told her everything. About your illness and being your first cousin."

"Come on dad. Let's get out of here." Thomas managed to say.

Thomas took one last look at his apartment and then left with his father. In the parking lot, Thomas put his luggage and his father's suitcases in the back seat of his Cadillac. His father designated himself driver and drove onto the highway. Thomas instructed him to drive pass Salisbury State College, the place where he first met Edith. When they were twenty miles from Salisbury, Thomas opened his wallet and retrieved Jessica's picture. *Could she be the one to replace Edith? She knew what his future held.*

167

Chapter Twenty

Edith was overdue. The doctor assured her she had nothing to worry about.

"Sometimes, your first child arrives late. If you don't have the baby in two weeks, we'll induce labor." Her doctor said.

Edith counted the days leading to her delivery. The baby was getting restless and her belly had dropped. Despite the doctors glowing report, she still feared the baby might be abnormal. They baby might have sickle-cell. She prayed every night her baby would be healthy. Still she had a nagging feeling inside, something was wrong. Maybe God didn't hear her petition.

Daniel stayed by her side. He slept on her couch at night instead of sleeping in his comfortable king size bed in his apartment. He dare not leave her alone. There was no telling when she would go into labor. And he wanted to be there when she needed him. Her bags were packed, sitting by the door. He had the number of a neighborhood taxi. Everything was set.

When Edith was asleep, he would sneak in her room and sit in the chair by her bed. She was a beautiful girl. She resembled a black Barbie doll snoozing on her cot. It took all his will power to reframe from touching her, caressing her, making love to her. Despite his efforts to keep emotions intact, he had fallen in love with her. His life revolved around her. He never felt about any woman the way he felt about her.

During the last week before her delivery, Edith pried into Daniel's personal life. He knew all about her but she knew little about him. One evening in late July, while they sat on a park bench watching children play on monkey bars, slide down sliding boards and play silly games in the sand, Edith commenced interrogating him.

"Where are you from?"

"Chicago." Daniel said.

"Born and raised?"

"Yes. My parents died when I was six in an automobile accident. I was raised by my grandparents. They worked in a shirt factory. They saw that I got a college education. At college I got a degree in liberal arts with emphasis in journalism. I got a job as a reporter in a local television station. I worked there for a couple years and then got a job with the magazine company I am working with now." There was his autobiography in one small paragraph.

"Any girl friends?" *A man as handsome as Daniel must have had a swarm of females clawing after him.*

Daniel sighed. "My love life is not interesting. I have had few romantic interludes but they never mounted too much. I have a tendency to want what is forbidden."

"Does that mean married women?" She was curious.

"No. I don't go that way. I mean falling for people who don't love me." He looked into her eyes. "Girls like you."

Edith realized she had crossed the border. She had to change the topic. "You and Edward

Met in college I gather."

"Yes we did and we kept in touch." Daniel said. "We get together when we are in each other's neck of the woods."

Edith stood up. "I believe I'm ready to go back and get some rest."

"Should I call a taxi?" Daniel asked.

"No. I can walk from here. It's only a block from our apartment. Besides, the walk might induce labor." Edith replied.

"OK."

As they walked toward their apartment, Edith realized what a wonderful man Daniel was. And she did appreciate him altering his work life to accommodate her. He could have stayed in Chicago and left her to fair for herself. Of course Edward would have been there but not nearly as ready as Daniel. He was there to satisfy her weird cravings in the middle of the night. He was there to massage her aching back or rub her swollen feet.

In the last few weeks, she began to develop warm feelings for Daniel. She began to feel guilty avoiding to hold his hand when the toured the neighborhood. It was not right to permit him to finger her stiff shoulders but not nibble her ears. It was not fair for her to lean against him for support when she was tired but yet it was taboo for him to embrace her before he tucked her in for the night. It was time she accepted the fact what she and Thomas had was forever finished. The only remnant left from their brief affair was a child.

As they approached the path leading to their residency, Edith decided to reveal her inner feelings. It was time Daniel knew where he stood in her life. "Daniel there is something you should know." Edith started.

Daniel wondered what she was leading up to. "I'm listening."

"In the last few weeks, I have developed feelings toward you that is more than friendship and appreciation." She confessed.

"What are you saying?" He asked as they continued to walk toward the building.

Edith took a deep breath. "I am ready to accept you as a boyfriend."

Daniel halted her and looked into her eyes. "Are you saying this because you are close to having the baby?"

"No." Edith replied gazing back into his eyes. "I want you to be more than a father to my child. I want you to be a part of my life."

Daniel kissed her. Having her in his arms was like a dream come true. No longer did he have to restrain his feelings and be careful of what he said or done. Finally he found a woman who felt about him the way he felt about her. Still he had to be certain. "Are you sure this is what you want. This is not your hormones talking."

Edith smiled as she held his neck in her hands. "Daniel I love you and I want you."

They kissed again.

That night they laid in bed beside each other. Daniel desired to make love to her, but that was not possible. She commenced experiencing labor pains, and he timed them with his watch. When they were eight minutes apart, Daniel called a taxi, and escorted her and her luggage outside to be tucked into the backseat. The driver, an elderly man, drove them to the hospital. Daniel tipped him handsomely for getting them there quickly.

When they walked into the hospital, an aid, a young white girl in blue, put Edith into a wheelchair and took her small bag. She gestured Daniel to the waiting solarium while she checked her in and prepared her for labor. Daniel went to the designated area ten yards from where he was standing.

The place was practically empty. There was a young Mexican man gazing out the window admiring the scenery when a nurse in white opened a door summoning him to come and see his son. Daniel sat down and watched the news on the set suspended from the ceiling. Then he remembered Edward. Surely he would want to know. He searched for a telephone. There was a pay phone in the hall across from the waiting area. He fished a dime from his pocket and went to the phone to contact Edward. Edward answered on the third ring.

"Hello." Edward was in his office. A client was sitting across from him.

"I was just letting you know, I brought Edith to the hospital. She's in labor," he explained.

"I will be there as soon as I finish here. Which hospital are you end?"

"The one ten blocks from where we live." Daniel had trouble remembering the name of the facility. He had never been there before.

"I know where it is. See you in a bit." Edward promised.

Daniel returned to the waiting area. He watched television for a few minutes, and then paced back and forth. Minutes turned into hours. He wondered how long it took for a woman to have a baby. Two hours later Edward joined him. At the time he was watching television.

"Still in labor I gather," Edward said sitting beside Daniel.

"I haven't heard or seen a soul since they took her back." Daniel's hands began to sweat.

Edward scoped out the room. There was nobody there but them. "I thought there would be more people here than us two."

A short Pilipino woman with straight black hair and small hands dressed in white wearing a mask came into the waiting area through the same door the previous man disappeared behind. She removed her mask and approached the men. "Which one of you men is Daniel? I forget the last name."

Daniel stood up. "It is me."

"I just want you to know it's going to be awhile, but she will have the baby tonight. She hasn't dilated enough for delivery yet. So if you want to go, get something to eat, and come back in a couple hours, that would be fine," the doctor said.

"Thank you." Daniel said quietly.

The lady disappeared behind the swinging door.

"Want to get some steak and fries. My treat." Edward volunteered.

"Sounds good to me." Daniel replied.

Edward took Daniel to a Steak House Restaurant about forty-five minute drive from the hospital. The place was crowded. The waitress, dressed in western attire took their order. She brought them cokes in two huge glass mugs. The men talked shop as they waited to be served.

"How are you doing with your column?" Edward started the discussion.

"My Boss likes the articles, but she's wondering when I'll be able to return to Chicago." Daniel filled him in.

"Well, after Edith has the baby, you're free to do as you please." Edward remarked.

"I'm going back to Chicago. But I want Edith and the baby to come with me."

Edward was shocked to hear the news. "What makes you think Edith would want to go to Chicago with you?"

"I don't know. But I do know she loves me. She told me so." Daniel said.

Edward pondered over what he heard before he commented. Then he said evenly. "I am glad that she loves you. And obviously from the expression on your face, you must love her too."

"After she has the baby, I will give her time to decide what she want to do. If she chooses to stay here, than I will have to do a lot of communing. I hope she comes back with me." Daniel figured she would. She already solicited him to be her baby's father.

In all the years he knew Daniel, he never seen him so happy and content. His cousin had certainly changed his life. "If you make her happy, and keep her mind off Thomas, than go for it."

"Sounds like you're giving me your blessing."

"Daniel, you're a good friend. I appreciate all that you have done. You stood by her all during this pregnancy. And I want to thank you for that even though I tilted the tables in her favor." Edward recollected how he used his influence to get Daniel to work from New York.

"I am glad you brought us together." Daniel was grateful. "If you had not intervened, none of this would have happened."

The waitress delivered their food. The men anxiously chowed their delicious steaks leaving nothing but bones and empty mugs. They finished off their dinner with a slice of sweet potato pie topped with a scoop of vanilla ice cream. Edward paid the bill with his credit card and left a ten dollar tip on the table.

When they returned to the hospital, a nurse met them at the door, and ushered them down a long hall to Edith's physician. The short Pilipino doctor was sitting behind her huge desk in street clothes, combing her hair. Immediately she beckoned the men to sit.

Daniel sensed the news was bad. "Doctor, what's wrong?"

The lady leaned forward in her chair tucking her comb in a drawer. She maintained eye contact with both men, observing their ambiguity. "She had the baby, but he has several birth defects and physical deformities. One of his lungs is under developed. Presently his on a respirator until we determine if his strong enough to breathe on his own. Eventually we will wean him off the machine. The next twenty-four hours are crucial. " She was blunt.

Daniel wanted to cry but fought back the tears. Everything was fine. Edith took terrific care of herself. She ate well, walked daily, and exercised faithfully. Her doctor, the lady sitting before him, gave her a clean bill of health. How could this awful thing happen? "What about the ultra-sonogram? Why didn't you pick this up before now?" Daniel questioned.

"Perhaps the baby's position hid the deformities. We had no way of knowing about the lungs until he was born. According to the pictures, the child looked normal. This is as much of a shock to us as it is to you. In all my years of practicing, I have never witnessed anything like this."

Edward was concerned about his cousin. "Does Edith know?"

"The nurse told her, but she has not seen the child. She refused to see her child without you two guys beside her." The doctor walked toward the door. "Follow me. I am going to take you to her room."

It was the longest stride in Daniel's life. His heart thumped in his throat with every footstep. Looking at his shoes, he calculated the tiles, ignoring his surroundings. People walked pass but he choked out their presence. Their conversation, a mystery to his ears. He stopped rationalizing. Silence became his empire. Was this a nightmare? He wanted to wake-up. No it was real and he was not dreaming.

The doctor escorted them into the room and Edith sat up in bed welcoming her support team. Edward noticed her eyes were red from crying. He immediately rushed to her and hugged her expressing his sorrow. Daniel kissed her tenderly and grasped her cold hands. Both men were at loss for words to alleviate her grief.

The doctor seized the moment. "When you're ready to see the baby, ring your bell, and one of the aids will take you to him. "She excused herself leaving Edith with her visitors.

"I don't understand how this happened. Why didn't the sonogram reveal this beforehand?"

Daniel wondered.

Edith reached for Edward with her free hand. "I feared this for weeks. I had this nagging pit in my stomach. No matter how hard I prayed, it never dissolved." Then she remembered what Sarah said. *"I am worried about you. I want you to be careful." Sarah prophesized. "I see things in your future, and I want you to know, whatever happen, God is in control." She shifted her feet and continued, "I know you've been with Thomas, but sometimes what we think is best, is not good for us. So again I say, be careful."* She wondered if that moment was what she was prophesizing about.

Edward squeezed her hand. "The question is where we go from here."

Edith took a deep breath. Observing Daniel, she sensed he was still bewildered. He wanted so much to be a father. Now there was a probability that would never happen. "First he has to be able to breathe independently. And then if he does survive, are we able to raise a child with special needs. Do you want that responsibility?" She focused on Daniel.

Daniel mulled over the challenge. It would be a great undertaking. But they had enough money to pacify his needs and wants. They could provide him with the love and moral support to live a normal life. He was up for the challenge. Daniel answered Edith's question with an affirmative headshake. Then she suggested, "Let's see the baby."

Edith pressed her bedside light. A few minutes later, the same girl who admitted her, rolled in a wheelchair. She saw Edith safely seated in the chair and strolled the crew down the hall to the huge window revealing the nursery. She instructed them to wait while she went inside to get the baby and roll him to the window where they could see him.

Edward examined the babies in the nursery resting in there cribs and incubators. They had all their limbs, resembling little people, healthy and alive. Why couldn't Edith's baby be normal? It was not fair. She was a good person. She didn't deserve this.

The girl rolled their baby to the window with a tube running into his little nose. He had a clef lip, and one of his arms was half the length of the other arm with four fingers. One leg was slightly shorter than the other one with four toes. One of his eyes was covered with a thin layer of skin. His right ear was slightly smaller than his left ear. All of his deformities was on the right side.

Despite how he looked, Edith loved him. He was flesh of her flesh, and blood of her blood. Even if he was abnormal, he was still her child. He had to live. Her doctor joined Edith, and her family as they stood looking at the infant.

"If he lives, which it appears he will. His good lung is doing better than he anticipated. We will send him to another hospital that can correct some of these deformities like his clef lips and the film of skin over the eye." The doctor was preparing to leave for the day. "Of course this won't be right away."

Edith spoke. "You said the next twenty-four hours were crucial."

"Because of his condition, we're going to keep him here for a week or so before transferring him for corrective surgery, but you will be discharged in a couple days. We're going to start weaning him off the breathing machine in the next twelve hours. According to my colleagues, his doing well. I checked with them a few minutes ago." She gave her a brief update.

"When will I be able to hold him?" Edith wanted to know. She could hardly wait to cuddle him in her arms.

"Probably tomorrow. We want to get him stable." She excused herself and wished them a blessed day.

Daniel rubbed Edith's back. "I believe he'll be alright. We can handle this." Daniel visualized what his son would look like ten years from now with his corrected deformities.

Edith turned to face Daniel. "I needed to hear that." She said.

Edward smiled and tapped the window trying to arouse his little cousin. He was grateful he was alive despite how he looked. "What is his name?"

"I haven't thought about that. I'll let you guys pick a name." Edith said.

The aid rolled the baby from the window back to his prospective spot after the men whispered pleasantries and silly remarks to the sleeping infant. Then she reappeared and escorted Edith and her ensemble back to her room. Her room was graced with several bouquets of flowers sparsely scattered about filling the area with a sweet aroma.

Nobody knew she was at the hospital except Daniel and Edward. She faced her comrades. "Which one of you is responsible for this?"

They both looked at each other and laughed.

Edward confessed. "I had them sent over when Daniel called me and told me you were in labor."

"Thank you cousin."

Edith was allowed to hold and breast feed her baby the next day. They removed him from the respirator and he was doing fine. She enjoyed having him nibble her breast seeking milk. Daniel sat near her writing an article for his column. Edward was working but assured her he would stop by after work.

Daniel looked up from his writing and gazed at Edith. Now was the appropriate time to ask her the important question that had been gnawing at his thoughts for the last twenty-four hours.

"Edith. I want to ask you something."

"I hear you." She said looking at her baby.

Daniel started. "I'm going to have to return to Chicago in a few weeks. I want you and the baby to come with me."

Edith was not shocked by his request. She knew he wanted to be with her and the baby. She wondered when he would gather up the nerve to ask. "I would be glad to go with you."

Daniel put down his pad and kissed Edith.

Now, when would he have the nerve to ask for her hand in marriage?

Edith was released from the hospital and her son was transferred to another hospital to correct his birth deformities. The couple made plans to leave New York and move to Chicago. Daniel rented a larger apartment closer to his job. An apartment for one would not suffice for three. The day before they picked-up little Daniel from the hospital following his surgery, Daniel proposed to Edith giving her a diamond engagement ring.

"Daniel I would love to be your wife."

When they carried little Daniel home, they were pleased with the results. His cleft lip was normal and the film over his eyes had been removed revealing a normal eye matching the other one. He had a beautiful face and a charming smile that melted Edith's and Daniel's heart.

They married in a New York Court house with Edward as a witness. He presented them a fifty thousand dollar check as a wedding gift. Four weeks after they married, they caught a plane from New York to Chicago where they started a new life as husband, wife and son.

Chapter Twenty-One

Ellen Bosworth maneuvered through a huddle of reporters asking questions, snapping pictures, as she entered the crowded courtroom. Spectators waited eagerly as the prosecuting attorney, an attractive blond with skinny legs, sporting a tight fitting blue dress accented by a white blouse hiding her broad shoulders, strategized. The lady, Elizabeth, was one of one of the best lawyer on the Eastern Shore.

She approached the jury preaching her opening statement. "Today we are presented with the case of John, Douglas, Bosworth verses the state of Maryland. I intent to prove, beyond all shadow of doubt, on July 28, 1971 John, Douglas, Bosworth premeditatedly murdered Stanly, Theodore, Cross on his yacht. John, Douglas, Bosworth lowered Stanly, Theodore, Cross to his ship, confronted him about having an affair with his wife, beat him to a pulp, and shoved him overboard. Then he allegedly rescued him, and instructed his wife to call for help to cover-up what he did. When you deliberate your verdict, forget that John Douglas Bosworth is a pillar of this community. Remember how he murdered an innocent man in cold blood. Remember how he sought vengeance by taking the life of another human being." She concluded her introductory statement and took her seat in front of a pile of folders waiting for her.

The defending attorney approached the jury box. He was a young Negro with a jerry curl hairdo. He was an apprentice to John's Brother, Luther. Luther sat beside his brother, watching his associate make his mark. "My client, John Douglas Bosworth had been a friend of Stanly Theodore Cross for many years. I am sure he was angry when he realized his lifelong friend was having an affair. But let me inform you, John knew about his affair for a long time and said or done nothing. When he invited

Stanly Theodore Cross and his wife on his yacht, it was not a ploy to get him on the ship so he could kill him. If he wanted to do that, he could have done it ages ago. He simply wanted to spend a relaxing evening with his friend and wife. Then his friend got drunk and told him about their affair. John was angry and hurt. Hurt because his friend told him what he did and attempted to justify his action. John lost it. They got into a heated confrontation which led to a fight. Stanly Theodore Cross assaulted John Douglas Cross with a lamp. John ran after him and the fight led to the upper deck. In the midst of the fight, Stanly Theodore Cross fell overboard. John immediately realized what happened and jumped overboard to rescue his friend. He managed to drag him aboard the fish platform of the ship where he yelled to his wife to call for help on the CB in the captain's control booth. Paramedics with a nearby rescue squad, took Stanly Theodore Cross to a nearby medical center where it was determined Stanly Theodore Cross died from drowning and not from the wounds inflicted from the fight. If John Douglas Bosworth wanted to kill Stanly Theodore Cross, why did he rescue him? Despite how angry and upset he was, he attempted to rescue him from a certain death. Stanly Theodore Cross' death was an accident and not murder. Thank you." The young man joined his judicial team.

The judge, a middle-aged Caucasian male with cold black hair, and thick eyebrows behind spectacles, made an announcement. "Because of the lateness of the hour, I dismiss court for today and we will commence again Monday at ten o'clock sharp. Jury I must remind you not to discuss this case with anyone in your absence. Court adjourn." The hit his desk with his gavel and left his post.

Ellen made an abrupt exit. She wanted to avoid the crowd. Reporters snapped picture as she plowed through swinging doors as the press hurled questions after her. When she was halfway down the corridor ready to descend stairs leading to the ground floor, she glanced backward discovering a relentless media engulfing her husband as his barristers struggled to fan them away. Thank God their focus of attention was off her. Quickly she walked from the historic courthouse onto the street spotting her car in the busy lot. She trotted to her vehicle, got inside and turned on the ignition. She inhaled deeply, relieved to escape an impending interrogation. Thank God for the weekend. She was scheduled to be an eye witness. Her husband's future rested in her hands. She was certain his brother would vindicate his innocence. It was a formality. There was no such thing as a partial jury in that case. Of course, Elizabeth was a touch prosecutor. It would be a grueling exploit defeating her. She had more tricks up her sleeves than Perry Mason. She would tear her to shreds during her cross examination. Elizabeth would twist her words to work in her favor.

Ellen drove home trying not to think about Monday. But that was impossible. All eyes would be on her. Her mother-in-law hated her for be unfaithful to her son. She was surprised when she discovered she remained in Wilmington, choosing to stay out of the courtroom. She had faith in her son. She knew he would get an acquittal for his brother. Her sisters came down to support her even though they were displeased with her behavior. *John was a good man. How could she have an affair with his best friend? What was she thinking?*

When Ellen walked into her kitchen, she was greeted by her two sisters sitting at the kitchen table drinking coffee and sharing the daily times. Olvera was the first to speak. "How did the trial go?"

"I didn't get the chance to testify." Ellen said resting her pocketbook on the table. Then she sat in a chair and removed her shoes. Her feet where sore.

Bessie spoke after sipping her coffee and sliding the rest of the paper to her sister. "I was afraid this was going to happen. Why did you allow this affair to linger?"

"I don't need your criticism. I need your support?" She reminded her sister.

Olvera scratched her premature graying head. She felt awkward without her hat. "Sis that's why we're here. Still it doesn't make it right what you did. You know it was wrong. John is a good man."

Ellen mellowed down. "Olvera you're right. I should not have allowed myself to fall for Stanly. And there is nothing I can say to justify my actions. Neither is there anything I can do to bring him back to life."

"Do you think John will be acquitted?" Bessie wondered.

"Well his brother is one of the best criminal lawyers in the country. If anyone can get him off, I'm sure he will."

"Yeah but that prosecuting attorney has an impeccable track record." Olvera, being an advent reader, informed them.

Ellen went to the refrigerator and seized a cold Pepsi from the top shelf. "I want this whole thing over so I can go on with my life."

"Monday, we will be in the courthouse with you." Bessie promised.

Monday came quicker than Ellen expected despite the multitude of activities she engaged in during the weekend to delay its arrival. Her day on the witness stand was predestined. There was no erasing the inevitable. She had to testify in her husband's behalf. She had to convince the jury Stanly's demise was an accidental. The questioned ringing in her ear was, did she honestly believe that. *After being exposed to the slide show of her infidelity and the picture Stanly revealed to her the day of his death, it all came together like a jigsaw puzzle. Was her quiet, soft spoken husband planning to murder her lover, his friend for many years? Was the yacht trip his way of exposing their secret? Was it his way of seeking revenge for their betrayal. But if that was the case why did he try to save him. He could have allowed him to drown and let his body wash ashore. There would be no proof linking him to his death. As far as the world knew, they were cohorts, good buddies and he got drunk and fell overboard.*

Ellen took the witness stand with her sisters sitting in the audience. Olvera was sporting a wide brim hat and a white suite for good luck. Bessie wore a navy blue pants suit Ellen gave her as a Christmas gift. John's brother Luther was decked out in a three piece white suit with a black tie. His associate was fashioned in casual dress pants and a dark blazer, absent the tie. He was dressed for work, not a fashion model. He approached Ellen holding a notepad and a pencil. He rallied his list of questions. "Mrs. Bosworth, how long have you know the deceased?"

"Since high school." She said evenly.

"How long has your husband known the deceased?"

"Since high school."

The young man paced about glancing at John and Luther. "Would you say that your husband and the deceased were good friends?"

"Certainly."

The student lawyer faced the jury box. "Is your husband capable of killing a man in cold blood—?

The prosecutor objected to his line of question. The judge sustained her objection.

The lawyer changed his line of questioning. "Would you tell the jury what happened on the evening of Stanly Theodore Cross's death?"

Ellen took a deep breath and began to recreate the events of the evening. "I heard a lot of fussing and swearing and tumbling on the upper deck. So I left my bedroom on the lower deck and went to the upper deck to see what the commotion was about. I saw my husband and Stanly fighting frantically. I yelled for them to stop but they didn't hear or see me. I saw my husband strike Stanly several times and Stanly stumbled backward and fell off the ship. My husband panicked and jumped overboard to rescue him. He managed to grab him as he surfaced for the second time and dragged him to the fishing platform on the lower deck below the captain's booth. At the time I was in the control room. He yelled and told me to call for help. I picked up the CB and telephoned for help. I told them a man had fallen overboard and needed medical attention. A nearby boater telephoned the national guards and they appeared from nowhere with medics on a small craft. John was frantic by now. He was crying and pleading for Stanly to hold on. The medics took Stanly from the yacht and headed to the nearest hospital. When we got to shore, the police took my husband in custody for murder."

"You said your husband told you to call for help." Todd, the young intern asked.

"That's correct." She was shaking from reliving the dreadful event.

"And you said your husband was mortified by Stanly falling overboard and pleading for him to stay alive." Todd paraphrased her testimony.

"He was quite upset and sobbing uncontrollably." She replied.

"And what did you do?" He wanted to know.

"I kept assuring him everything was going to be alright."

"Thank you Mrs. Bosworth." He took his place beside Luther.

The prosecuting attorney approached Ellen. She kept her hands to her side. "You said Mrs. Bosworth that you heard a commotion and went to the upper deck to investigate. Is that true?"

"Yes." She said, collecting her thoughts.

"You said you saw your husband hitting, or fighting with the deceased, yes." Elizabeth said firmly

"Yes," she agreed.

"You said your husband struck Stanly Theodore Cross forcing him to fall off the balcony" She reminded her.

"Yes."

"Was Stanly Theodore Cross alive when rescued him from his fall?" She asked.

"I don't know."

"According to the medical records Stanly Theodore Cross was dead when the medics and National Guard brought him to hospital. Did you know that Mrs. Bosworth?"

"No." Ellen confessed.

"For all intent purpose jury and your honor, the beating John Douglas Bosworth inflicted on Stanly Theodore Cross is what killed him. Yes, he may have tried to----rescue him but he was dead. The defendant had already killed him'"

The intern strongly objected interrupting the prosecutor's statement. "Objection your honor! We have facts proving the contrary! Objection!"

"I have no further questions." Elizabeth walked back to her bench while the judge pounded his mallet shouting, "Order in the courtroom." The crowd was aroused by the prosecutor's last remark. People whispered to each other, glancing from juries, to the attorneys. A volatile point had been made. Now it was time for a rematch.

When the crowd simmered down, the judge asked the defendant if he had any further questions for the witness. Todd said no but he wanted to call another witness to the stand. The judge dismissed Ellen and she joined her sisters in the audience. "I want to call Doctor Benjamin Franklin to the stand at this time."

Doctor Benjamin Franklin was a heavy set black man with a huge afro and dark penetrating pupils. He was wearing blue jeans and a polo shirt. The bailiff, a short white headed gentlemen wearing glasses, swore him in. Todd approached him. He left his writing pad behind. "Dr. Benjamin Franklin, you were the on call physician when Stanly Cross was bought into the hospital, is that correct?"

"Yes sir." The doctor was mannerly.

"After you examined his body, what did you determine was his cause of death?" Todd asked.

"Drowning."

Todd looked at the stenographer. "Let the court records show the deceased's death was contributed to drowning." Todd turned away from his witness. "I have no more questions."

Elizabeth rose to her feet. "Your honor I would like to cross exam."

"Proceed." The judge nodded.

"Mr. Benjamin Franklin, what was the shape of the victim's body when you saw him?"

"He had several bruises and contusions. He was a bloody mess—"

"From where he was battened brutally." Elizabeth finished his statement.

"He did take a pounding." The doctor agreed.

"Would not the condition he was in when he algidity fell overboard contributed to his water affixation?"

"Sure it did," the doctor agreed.

"Let the records show Dr. Benjamin Franklin's conclusion the injuries inflicted on the deceased contributed to his death." Elizabeth smiled. She supplied the jury reasonable doubt about the defendant's innocence. She returned to her seat.

Todd rose to his feet and approached the witness box. "Doctor, if John Bosworth failed to rescue Stanly Cross from his fall, what would have happened to him?"

"He would have drowned."

"Was Stanly alive when the paramedics arrived on the scene?" Todd asked with one eye on his witness and the other eye on the jury.

"The report said as much."

"When he arrived at the hospital, was an autopsy done?" Todd asked holding his breath.

"No. It was not deemed necessary." Benjamin said, not knowing where the lining of questioning would lead.

"So it was obvious Stanly's death was from downing?"

Benjamin realized what the young lawyer was gearing toward. "Yes." Benjamin said easily. The courtroom went silent.

"Therefore injuries sustained from the fight were not responsible for his death, yes."

"Unlikely."

"Let the records show Stanly Cross died from water affixation in accordance to the report submitted by doctors on call." Todd went to his desk, grabbed a small stack of papers and presented it to the judge. "I am submitting this report as evidence."

The judge glanced over the papers and then handed it to the bailiff who placed it on a table with other paraphernalia collected during the trial. Then he reclaimed his focus back to Todd who had taken his seat. "Do you have more questions?"

"No your honor."

The judge looked at a defeated Elizabeth. Her opponent had robbed her of her thunder. "Would you like to cross examine the witness?" The judge asked.

"No."

"I am adjourning until 2:00 pm for final summations." He reminded the jury of their responsibilities and hampered his desk for dismissal.

Ellen and her sisters left the courtroom immediately, trying to avoid the crowd. Reporters snapped pictures and asked questions but they pushed through the press ignoring their questions and flashing lights. The press quickly faded from Ellen and her sisters to her dismal husband with his head low and his impressive legal Team exiting the courtroom.

Ellen and her sisters walked the short distance from the courthouse to the parking lot behind the courthouse where they climbed inside Ellen's Volvo and headed to English Grill for lunch. As usual the place was packed with seniors and dignitaries. Luckily they located seating for three in the Alpine room. A young white girl, in her early twenties, severed them. After taking their order, she went to gather their drinks.

"This trial is going fast." Olvera said, tipping her hat to the side. "It's only been in session for a few days."

"Yeah but they had a slew of character witnesses the first few days." Bessie reminded her.

"Yeah, you're right about that." Olvera agreed.

"Do you think John will get off?" Bessie wondered.

"I think so." Ellen said.

"Have you spoke to John since the trial started?" Bessie wondered. Despite what happened, she liked John and hated how her sister betrayed him.

"He talked to me about the business but that's it." Ellen placed her pocketbook on the floor beside herself. Even though she dreaded admitting it, she felt guilty for her actions "I hurt him something terrible, we both did. I cannot get it out of my head how he cried and pleaded for Stanly to live after he rescued him from his fall. He was upset."

"I imagine he was." Bessie commented.

Olvera changed the subject. "Where is your daughter?" Olvera asked.

"Edith moved to New York, had a child with special needs, got married and moved to Chicago with her husband." Ellen summarized everything up in one sentence.

"So she married that man we saw during the holidays?" Olvera assumed.

"No. They separated." Ellen said.

"Separated," Olvera echoed.

"Let me bring you both up to speed to what happened since Christmas." She told them about a visit from Thomas' father; a visit which revealed her husband and Thomas' father, Phillip, being brothers which lead her to reveal to her daughter Thomas was her first cousin suffering from sickle-cell anemia. She cautioned her sisters not to tell anyone about Phillip and her husband being brothers.

"After you told her this, she left home and went to New York pregnant with his baby."

Olvera guessed.

"I didn't know she was pregnant until after she had the baby. I didn't know where she was until her cousin, Edward, called and told me she had Thomas' baby, which was deformed, married his a college buddy of his, and moved to Chicago. It was a shock to me." Ellen said.

"Does Thomas know Edith and him are first cousins?" Bessie asked.

"He does now. But Edith didn't tell him. I don't know what he was thinking when Edith broke off with him. His father told him a few weeks ago."

"And where is he now?" Olvera was curious.

"I received a call from Phillip. He said they were leaving town. Where they were going, he said nothing."

"Have you heard from Edith?" Olvera asked.

"Not word. And now all this happened."

The waitress brought their food and drinks on one large tray. The ladies chowed their meal slowly savoring the flavor. Before they realized it, it was twenty- minutes before the hour. Together they piled bills on the table blessing the waitress with a hefty tip. Ellen took the bill and paid at the cash register with a credit card.

When they reconvened in the courtroom, the trial was underway. Heavy Traffic and stubborn lights hindered them for fifteen minutes making them tardy. Elizabeth was in the middle of her closing summations grandstanding to alter the jury's mindset. Jurors mopped her movements and gestures as she strived to prove her point.

"I know you have heard several character witnesses testifying about John Douglas Bosworth's character. Yes, indeed he is a prominent citizen in the community. But the question that bothers me is why John Douglas Bosworth arranged for Stanly Theodore Cross and his wife to accompany him on the yacht. He knew about the affair for some time. At least a year. Once they were on the ship, he confronted his wife and her lover about the affair. He viciously and maliciously attacked Stanly Theodore Cross. They got into a fight. Stanly Theodore Cross tried to escape his madness. He ran to the upper deck. John Douglas Bosworth trailed him and struck him numerous times. One of those strikes sent him sailing off the balcony. He panicked and jumped overboard to rescue him. When he got him back on the ship he had his wife call for help which she did. But the damage had already been done. On route to the hospital, he died. He died of drowning where the defendant struck him forcing him to fall overboard. If he had not struck him, and beat him as savagely as he did, Stanly Theodore Cross would be alive today. It does not matter where he died. The fact is he died as a result of a beating inflicted by his old friend, Stanly Theodore Cross, who betrayed him. I am sure the defendant will tell you John tried to save the decease, and perhaps he did, but if he had not attacked, Stanly Theodore Cross, forcing him to stagger and fall overboard, we would not be here today. A man, regardless of his behavior, is dead today because of John Douglas Bosworth; A meaningless death. No action on earth can justify one man taking the life of another man despite the circumstances. Think about that when you render your verdict." Elizabeth rubbed her hands against her pants and took her seat.

Todd, who had been groomed by Luther, approached the stoned faced jurors. They were not moved by Elizabeth's plea for a conviction. Now it was his chance to seek an acquittal. His boss's brother's life was hanging in the balance. "Today you are asked to decide the fate of John Douglas Bosworth. A man who acted irrational after keeping a secret that hurt him to the core. A secret that exploded in a moment of rage. Yes, John Douglas attacked Stanly Theodore Cross and he did beat him something terrible. For the moment he lost himself and with just reason. His best friend was sleeping with his wife. It was too much to swallow. So they got into a fight. A fight which transpired to the top deck. It was during that fight, Stanly Theodore Cross fell overboard. My client did not push him. The minute he fell overboard, he realized his life was in danger and he jumped overboard and rescued him. He drug him to a lower deck and had his wife call for help. According to his wife's testimony he was obviously upset about what happened. He was pleading and sobbing for his life. Stanly Theodore Cross's death was accidental and not murder. Sure John Douglas Bosworth was angry with him and wanted to do him bodily harm but not murder. My client is not a murderer. Remember he rescued him from a certain death. If he wanted him dead, why didn't he leave him in the bay to die? No, he tried to save his life. When you reach your verdict, keep that in mind. I rest my case."

The judge took over after Todd took his seat. "You have heard from both sides. At this time I am going to ask the jury to retire to their chambers and decide whether John Douglas Bosworth is guilty or innocent of the charges brought against him."

Jurors exited through a side door trailing the bailiff.

Ellen and her sisters left the courthouse and walked to the downtown plaza. They wanted to be nearby when the verdict was rendered.

It was a warm evening. They sat on a bench accommodating three. Olvera went to a vender near the end of the plaza where she purchased a hotdog from a tall slim white man wearing an apron. He offered her condiments while he pulled the beef frank from the steaming water and placed it on a bun with a prong. When she rejoined her sisters, she offered them a bite but they declined. Ellen loathed hotdogs with a passion and Bessie loved then but they gave her indigestion.

"I'll be glad when this is over." Ellen commented.

"Well, it won't be long now." Olvera. said between bites.

"John looks like a zombie staring out in space." Bessie said.

"That's the way he's been since he was arrested." Ellen said. "He talks when he has to. He keeps reliving that day over and over. He says it's like a reoccurring nightmare."

"He told you that?" Olvera asked.

"I did get that much out of him."

Bessie stood up. "Let's go into Hess Apparel. I wonder what they have on sale."

Olvera was still nibbling on her hotdog. "You two go ahead. I am going to sit right here and enjoy my dog."

"Are you sure?" Ellen asked.

"Yeah, go ahead."

Ellen and Bessie went into the shop. An elderly woman offered her services but Ellen declined relaying they were window shopping. The lady made herself available if needed. While cruising the store admiring the outfits, and checking the tags for bargains, they lost conception of time. A few minutes later, Olvera popped it questioning if they found anything. Ellen admitted she found a few items she was considering purchasing. Bessie complained about the prices. Olvera reminded them it was almost three thirty, and suggested they return to the courthouse before the trial resumed. Bessie agreed with her.

When the ladies entered the courtroom, the judge accepted a piece of paper from his bailiff. He nodded and the bailiff went to the back of the courtroom, opened the door, and said to the people gathered in the corridors, "The jury was ready to issue their decision." Inside five minutes, the courtroom was crammed with spectators and reporters. The jurors came from their chambers and took their respective places in their chamber.

The judge slammed his mallet and the room went silent. "Have you reached a verdict?"

The spokesman for the jury, a short black man with gray hair and a pot belly stood up. "Yes sir your honor."

"What is your verdict?"

"We find John Douglas Bosworth not guilty for the murder of Stanly Theodore Cross in the first degree."

Mumbling and loud chatter rambled the tense atmosphere. Elizabeth was disillusioned with the outcome. She lost her case. All she could do was pack up and leave. Todd and Luther were overjoyed. Luther thanked Todd for defending his brother. Yet John was not moved by the verdict. It was if he was in a daze, and a blank expression remained plastered on his face.

The judge flocked through a stack of papers resurfacing the document prepared for the outcome. He instructed John and his team to stand while he read his sentence. "John Douglas Bosworth, as of this day, August 29 1971, you are sentenced to ten years' probation for manslaughter. You cannot leave the state of Maryland for any reason at that time. You have to report to your probation officer every three months. If you violate your probation, you will be incarcerated for thirty days and fined $50,000. Case dismissed." He hammered his desk with the mallet. The trial was over.

Bessie was pleased. She left her sister and rushed to John's side. She hugged him, catching him off guard, grabbed his hands and looked into his bewildered eyes. "It's going to be alright."

When Luther ushered his brother into his home, Ellen and her sisters greeted him in the lobby. But John was not the man they once knew. He was withdrawn and aloft. He walked into the parlor and collapsed into his favorite chair without acknowledging anyone. He was like a zombie displaying no emotion. Luther signaled Ellen and her sisters to remain behind and not pursue him.

"His been this way ever since he was arrested. If I ask him a question, he will answer but not initiate any conversation. He did tell me, he wished the jury found him guilty. He blames himself for what happened to Stanly. He believes he should be punished." Luther explained.

"He should hate me. I am responsible for this. "Ellen confessed. She wanted her husband back, not a hollow being in a shell. *If only she could draw him out of his trance.*

Luther seized Ellen's elbow escorting her into the kitchen. Bessie and Olvera trailed them. Luther gestured her to sit and sat opposite her. Her sisters accompanied them at the oval table.

"There's something you should know." Luther started.

The doorbell chimed. Bessie volunteered to answer it.

"What is it?" Ellen was worried. *What was going on?*

"Wait a minute." Luther suggested.

Bessie returned with Todd and Stanly Theodore Cross.

Ellen was shocked. Her sisters were speechless. They gawked at each other.

"What's going on?" Ellen asked.

"I'll let Stanly explain." Luther said.

Stanly focused on Todd. "Todd is my cousin as well as Luther's associate. You all know John rescued me from drowning and I was taken to a nearby hospital where I was pronounced dead. Todd was notified and he made arrangements for my body to be sent to a family mortician. The mortician was about to embalm my body when he discovered I was still breathing, ever so lightly. The mortician was my grandmother's brother. Instead of telling Todd I was alive, he led him to believe he buried me in the family cemetery per my request. I chose to stay hidden. I didn't want anyone to know I was alive. I knew John was furious with me and I could not blame him. I hated myself for falling in love with his wife. With me out of the picture, that was best for all of us. I knew my murder trial was underway. If John was convicted, I would have come forward. I would not stand by and watch him go to prison for a crime he never committed. But I believed my cousin and John's brother would get him exonerated. I called Todd when the trial was over. He was shocked to hear my voice. I saw pictures of John looking bewildered and displaced. I had to know how he was doing. That's when Todd told me John was withdrawn and quiet since he was arrested for my death. I knew what I had to do. I could not allow him to think he murdered his best friend. I owed him that much."

John walked into the kitchen. Stanly turned facing him. When John saw him, he started crying and embraced him. All he could say was, "You're alive. My God you're alive. Thank God you're alive."

"Yes, John, I am alive. You didn't kill me."

John stood back and took a long look at him. "How can this be? They said I killed you. I went on trial for your murder."

"It's a long story. I will tell you about it." Todd intervened.

"I'm going to leave. I just want you to know you did not kill me." Stanly walked passed John.

John grabbed his arm. "Where are you going?"

"Out of your life. I have caused you enough trouble." Stanly eased loose and paced into the foyer where he exited leaving John and his wife behind. *With him out of the picture, they could start a new life together. The affair was over. He would go back into hiding. He knew John would never forgive him. Hell, he would never forgive himself. What was he thinking; an affair with his best friend's wife.*

Chapter Twenty-Two

Another autumn day swept into Salisbury Maryland. It was Thanksgiving. Ellen dressed the dining table with harvest china. John watched football game with a host of male guest. His brother Luther, and his son Edward, were cheering for the Steelers. His brother Bill, and brother-in-law Justin, polluted the room with smoke as they yelled when their favorite player made a touchdown. Bernard joined the festivities asking the score. His friend had to work and was unable to accompany him. He felt strange not having her at his side.

Olvera accompanied Ellen in the kitchen sashaying her famous sweet potato pie, and placed it in the refrigerator. Bessie and Florence hung their coats on the rack in the foyer, and went to the kitchen holding paper bags with an assortment of beverages. They laid the drinks on a counter. The refrigerator was packed. Bessel joined her daughter-in-law in the dining area. She was admiring her centerpiece.

"Everything looks good." Bessel commented.

"Thank you." Ellen replied.

"I see the maid cooked the turkey and stuffing." Bessel was disappointed. Usually she was bestowed cooking the main dish. Her job was gone.

Ellen placed her hands to her lips. "Bessel I had no idea she did that. I am truly sorry." She apologized. She thought she told Eleanor not to cook the turkey, but obviously she forgot. She was excited about the holidays.

"What can I do?" Bessel asked.

"Well," Ellen thought for a moment. "Why don't you cook some greens? John tells me your greens are delicious."

"Do you have any?"

"We have several bags in the freezer." Ellen assured her.

Bessel was leaving when she remembered something. "I hear Edith and her husband are coming for Thanksgiving."

"Yes, they should be here anytime."

"That's a long ride. Why didn't they take a plane?" Bessel wondered. "Especially with the baby."

"I don't know."

Daniel and Edith disembarked their black cavalier. It was windy. She studied her home with vehicles in the driveway and on the street in front of the estate. So much had occurred since she left. She was a mother. Thomas was gone. Daniel was her husband.

She opened the rear door unstrapping her deformed infant from his seat. Snuggly she secured him in a blanket hampering the frigid air from his fragile body. Eastern Shore Autumns were brutal. With Daniel beside her, they approached her homestead. A breeze shuffled Autumn Leaves from place to place.

THE END

Printed in the United States
By Bookmasters